ADVANCE PRAISE

M000165252

searing stories told in rough and poetic language. Unforgettable and necessary.

– Lee Smith

Here is a vision and voice that your heart and blood will never forget. It is about the forgotten, the hurt, and the helpless, but Peter Christopher's magic makes these people whole again. I am grateful for finding this book.

– Harry Crews

If we could all look at the world the way the stories of Peter Christopher do, maybe we would be kinder to each other. I'm continuously impressed with the rendering of language in his work: every bit brings me to my knees. *Campfires of the Dead and The Living* is so good it makes you truly realize you really can do anything in a short story, whatever the fuck you want, as long as each sentence leads the reader to the perfect point of heartbreak.

– Elle Nash

Peter Christopher was a deep-hearted and clear-eyed beholder of every rank loveliness of the human estate. He was a master of the slang-shot sentence of manic downtroddendom, a genius of the nerve-stretching violent quiets of the failing and the failed. Here in one abounding volume are the long-overdue début of one collection of soul-boiling fictions and a return to circulation of another—the legacy of an extraordinary writer reworking the American short story with full, determining force.

– Garielle Lutz

Hilariously raw, chiseled and brilliant, the posthumously collected work of Peter Christopher hitchhikes the outskirts of lives lived on a hardest edge—Hey, ninja beauties and Mr. Death, stray cats and ghost-face killers, wow. I loved these stories, their heart and illuminate lightning. This is maximalist fiction at its sonic best.

– William Tester

How exquisitely Peter Christopher hears—how exacting and cussed and tender and pitch-perfect are the voices. Sentence after luminous sentence I'm reminded of all the ways cadence restores us. This is a rewilding by language's music: hushed lowlands, incandescent riffs, and "whippoorwill harmonics." I would listen to these stories forever.

– Geri Doran

For years I've been xeroxing Peter Christopher's stories for my writing students. Finally, here are Christopher's collected stories, a book so full of grit and heart, compassion and rage, that I challenge you to read his stories without being changed as a person walking the earth. *Campfires of the Dead and the Living* is a remarkable, muscular book by a brilliant and fearless writer.

– Victoria Redel

Peter Christopher? A case wherein it's the man, not the littérateur, that demands remark—to wit, never knew, will never know, an instance of better, dearer, sweeter. That was Peter, none greater, not just a mensch but a mensch and a half.

– Gordon Lish

I read Peter Christopher's *Campfires of the Dead and the Living* in front of a space heater (an indoor campfire) in Chattanooga, Tennessee where the raccoons have come out from the dark to play with the chipmunks. Gently and unapologetically surged with domestic wild animal life and everyday tedium, Christopher's ever unrestrainable, shifting stories dare us to care. His stories are leisurely compassionate, spermatically original, and deftly defiant of all caustic arrogance by faithfully recording the comic discord and consonance in our humanity. The titles to his stories are a riot! He is funny. He is wild. He is unexpected. He does not pontificate. He does not flicker nor flinch nor whinge like a frightened cat, but boldly tugs and pulls and ticks and flips our imagination with an eye for conversation and an eye for quotidian details. His suave, sidesplitting stories will warm your bittered hearts up like a shot of whiskey aged over night by the distilled malted grain of his work's transient timelessly and keep them sober until your heart and mind become hysterical with petrified fever for the unknown.

– Vi Khi Nao

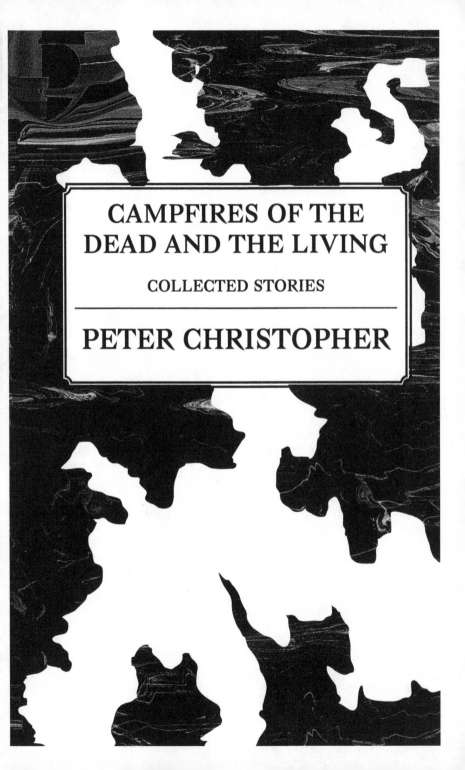

CAMPFIRES OF THE DEAD AND THE LIVING

COLLECTED STORIES

PETER CHRISTOPHER

Copyright © 2022 The Estate of Peter Christopher
c/o Carolyn Altman
All rights reserved

This book may not be reproduced in whole or in part, except for the inclusion of brief quotations in a review, without permission in writing from the author or publisher. No part of this publication may be reproduced, stored in or introduced into a retrieval system, or transmitted, in any form, or by any means (electronic, mechanical, photocopying, recording, or otherwise), without prior permission of the publisher.

Requests for permission should be directed to 1111@1111press.com, or mailed to 11:11 Press LLC, 4732 13th Ave S, Minneapolis, MN 55407.

Typeset by Mike Corrao

ISBN: 9781948687447 (paperback)
ISBN: 9781948687911 (ebook)
LCCN: 2021905442

Printed in the United States of America

FIRST AMERICAN EDITION

9 8 7 6 5 4 3 2

CAMPFIRES OF THE DEAD AND THE LIVING

COLLECTED STORIES

PETER CHRISTOPHER

THIS IS FOR FRANCES MARIE CARON FOR BLACK-
ENING THE INDIAN CORN JUST RIGHT, MAKING
SURE THE MISTLETOE IS KEPT REFRIGERATOR
COOL, BATHING RUSSELL LITTLE WITHOUT COM-
PLAINT WITH CAN AFTER CAN OF TOMATO JUICE
AFTER SMELLING SKUNK AND FINDING HIS OLD
HEAD–REMEMBER HIS DOWN TO THE BONE NICKS
AND SCARS?–DREAMING ODORIFEROUS DREAMS
ON MY PILLOW, FINDING IN THE HOLLOWED OUT P.
G. WODEHOUSE THE SQUIRREL TAIL HACKED OFF
WITH THE SKINNING KNIFE WITH THE BONE HAN-
DLE THAT WAS–ALONG WITH HIS MARINE CORPS
MEDAL FOR SHARP SHOOTING AND THE AIRPLANE
RIDE OVER SADDLE BACK–ONE OF THE GREAT
GIFTS FROM UNCLE BOBBY, BRAVING THE CEL-
LAR BECAUSE OF THE GARTER SNAKE LOST IN THE
TORN LINING OF BUB'S WELCOME HAND-ME-DOWN
OF A WINTER COAT, CROSSING A CREEK BAREFOOT
IN DECEMBER, DRIVING OVER THE WEIGHTS, PED-
ALING A BICYCLE INTO HEADSTONES DOWN AT
SOUTHVIEW CEMETERY, HAVING HAMBURGERS AND
SHAKES ON THOSE SAM AND BEAR BIRTHDAYS AT
A PICNIC TABLE ON THE SIDE OF THE ROAD; FOR
NOT TRADING ME FOR DAVE LIBARDI; FOR TAKING
BECKY IN WHEN BECKY WAS HUNGRY AND COLD
FROM LIVING IN A HOLE IN THE GROUND; FOR TAK-
ING ALL OF US IN FOR THESE OUR LIVES.

AND FOR MY FATHER,
WHEN I THOUGHT OF THE CHILD ALONE
IN THE DARKENED HOUSE,
IN THE WHITE-FLOWERED GARDEN.

TABLE OF CONTENTS

INTRODUCTION 17

THE LIVING

LOST DOGS 23

FISHING, WITH WHAT I HAVE 50

THE LIVING 58

THE YEAR OF THE PURCHASE 77

HUNGER 80

FLIGHT 95

SON OF MAN 100

MARISA, YOU WERE RIGHT ABOUT HEARING WE MADE THE PAPER AND SO I THOUGHT I WOULD SEND YOU THIS FOR OLD TIMES AND ALSO TO SAY PLEASE, PLEASE, PLEASE, DO NOT BURN UP ANY

THING MORE OF MINE IF YOU HAPPEN TO COME ACROSS MY SILK BOXER SHORTS AND DISCHARGE PAPERS AND A BOOK BY HARRY CREWS WITH CREWS ON THE COVER SHOWING OFF HIS BEAUTIFUL TAT-TOO HAT READS, HOW DO YOU LIKE YOUR BLUE-EYED BOY NOW, MR. DEATH? 115

DROPPING YOU ANOTHER LINE, MARISA, TO LET YOU KNOW THAT YOU ARE TERRIFIC AT KILLING A DREAM WITH X-RATED POETRY AS REAL AS THE REPO MAN KICKING IN THE DOOR AT 7:43 THIS A.M. BEFORE HE TOOK THE CLOCK, TV, COUCH, ETC., BUT HE LEFT ME, TRYING TO MAKE THE PRICE OF A SIX-PACK AND WONDERING OVER MY LUCK AT HOW MY MISSING CREDIT CARD HAPPENED NOT TO BURN UP TOO 118

MARISA, IT'S ME AGAIN, ASKING IF YOU COULD FIND IT IN YOUR HEART TO STOP BY THE LIBRARY ON YOUR WAY TO WHEREVER YOU WANT TO GO NOW THAT I HAVE CUT-UP MY CREDIT CARD WITH YOUR SKID MARKS FROM WHEN YOU BOMBED YOUR SKANKY FAT ANGER ALL OVER TOWN WHILE SOME-HOW MISSING A CHARGE-UP AT DELPHINA'S DIET AND WEIGHT LOSS CENTER 120

HEY, MARISA, THIS IS ME FINALLY GETTING MY LIFE TOGETHER AND I WANTED TO TELL YOU HOW AFTER CHEWING OVER YOUR ADVICE ABOUT DOING SOME-THING DECENT WITH MYSELF I DECIDED THAT EX-CEPT FOR THE DRIPPING POISON YOU WERE RIGHT AGAIN SO NOW I'M TRYING TO LAY OFF THE POTATO CRISPS, THE BEEF JERKY, EVEN THE SCHLITZ, WHILE GOING FULL BLAST ON THE ERNEST & JULIO GALLO

HEARTY BURGUNDY, REALLY, NO SHIT...................122

THAT HEAVY RIDER 124

LEGS 145

LET IT LOOSE 151

THE VISITOR 161

CAMPFIRES OF THE DEAD

BLOOD AND SEED 167

ROSIE AND DELLA, SANDY AND BESSIE, SISTER AND
DINAH 169

THE CAREERIST 176

CAMPFIRES OF THE DEAD 186

HUNGRY IN AMERICA 192

THE REPORTER 204

WAYS OF SEEING..207

FLAMINGOES AND OTHER SELF-CURES, ALMOST ...211

DEAR TO WHOEVER FINDS AND READS THIS SO THAT
YOU SHOULD KNOW DOZIER AND ME ARE NOT ALL
BAD, AT LEAST NOT DOZIER 221

THE MAN WHO FAILED TO WHACK OFF 233

INDIA, WHEN YOUR PHONE DOESN'T RING, IT'S ME, POMP 236

LEGENDS..244

ON RISING AND SINGING: A GUIDE TO WHALE RIDING 249

PASTORAL 252

I DON'T CARE IF I EVER GET BACK 258

The beauty forcing us as much as the harshness.
Our spirits forged in that wilderness, our minds
forged by the heart.

— Jack Gilbert

INTRODUCTION

Peter Christopher popped my cherry. Reading-wise.

Until Peter, I'd tell you that so-and-so was good reading. You know, the writer with his own shelf at Blockbuster Video. The third-person patch on what H. P. Lovecraft used to do. That billion-selling, second-rate Hemingway. What did I know?

I say Blockbuster because this was 1991? 92? Peter had gone to Columbia to study under Gordon Lish with writers such as Amy Hempel and Mark Richard and Tom Spanbauer. Tom had moved to Portland and taught the style of Minimalism in a workshop he called "Dangerous Writing." Tom invited Peter to come west, and what Peter came to teach us, he called "submerging the I." His theory being that fiction told in the first-person – *I walked... I read...* – held the most power and authority because a personality seemed present and accountable for the how-and-why the story was *being* told. The context.

That's something that third-person omniscient "voice of God" narration can't do. As per Peter, the modern reader is smart enough to know that the storyteller – even a fictitious storyteller, especially a fictitious storyteller – has her motives and slant on the truth. So if a story took place in that old-fashioned, third-person, *once upon a time* it was bullshit.

The catch was, Peter Christopher warned us that readers hate a story riddled with the first-person pronoun "I." That "I" reminded the reader that she was only a witness. The story was happening to someone else. The solution? Peter called it "submerging the I." Simply put, you told the story in first-person but used the first-person pronoun seldom if ever. Doing so you side-stepped the thudding I...I...I... sound of a self-obsessed bore. What's more you're forced to point the camera at everything else. Submerging the I breaks your work open.

Take Cory-Anne. For months she'd brought the same story into Tom's workshop. It was always about her nephew dying, and she'd cry when she read it aloud. In short, it was about Cory-Anne. Her writing wasn't getting any better, and she cried harder each week so it didn't seem that Cory-Anne was getting any better, either. Peter came west at Tom's invitation and asked us to submerge the I. He urged Cory-Anne to write something new.

Within a month she broke out. It was by submerging the I, or reading the work of Amy Hempel and Mark Richard. Or it was reading Peter's work, the stories in this book. But Cory-Anne wrote us a story that left Tom's workshop in silent awe for a moment.

At that Peter knelt on the floor and began to kowtow at her feet. He led the writers in a chant of her name as he continued to bow before her. And this time Cory-Anne didn't cry. She glowed. She'd written an astounding short story. She'd taken herself almost entirely out of the drama and given us a story in which we felt like characters.

It's a glorious moment, when a student writer breaks out their own voice. One day they're writing mawkish, tedious stuff. And the next week they're being cheered. And that moment wouldn't have happened without the advice and the patience of Peter Christopher.

Me, I once sublet a huge loft at 14th and Hudson in Manhattan with Peter. At the time it was a district of meat packers, where pigeons ate the raw fat and waded through the beef blood in the gutters. Nights, the area teemed with trans-gender sex workers. A half-block west of our door, the old West Side Elevated Line ran as a ruined no man's land as far uptown as 35th Street. It was a fast way to walk uptown, but so dangerous no one ever used it. It's now the ritzy New York High Line. Years later, the *New Yorker* magazine hosted a party for me at a lux nightclub named *Apartment*, and I attended, shocked to find that the space was the same one Peter and I had rented.

During our shared sublet it was winter, and I drank coffee all day so I could go out all night. Every evening the Italian restaurant below our place held a different bachelor party, but you could set your watch by it. Promptly at 9:30, the stripper would begin to dance to Madonna's *Material Girl*. The song list never varied and as long as the party lasted, the male crowds cheered up through the floors. Even once the night's party died down, I could blink awake after midnight to see sex workers on the roof, staring down at me through the skylights.

Peter told me how he'd once worked for Big Golden Books, a children's imprint at Penguin Random House. It was strange to think of Peter working on books like *The Poky Little Puppy* and *The Little Red Hen*. He'd already lost an eye to cancer and always worried the cancer might come back. Tom told me that Peter had always clung to university teaching jobs because he wanted the health insurance – in case the cancer came back. That's why Peter had published so little of his own fiction.

Peter brought so many people fully into the world. First by writing and thus showing us what excellent storytelling could be. And second, by teaching. Me and Cory-Anne, we're better writers due to him. And we're better readers thanks to Peter Christopher.

For twenty years I've pushed people to find and read his

collection *Campfires of the Dead*. It was out of print for so long that getting a copy was near impossible. And now, here it is. In your hands. And here I am writing to repay an old, old debt to the man who taught us all.

May this book make you a better reader. If you write, may it make you a better writer.

I'll shut up now.

Chuck Palahniuk April 7th, 2022

THE LIVING

The Living was written between 1990 and 2004. The stories are published in the order they appear in the manuscript Peter arranged before his passing.

LOST DOGS

They are along the highway. I mean the dogs, the cats too, but mostly the dogs. They trot the blacktop. They lie dusty in the blowing grass between the two lanes coming and the two lanes going. I sometimes see them crossing the highway with their eyes rolling in terror at the cars and trucks blaring horns at them and them running faster. They get to the tall grass. They slink into a ditch. They make the parking lot at Sonny's with the big dumpster out back.

Most of the cats I know come out at night. When I see a cat during the day, it's usually when the flies are already in a whirling feast. The flies blow off as if in a soft explosion of buzzing cat. The flies come back, travel the tongue curled black, fill an eye socket.

The dogs watch me walk the highway. They watch from the deep grass, panting, ready to run. Most are mutt dogs. Most are alone. Some are starving. Some are pregnant or slinging rows of pink teats. Not too long ago, I saw a litter tumbling over one another from a concrete culvert trickling water under the highway. Some bigger dog watched over while the litter of four played and the tractor trailer rigs rumbled above. A day after I saw those dogs, I went back out along the highway with another kind of feast. I swung a plastic bag holding half a pepperoni pie, a few fatty rib bones, the little miracle of an okay-smelling tuna roll I had pulled from dumpsters. When I got to the big culvert they were gone, as if they had never been. All four pups and the bigger dog, the mother dog, whatever they were or were not, were all swallowed up.

Some of the best diving around is done at Four Star. About midnight, I start watching from across the street. I stand in low hedges stomped lower as the night delivers a cheesy-pizza-of-a-moon all of us can eat. A cat crosses the parking lot in the moonlight. The cat slips around a corner, heading–I would bet–for Four Star's dumpster and some diving of his own.

Not long after I see the cat, a dog crosses the parking lot. The dog looks skinny hungry and all business by the way he trots. The dog disappears in the direction the cat disappeared when the lights at Four Star cut out. The oven boy fires up a doobie twist as he floats out the front door. Oven boy poots off on his scooter. Four Star Pizza's manager, wearing his sanitary-pizza-paper hat, is in such a hurry when he leaves that he runs a red light. I take my time going through the parking lot and out back.

Up on his hind legs at the big dumpster is the skinny dog. He tries to claw himself closer to the pizza boxes left stacked on top of the heap. Skinny dog looks at me, shows me his dirty yellow teeth, his long ones.

"Don't mess with me," I growl. "I'm the bigger dog."

I show him my broken teeth. Skinny dog moves off, sits under a tree trailing down Spanish moss. The cat I saw crossing the parking lot sits up a branch in that tree. The cat's tail hangs as if diseased, dying moss. Both the cat and the dog look at me as if I might know something better.

"I'm the bigger dog only for now," is what I tell them.

I don't have to tell them how after diving some you almost forget the shit-soup smell of the draining muck at the bottom of the dumpsters. Tossed into the smell of Four Star's dumpster are the usual bundles of cardboard and paper, loose diapers, ripped and leaking plastic trash bags, and on top, a tottering stack of taped pizza boxes holding tonight's mistakes: maybe an anchovy and pineapple pie that caught on fire while oven boy nodded in doper dreams, or pies delivered cold nobody would pay for, or a bored baby-sitter's prank order. I take a peek. Two eggplant and a lobster is tonight's haul still warm through the boxes. Two eggplant beauties and what looks to me like melted runny chunks of Taiwan-plastic-lobster toys poked loose from the gumball machines at Winn Dixie, what smells to me like rotting-fish-stinking-blue-cheese-moldering-rat puke so strong that your stomach twists away faster than your mind can begin to say to itself, "Jesus H. Christ, *no*, there is no way I can even *think* about taste testing this one!"

Skinny dog clicks his teeth, slings drool, as he snags in mid-air the eggplant slice I toss him. The slice is gone in two quick chokes. Chops are licked. Skinny dog slows somewhat after his fourth slice. Both skinny dog and the cat ignore what might pass as lobster at some other party. The cat sniffs at the eggplant slice I flop up into a nearby branch, bats a paw at it. The cat, owned by neither hunger nor fear, looks down at skinny dog and me looking up at him in all the moonlight.

People say I'm crazy doing what I'm doing. Nearly everybody I know figures anybody living the way I do–the long quiet, the always looking for some luck–is short a baked bean side order of a full lunch. Most everybody has called this one right. Every morning I start out walking from zero toward the possibility of making it work for one more day. I kick up dead palm fronds along the side of the highway and see what happens to those of us not behind the steering wheel of a big machine cranked up.

Now that I've said that I should say this, I was walking the highway this morning when I heard something, some whining. Down on the other side of a ditch, on the hood of a wrecked bus long captured by kudzu and weeds, I saw something move. Up closer, crouching, carefully parting long leaves sharp as a suicide's straight razor, I saw a little dog twitching in the day's growing heat. Her burred-thick coat was mostly black, but for a splash of white at the chest and throat. Her four, long, pale paw stockings and her tail tip were also white.

Sometimes you know right away when your luck has changed. Sometimes you feel as if something bigger and better than yourself, something lighter than air, is gathering itself in your lungs.

She yawned. When she was done, the little dog lifted her head into looking around. When she saw me, she thumped her tail hard, whacking metal, the sound like some ghosting big engine still running fast under that bus hood.

Don't get me wrong, I'm not yet so fruit loopy, so rotten with self regard, that I don't know what's going on. I know that I'm nobody's dreamboat. Most women don't go for me. I should say that, for a long time now, most has not amounted to any, but that doesn't stop me from giving my best shot.

I walk the wide, air-conditioned aisles of Pick-N-Save. I doodle dong around HARDWARE. I pick up a hammer. I squeeze the trigger on an electric drill. I sword fight with a wooden-handled toilet plunger when I see the woman I'm looking for in HOUSEWARES.

She is even better looking than her employee-of-the-month picture posted by the cash registers: less glossy, more fleshy around the jaw, more hair teased up higher than I have ever seen hair teased, and I have been a hair freak for a long time now, more confidence in the way she holds her mouth and in the way she looks at me, who once started out tiny and pink and who is now swollen and hairy.

"May I help you?" she asks.

Her kind of confidence up close, the way her mouth

moves when she talks, speaks to me of fear.

"Yes, yes, you can, but first I want to congratulate you on your Pick-N-Save employee of the month merit award, Mrs. Melissa Carter, Customer Service Representative," I say.

"Well, ummmmm, thanks," she says, the little crack already starting to widen.

"No, I should thank *you* and by the way, your official winner's picture doesn't do you justice. Really. I mean it. Your hair, your. . ."

"Thanks, but what can I help you with?" she says, looking around so that I know she knows and that I have to work faster, or smarter.

"Well, I just wanted to ask you about something," I say.

"Yes, go ahead, how can I help you?" she says.

"Okay, all right, you know how people, whether customers or just regular human types, are strange," I say. "I mean, how you are with one person for a while, eating and sleeping and living with them, hearing the little noises they make when they are in the bathroom the first thing in the morning or right after making love, and you are talking to them, maybe complaining a little about only a few of the smaller things, or later sometimes going places together, sometimes holding hands as if holding hands still really meant something, truly loving them, and then it stops. . ."

"That's enough right there, mister," she says.

"Roland, you can call me Roland," I say.

"That's enough," she says. "Now, do you leave on your own, or do I have to holler for *Merton* to come to HOUSE-WARES?"

"Merton?" I say.

"Yes, Merton," she says.

She looks over to **SPORTING GOODS**, three cool and clean aisles away. A big brother wearing the red Pick-N-Save smock stands among the bowling balls, the big three-holed bowling balls. His huge hands hold one in a way that makes it look like one of the little bowling balls used for candle pins in a beer joint.

She says to me, "It's your call. . ."

"As I was saying, you know how after they have gone and you are in the bathroom and you happen to look down at their toothbrush hanging there as if the dang thing is waiting for the loved one to come back and you take a closer look and see the bristles all bent from the little grooves in their teeth that you have run the tip of your tongue over and over and never will again when. . ."

"Merton!" she sings out. "Merton, can you come over here for a minute?"

Merton moves the way you would imagine a Merton moving, fast on his feet for such a big guy, all ass muscle and arms working very well together.

"Merton, this gentleman was just leaving and I was wondering if you could show him the way out," she says.

"This way is the way, my man," Merton says, nodding toward the double doors at the front of the store.

She gives me a little wave good-bye, not in an unkind or sarcastic way, and goes back to folding very thin dish towels on sale, three for a dollar.

I want my money's worth so I start throwing air punches, an uppercut or two. I shuffle. I pretend I'm making something happen. I know I'm not fooling anybody, not even myself. My hands are too small and I have no real thing for fighting. I stop with the late round action. I mostly go meekly.

"Merton, you know how people, human beings, are really kind of strange," I say, a little out of breath. "You know how you are with one person for a while, eating and sleeping and . . ."

"I know, my man, I know," Merton says. "And ain't it something? Ain't it really something the way it all goes down?"

"Yes!" I say. "Yes, it is!"

Out in the ferocious heat rising off the tar of the parking lot sticking to my one wingtip worn down at the heel and my one basketball sneaker needing a new lace, I say to Merton, "Oh yeah, right, okay, and there's one more thing."

Merton is just as cool looking in his smock as if he was standing over an open freezer, smoking cold, in the Pick-N-Save frozen food section, if Pick-N-Save had a frozen food section. He is one smart dude with job security, as much forty-hour week as anybody has nowadays.

"You can tell Mrs. Melissa Carter, our Customer Service Representative, fucking merit award winner for the month, that she can. . ."

"Yes?" Merton says to me.

Merton is big and smart and icy cool and also not unkind. His smile is real.

"You can tell her, if she wants to, she can still call me Roland."

I'm giving it another shot.

Out back of the Sawamura Japanese Steak & Sushi House, in the parking lot with the potholes and the chunks of busted-up asphalt, is where Nishi usually goes during her breaks to take quick and quiet puffs on her slim cigarettes one after another. While I wait for her, I gurgle at a pint of Old Grandad. I go through the dumpster, a Boone deluxe model. I do so to keep my chops up. My diving has become not so much taking what I can as what I need. The amateurs, or worse, the monkey walkers, are the ones in a long sweat, mixing everything up all the way to the bottom while looking for cans to cash in for a quick taste or sniff. In their hurry, they lose or mess up every decent thing they happen to come across—I have found nearly new lava lamps, dart-boards, coffee makers, computers, and more—whether they can use it or not, whether anyone else can use it or not.

Eating what you find, finding what you eat, is what separates the professionals from the part timers, the men from the boys, the big dogs from the littler dogs. Finding a pepperoni pizza hot in its box stacked out on the nightly heap by a college kid with feeling, or coming across cans sometimes a little dented or missing a label for Vienna sausage, deviled ham, tuna fish and such, is one thing. Moving on to the dry foods: chips, cereal, cookies, pasta, while making sure they are, for the most part, crisp and ungreen, is something else. So is fruit with the skin bruised, cheese gone a little moldy blue, chocolate with the cocoa butter turning white--more food than I can ever eat. No wonder I've gained forty-three pounds. No wonder I get the nasty runs, usually during hot weather. Sure, I watch for every elbow macaroni to squirm around into a maggot. Sure, Tex-Mex is always questionable. A lot of ethnic food is not always what you at first might think. Only the best and the bravest dive at the Chinese and Japanese joints. Like most things though, you have to pick and choose, study the take-out menu, and go with the best. In Hogtown, hands down, the best is Sawamura, home of the dumpster with the baddest smell. Once you get past that smell, baby, you got it licked. That shit is the Olive Garden.

"Roland," Nishi whispers from the shadows near the high wooden fence. "I have something for you."

Nishi's pale face is a little hidden moon under her scudding cloud of long black hair. No it's not, but she is really something, as Merton would say, with her hair almost as long as she is tiny, her silky Sawamura kimono and ornate sash, her chunky high-heeled sneakers. Did I say how Nishi sometimes reminds me of somebody I knew a long time ago? To look at her is nearly feast and memory enough.

"Roland," she whispers. "Come get some stir-fry before the boss misses me."

She also has chop sticks and her ciggies that she smokes

while I eat.

"Nishi, let me lick your ankles when I'm done," I say.

"Roland, don't start," she says.

"Your tiny ankles, your tiny knees. . ."

"Roland, please," she says, puffing faster. "I like you, Roland, but it is not there for me in that way."

I said nearly.

"Maybe some day it could be." I say, burping some shrimp, some dear Old Gramps. "Maybe after I get less swollen?"

"No, Loland."

"Did you say Loland?"

"I said Roland," Nishi says.

"Oh, I thought I heard you say Loland, but anyway, why?"

"Why what?" Nishi says.

"Why won't you maybe go for me after I get back on track and everything else comes into play?" I ask.

"Why, because I love another woman," Nishi says. "Because we live together and we are sometimes in love with each other at the same time."

Did I say before how only the best and the bravest do triple gainers at the Japanese joints? Did I say you have to quiz yourself on the take-out menu? Did I say once you get way, way, way past the smell you got it licked?

"I'm a sushi eater myself," I say.

In the quiet, I hear the tree peeper toads. I hear the traffic off on the highway.

"Well, you know, that is, when I can get some, any," I say, "you know. . ."

More toad clamor: whump, wheep, whump. More traffic slushing past.

"I'm sorry I said that," I say. "Well, not that I said what I said about sushi diving so much as that I hurt you and that, you know. . ."

"I know, Roland."

"I'm sorry," I say.

"I know you're sorry," Nishi says. "How's your poo-poo shrimp?"

Nishi is tiny, but her heart is huge. Nishi's heart fills the parking lot to overflowing with her goodness. Her kindness is such that she flies us through the darkness above the headlights of the cars and the trucks whining along the highway and over a thunderstorm flashing in the distance. She leads us on through the widening night that feels as close and as heavy and as alive to me as my own panting heart.

I'm smashed, so go ahead, laugh at those sentences.

I'm really such an amateur drunk.

So what? So go ahead and run me over in a Lincoln Town Car. Give me impetigo. Send me into the jungle to take all the fiery heat whatever little sincere guys want to throw my way.

On second thought, I'm not that drunk. I'm not so gone as to forget that I have seen all that, done all that, bought the fast-shrinking, shrunk too tight, XXL T-shirt. Nobody has to tell me my best shot has never been none too good.

Another day, another Grandad hangover. Even so, I'm out earlier than usual, before the sun machineguns the asphalt and what is left of my brain. Southwest Sixth Street is quiet, but for the locusts power drilling their electric buzz song into my head. Those locusts and the 6:13 Cotton Belt thrumming the rusty rails through town. Others of us are also up and about. Sam the Dealer Man sits on a picnic table near the basketball court waiting for a young blood to show up for the next shift. A somebody or other, a Laotian-Manchurian-Laplander on a bicycle, rattles chain on his way to school or work.

"Are you with me, Doctor Woo?" I call after him.

A catbird watches and calls the play-by-play from his

seat among the waxy leaves of a Chinaberry tree. Mighty Casey crawls to the plate. Actually, I'm wingtipping and dribbling along in my sloping-worn shoes when a van goes by fast. The van slams to a stop about a quarter mile up street. The van's side door bangs back and a woman is thrown out. She lands hard. Her head takes a couple of bounces among the weeds, but she comes up working her mouth in a way that shows her spirit is not yet completely eaten out, "JERK-OFFS! ASSHOLES! DUMB PRICKS!"

By the time I get to her she is on to a different game. She is on her knees, gacking.

The sun shoots me a little more while I wait on her. My eyes boil in a big pot out in the front yard of the shotgun shack that is behind my eyelids. My brain squats heavy and thuggish. My skin flakes off as crumbly-old as the yellow newspapers that failed to keep the freezing cold from the attic of my boyhood.

So, maybe I'm still a little drunk, okay? Or maybe I wish I was, okay?

"Mickey Mantle Liver Shots all around!" I scream to no one in particular.

The catbird imitates her heaves and my groans.

Another Samoan-Somalian-Croatian-type person bikes past. Everything is too hot and hazy for me, a little too oriental, a little too. . .

"You all right?" is what I say when she stops puking long enough to dab the back of a hand at her lips punched fat.

"Do I look all right?" she croaks.

One of her flip-flops has flipped off. Her T-shirt and stretch pants are rags showing her ass meat. She looks like a curb whore, worn-out, busted down, thrown away by just about everybody she has ever met. She is skeleton still dying with filthy hair matted to her head.

"Is there anything I can do for you?" I ask her.

"You got any money?" she asks me.

I fist around in my pockets for $1.47, all in change, which I tell her about.

"That'll do you, Bud," she says. "Follow me."

She staggers up and slaps one flip-flop across Southwest Sixth and into the jungle growing along the creek. The catbird follows too, swooping from branch to telephone pole to shopping cart overturned in the little clearing. Beside the cart, there are overturned boxes, a ripped blue pool tarp, a big lounger chair with the legs snapped even stubbier around a heap of ashes and charred wood.

She has me sit in the angled Easy Boy lounger while she kneels in front of me. My head bangs around pretty good. Bases are loaded and Casey is at bat. Stuffing, musty and piss smelling, scratches at the back of my neck as if some hairy animal, a rotting dog, is somehow hiding in the lounger and snuffling around with its bristly snout for some last air. The curbie heaves and catches herself before getting me out. My little stray is hidden by hair and a roller of fat.

When I open my fist I can smell the copper smell of sweaty coins. She takes the change without missing a beat. Slup, slup, slup. I stroke chairdog's chinny-chin-chin in time with the slupping.

While we were crossing Sixth, I think I remember she soft drawled that her name was Suzette. I let myself go with Suzette and sink further into some of the old, boundless ignorance. The old spooky tooth I have become shoots my very own death rays. My head sizzles from the blasts and I pump a splooge monster. I too join in the destruction lying just about everywhere under the balding hot sun.

The catbird, perched on the cart, calls balls and strikes, calls it right alright—warbling, laughing, crying softly as a baby.

The great thing about her is she is not as scared as the rest of us. Well, maybe a little bit, but most dogs will have nothing to do with strangers. Given any kind of chance, most strays will run off, or ignore you if you don't have food. This one lets me come up to her hanging around the old bus wreck whether I have a half-eaten hoagie hero or waffles dripping with syrup or even when I don't have anything at all. She whispers hello. She lets me stroke her head. I put my arm around her and we are in the catbird seat. We lazily watch the dragonflies and the little lizards. The lizards are really tiny dinosaurs running over the flaking prehistoric plain of the bus hood that once housed a big driving load. I look down into her brown eyes carrying love and a certain helplessness. I pinch off a seed tick and mash it. I scratch her along her mottled throat and do all the worst chit-chatting.

". . . And believe me when I tell you I was giving it to her straight and hard as in jab, move, jab, big right word hook to the bigger brain lobe of one Mrs. Melissa Carter, our Pick-N-Save Customer Service Representative and employee standout for the month of May. I was, after all, a customer. Well, I was almost a customer. I had thought about buying something, a so-called plumber's friend, if I had had the bread, which I didn't, but I would have if I did, when I asked her, our dear Mrs. Carter that is, with the stacked-high beehive do, a decorated expert in dealing with the human species, how, I asked, can we connect with somebody in a way that lasts longer than a salami and onion sandwich a la dumpster when the monkey walkers haven't had a good goddamn hike from Sam and his boys in three days and they are wild in their agony . . ."

She looks at me with those sweet brown eyes like all the good ones have and listens to every crazy word I say.

Not that nothing is easy for nobody. Cars and trucks are stopped at the traffic light. The shiny new zipsters and the old pickup trucks clunking as if trying to throw a piston, the smashed and smashing rocket ships and battleships, are backed up hot inches from one another filled with people waiting patiently. These are men and women looking straight ahead, not talking to each other, not seeing me, or if they do, they see a hunk of walking trash with thirteen cents in his pocket. They act as if I'm just another something to look through, more oily air, a flawed nothing farting past them.

A young woman in an old Nova doesn't move her head, her eyes, not even a little, when I knock knuckles on her beater's rear window. I smile. She acts as if nothing is happening in her rearview. I flash my psycho-zombie-drooler's face. I bare my broken monkey teeth. She fast wheels the old car onto the grassy shoulder, fishtail skids and guns it through the light, keeps on going up the long highway.

Now there is someone more than just me owned by all our big and little fears, at least one woman speed jock not just breathing chilled air and looking straight ahead as if paid to shut up and not see, just keep driving, keep going, only to wait and wait and wait somewhere else; a broken toilet seat, a creaking chair at a desk in an otherwise empty office, a supermarket check-out line, a packed jail cell smelling of rampant sweaty fear, a small restaurant table where one night's leftover food could feed a family of three for a week, a stool in a bar near the tracks where the soapy-flat beer sloshes every time a freight train blows by, a hospital bed with restraining straps, a sofa in front of a very tiny television set showing, *The Price is Right* where we all wait locked-down, jacked-off, chopped-up for the grand prize–grinning old dog death himself.

I tell myself that I have tried not to let women and money run my life.

I mumble something about how I was never much good at waiting, dangling, pretending the fix wasn't in. I pretend to take only what I need. Until then, I flop on a broken bed in a room so small I had to lie down to pull my shirt over my head. I listen to Aretha Franklin and other soul survivors on the boom box I found behind Sound Shack.

I know I am just another cat in a tree, only not as good as a cat. I am a monkey, no, worse than that, a bloated man hairy in all the wrong places, up that branch, falling into the waiting mouths of those with nothing more to do than drink, eat, fuck, kill—all of it in the name of getting more money and power over Little Red Riding Hood running through the darkening woods and Brutus chuckling while pile driving Popeye and Davey Crockett eating Mexican musket balls at the Alamo and Tarzan of the Apes whirling around underwater while knifing a giant crocodile and my old man holding me underwater until my soul floated out limp and Dennis Prevey the Houghton School bully kneeling on my shoulders while belting home run punches off my face and my first job where I killed rats in the stinking wet hell of that tannery for a nickel a rat and the nuns chasing me out of the Catholic Church for eating a meatball sandwich in catechism class and stomping fourteen miles of fence in shale stone blistering the skin raw from my hands while the old timers laughed and the dizzying hunger as I walked all night that one winter night down by the docks to keep warm and watching the Vietnamese boys coming toward us knowing it was either deal them a good hand of death or die trying and lying on a hospital cot for two days after they micro-waved my eyeball so my eye dripped down my face sunny side up and. . . . Claire. . . my God, Claire. . . she is the only something I would have done differently, harder, more of.

Inside my head is woofing like a dog.

A fly flies around in this cardboard box of a room.

The fly lights on my foot.

There is more than enough room in here for all of us, the Queen of Soul, Tarzan swinging through the trees, the pomp and splash of the Catholic Church, all the big and little eaters.

Jesus Christ, I'm so fucking fat.

I'm fat and tired of talking to myself.

No, I'm not talking about my first sushi-nookie-teriyaki or the lying television soap opera in this late afternoon that is memory. If Merton had known Claire, then even Mr. Super Cool himself would have said right on, that is one hell of a hitter, somebody who knows how to stroke that low, hard, inside pitch out of any park. When she swung her long hair away from her face and pulled me down and kissed me, I was kissed. I know nobody not in love wants to hear this shit. No one cares about how one time when she kissed me, a hairy-sloppy-teetering-ass-grabbing-swooning-wet kiss, we fell, cracked our teeth together in such a way that I saw brain stars. When I tried to get up she grabbed me by my belt and I farted. No woman I know wants to have anything to do with men and their thing with farting, but Claire looked me right in my eyes and tugged at my belt again. I farted again.

We were in love.

Most of us are skinny dogs on the hunt. Sometimes, if we are lucky, really lucky, we might come across someone who gives us some big real of themselves.

Claire and me did the farting thing again and again until we laughed ourselves crazy sick.

Hey, maybe this guy, me, myself, I, really is crazy?

Is or are?

Hello?

Doctor Woo?

You want to see crazy?

Skip the grandstanding. Skip the flashy fisticuffs. Head straight for go and playing with yourself as if you are sitting in a nest of angry scorpions while wearing your mother's favorite butt plug. Eat hot gasoline-soaked chimichangas from Olé El Toro and light your ass on fire for dessert. Do what *you* have to do. I want to make it clear that for me, some twenty-two years ago already, Claire was the original something, my deluxe model, the one who turned on the lights.

I mean, I just slept. Now I'm awake and on my hand is the same fly from before. I recognize him and his scrawny fly arms and legs.

"Hey, fly, still hanging around, huh? Well, hang around long enough, fly, and I'm going to name you Leopold."

Moving fast, I use a boxing combo Benny at the New Rochelle Y taught me at five bucks a pop when that was one hell of a pop. Hook them to the body, hook them to the head, then bang, hang up the phone, put out the lights. Benny at seventy-nine was still booming with life. That was Benny for you, then Benny croaked.

I catch Leopold with Benny's old move.

"You *are* Leopold and you know something, Leopold, I could croak you too, but I'm not going to. Flies are but gods to children. Didn't Bill Shakespeare, or somebody else old and croaked, say something like that?"

I know I'm messing with Leopold. I know I've aged like a punk in an old movie. I got the bad teeth, a gut, and only a little understanding of making my way.

"You too, Leopold? You want to believe, Leopold?"

I want to believe.

"You can believe, baby, when I tell you it's not going to end for you in this place, not now, not today. No Vietnamese boys are out in the open losing their heads from the fire we lay down. Not on this one. No body is wrapped in a rug left on the side of the road. No bloody butcher paper is ripping open in the bottom of a dumpster to show a dead baby's tiny hand."

I let him loose.

Leopold buzzes around for the longest time before landing on Mrs. Melissa Carter's liberated employee-of-the-month mug shot somehow found decorating one bent wall of this box I call home.

"Okay, Leopold, if that didn't grab you, how about the

news that the little dog I love is everything I need. Yeah, I said love. I sometimes tongue her before I take off. Don't look so disgusted for Christ sakes, Leopold, you're a fly. Lucky for you, Leopold, I'm easy going because you are somebody, one fly, who is going to make it if I can help it, at least for one more day.

I know I have got to cool out.

I know, Doctor Woo, I know, but I just remembered another one. I remember how one hot night we sat on Claire's bed. We ate oranges for dinner and we talked about every big and little thing from our day. She had taken off everything and sweat ran in streaks down her throat and between her little breasts with the shouting nipples. When we could no longer take the heat and noise cramming her small room, we dragged the mattress onto the roof. The wind around our heads was a moan as if the sound and feel of night itself. I lay down and again and again she swept her long hair over my skin. Sleep was furious, as if I was flying with the wind. The city horns and the sirens were far away and yet we heard them so clearly. The clouds were close to our heads. The sheets were blowing. I held her and we flew while her hair surrounding us was a darkness that was a better night.

When Claire went, she went fast. By the end, I carried her everywhere. She weighed sixty-eight pounds. Her teeth fell fast out of her black gums. She was her long hair that had gone white from what they dripped into her to save her. She gave me, with all her suffering, hair by hair, cell by cell, moment by moment, the best death she could give.

Inside my head is a big want for a paper bucket of Sonny's baked beans, a side of some of those delicious smoked ribs. Sometimes one of the brothers working over the hickory pit will hand me a paper bag out the back door. Most of the time I look for us myself.

Mist rises from the pavement tonight. Mist and hunger and memory are everywhere. I can't remember seeing many flies at night. I can't remember seeing any, at least not while night diving. Where do they go? Do they get stuck in fly traffic and stare straight ahead? I bet flies know better. I know Leopold knows better, but I'll have to ask him. Sure, I hear a little dumpster buzzing now and then at night, but those are most likely the fly divers like myself, checking out what people and the other flies have left.

I stir around in the big dumpster at Sonny's with a wire shirt hanger. I come up with somebody's doggie bag. They most probably had the waitress pack it for them and forgot to take it home. Inside the bag, there are some nice smoked pork slices, a fat knobbed bone, a three piece. . .

"Yo, scrapper, what you got for me?

He is a big one, gaunt, but big. He has a long antenna. He has that monkey-walker need coming off him hard.

"What do you want, Daddy?" I say to him.

"Didn't your motherfucking mama ever teach you not to answer a question with a question?" he says. "I say what you got there for Kingsley?"

"I've got thirteen cents if you want it," I say.

"Thirteen cents, sheeeeet, old timer, don't you lie to your bigger."

"I've got change and pork slices and. . .

"Sheeeet, scrapper," says Monkey Walker, " I'm not going to ask you but one time more before I. . ."

Monkey Walker catches me with the truck antenna.

For me, it is no longer the fear of most things so much as the strangeness of them. Really, most things we do as people are so very strange.

He is fast and he catches me again, this time across the neck. He takes me down. As I go, I take his antenna. I snag it from his hands and lie on it. I doggie whimper. I beg for mercy. When Monkey Walker comes over muttering to get his piece of me, when he is close enough that I can smell the teeth rotting in his head, is when I have my good steel blade at his throat.

He slathers and wrestles a little in the sleeper hold I have on him. I shave him. I crease him a little line under his chin. He understands blood. He quits.

"Now do you run or do I slice your lungs out?" I say.

"You'd be doing me a favor," he says softly, bloody spit foaming from his lips.

"I know," I say softer.

We whisper while looking into each other's eyes. I turn him loose hard and fast, stomp him a little more. He takes it. I step on his antenna, bend it, snap it into small pieces that I throw into the tall darkness of the trees. None of it means nothing. We're a couple of bums on parade.

I walk bleeding through the mist rising like my ghost wanting out into the Spanish moss.

When I look back, we are gone.

I wake having my neck licked.

I try to move s----l----o----w.

I move s--------l--------ooooooo------w------e------r.

She laps my face. I soft dent my weight around on the hood of the old bus. I lean up. My shirt, crusty with dried blood, puckers open. The gash between my ribs has also been licked clean.

I really have gone zombie not knowing how I got this far. Most of me is hot and throbbing. All of me is hot and thirsty. I can barely breathe I'm so fevered hot.

She licks me more and I look into her loving eyes.

Why of course, Roland, you rusting-can-of-Spam-for-brains, you idjit, you fuckhead.

So I'm not the smartest guy in the world.

So this whole time it has lapped me right in the face and I never got it. Of course, she has known all along, and has just kept going with it, not letting on, enjoying it, making nothing of the mystery.

"Welcome back, darling, I missed you so," I say to this lit-tle bitch with the beautiful brown eyes. "I knew you would come back to me, but I never thought you would come as a bus-living stray."

She rests her head in my lap. I touch her soft ears, her muzzle, and I talk to her. I tell her all the things that I have wanted to tell her for so long now.

I monkey yammer all the big and little things I know she likes to hear.

I buzz.

I meow.

I talk in the voice of a flophouse down-and-outer drinking and hooting all night through the rotted canvas slung over a rope hanging between our cribs. . .

"And don't think there ain't some gamer left in me, boy, with the way this mug of mine is a pitted fright mask like I don't know it every time you and everybody else looks away from the night I jumped a flying fast train and got landed in behind an open boxcar of wood slash. By the time I caught on what was happening, I was moving too hurried to do anything other than hang on and take it, them wind-whipping splinters, for the next nineteen towns, them driven wooden needles sticking in me ev-erywhere my skin was not covered by the long sleeves of my moth-er's own work shirt."

"No tickee, Doc, no laundee."

I talk until all the voices in me give out and then I hold her. I mean, I hold her again.

When everything gets too hot for her she moves down to my feet like a dog instead of the woman I know she is. We sleep touching and unafraid. I sleep knowing we again have the chance to happily fail at our lives.

After three days and three nights of rain my cardboard

shack is soaked through and through. I watch drops running down the wall as if racing one another. I trace a finger over the welt on my neck. I watch Leopold twist together his two front legs as if thinking, worrying too.

The rain has turned the parking lot into a pond. A picnic table in back of the nursing home has been stranded by the rising water. A cat crouches on the table, an old gray cat. His tail is splayed wet and muddy.

"Hey, Leopold, I'll bet you somebody let that cat off. You want to bet that some student going home for the holidays tossed the old guy from his BMW after seeing the brothers and sisters having lunch under the trees? Some law student most likely saw a few of the brothers and sisters dressed in their nursing clothes when they were laughing it up around the picnic table because it was Friday and they were happy collecting some of the green, even if it was for taking care of old ones warehoused for death. Maybe that same budding law student named Kip or Brent or Kent thought, Hey, those easy-going nigs might also have it somewhere in their hearts to take care of an old tomcat.

"Puss, puss, puss!"

I hold up a can of meatball appetizers. I short whistle as if for a dog.

The cat watches me without moving, doubtful, even when the rain comes harder, the thunder rolls closer.

"Leopold, you can believe me, man, when I tell you I'm *really* trying. Every day I visit her and every day I try my best to get her to come back to live with us. Sure, I don't play up the fly part, no offense, but you understand. Even so, Claire won't come. She only goes so far as if she is on an invisible leash. I have even tried leading her on a rope, but she spins and leaps, chews her way loose, barks, barks, barks. She is as scared as the rest of us. She won't leave the bus. I might as well move in with her. Now don't get nervous, Leopold, I'll ask her if you can move in too.

We'll set up a tarp, lay down some boards. Her and me will get married and head straight for that place of living together where you accept so many things as if they are not really happening. Hell, I'm already there. Am I right or am I right?" Leopold flies off and lands on my cleanest dirty pants wadded up and thrown in a wet corner.

The rain is more water standing around deeper.

The cat is gone.

Claire is not where she usually is. The rain-drenched air is filled with the weeping of something wrong. No, it's not, but there is something not right. She doesn't come greet me from out of the bus and she is not standing on the moldy green upholstery and she is not barking on the bus hood or roof or climbed into the trees with the Spanish moss almost touching the rising swamp water.

"Claire!"

Snakes are in the trees, wrapping through and over and around the higher branches and each other. The snakes wriggle around, hissing when I come close.

"Where are you, Claire!"

The rain splatters on everything. I push my way back through the wet heaviness of the leaves to the highway. The slower traffic plows water. A tractor trailer blasts by with a big watery tornado of wind.

Down the highway, I see something. In the whipping grass, I see her try to get up, try to drag herself away.

"Claire, it's me, don't be afraid!"

I sit in the beaten down grass and mud. I take her in my arms and hold her. With her fur wet she is so much smaller than she looks, so much more delicate. She lays her head on my leg. Blood seeps into my pants and shoes.

"Easy, darling."

Her back end is crushed. Her breathing is bubbles of

blood. Her eyes look into my eyes as I hold her. I stroke her. I touch at her soft ears and I start to tell her. . .

"Darling, I've been making all the stops. I went to Four Star looking for something special for you, a little pepperoni pie. Leopold sends his love. He's not doing much today, you know, hanging around, doing his thing, getting in the usual shit. I saw Mrs. Melissa Carter who is in charge of the COSMETICS aisle now and asking me what happened to her Employee-of-the-Month picture that is mysteriously missing from near the cash registers, and I saw Merton, who said his home on the west side is almost all paid for. Merton said he is going to try and take it a little easier from here on in. I said to Merton I'll believe it when I see it. Don't quit on me, darling. Nishi has quit her job. Bobby, you remember Bobby in the kitchen at Sawamura, said Nishi quit and went with Trish to California. They took off just like that. Please don't, darling. That's what we should do. Bobby got a post-card from Nishi saying things are really looking up for her. Nishi wrote how she and Trish want to open a Russian, or Hawaiian, or Slovakian coffee house, I'm not sure I'm remembering right what was which. I do remember he said she wrote that they now want to spend all their time together. Please, Claire. I haven't seen the monkey walker. I haven't seen him at Sonny's or anywhere else. Please, darling. Not again, darling. I wish I could see the moon again. I want us to see the moon shining in puddles in the parking lot of Winn Dixie and believe we see the face of God. Please, darling, please. I know the rain has soaked everything, but I'll get us a better place. We can move in together like we talked about. I'll make it nice, or I can move in with you if you want. Do you remember the time Tom had to move out from his brick hole on the lower East side and we moved him in the middle of the night so the landlord wouldn't. . . Please. . ."

I forget the words.

For a moment I almost forgot how I'm going to die alone

in a room far from where I was born.

Is it okay to forget?

I know how hard it is to watch what death does to those once living. I cleaned the blood from her. I combed her hair with my fingers. I carried her back to the old bus. And for two days, like an old dog, I slept by her side.

Why wait any longer to let the world begin?

I say you can have your maggoty cake and you can eat it too. I wish I had something more to drink, paint thinner to huff up. I wish I was really hammered as I walk Southwest Sixth Street this early morning. The greed, the fear, the anger, the wild sadness are already racing around, zipping and zinging all over the place. Sam the Dealer Man is doing his job that might as well serve up as a nine to five thing the same as the keeping-on plan that Merton is on. The little dino lizards are racing around, flowing fast as nature, trying to get big so they can eat us again. The catbird is dive bombing the world.

I have come to watch the world from the lounger. I stroke tufts of rotting chair hair. I'm catching all of this morning that I can right in the chops when Suzette comes down the street. I can tell by the way she walks that she is drunk, high, that she is in a lot of pain limping along. She stumbles hard just as the sun coming up, catches her from behind, lights her up, as if her head and hair are on fire, as if she is wearing a halo of fire.

"Hey, Suzette!"

Babylon Sister looks around as if blind, as if the radiance is too great for her to see with.

"Over here, Suzette!"

"Yo, Bud," Suzette says, not really looking at me as she says it, wobbling some on her way over.

"Buddy," she says, gobbing spit for a while, stringing it down to the street. "Got any?"

"Twenty-seven cents worth," I say to her.

"You want a donate or take it out of me?" she says.

"What I got is yours," I say.

She doesn't say anything. She sways in the breeze.

"It's yours if you want it," I say. "And everything else I got too."

She laughs. She looks at me and says, "I got too much of most of everything as it is, but I could use a little more jingle jangle."

When she bends to take the change from my hand, I look at the light licking though her hair as if a grass fire sprung up again alongside the highway, or fire on a far mountain.

Once, while hitchhiking, I was picked up by a family driving an old station wagon. I remember trying to talk to the man and woman sitting in the front seat, but no matter how I tried, they would not say anything to me as if I was I-talian in their eyes. I soon fell asleep in the backseat, the little girl sleeping with her head on my lap, while the man drove us. I slept and slept. When we stopped some where deep in that night, I remember coming to and looking out the window. There were other cars and trucks stopped, right in the dusty road. The little girl was awake too. She pointed out the window and said something I could not understand. I looked some more and saw that the mountain far below was on fire. Smoke drifted over us. People got out of their cars and trucks with crates of squawking chickens in the back. We got out too, the little girl and me, while the man and the woman and the boy stayed back waiting in the station wagon. The little girl and me were out among the others not saying anything either, not doing anything other than watching the fire. I remember watching for a long time, nobody going nowhere, nobody saying nothing, when cattle began coming up the road. Bellowing cattle herded up the dirt road around the cars and farm trucks stopped in the darkness. The little girl began to cry, and for the first time in a long time, too long really for me to remember when, I cried.

Suzette strolls away, coughing and laughing.

Her hair ablaze, Suzette walks without looking back.

The old grey cat is still hanging on, hanging around. I see him lying on the picnic table in the late afternoon sunlight. I talk to him from out my cardboard back door sawed crooked with a broken-tipped steak knife. The cat takes his time, stretches. The cat comes over when he wants to come over. He purrs and rubs against my legs. His hide is salted lumpy with buckshot. His big yellow eyes burn as if smaller suns.

"This is Leopold," I tell him. "Now be nice."

The cat acts as if he is listening to me, but I know better. Leopold knows better too and keeps his distance.

I get the dented can I fished loose from one of the dumpsters at Winn Dixie. I open the twelve-ounces of chunk light tuna in water and I set the can on the floor. I step back.

The cat looks at me, at Leopold buzzing around.

The cat eats.

FISHING, WITH WHAT I HAVE

My grandfather, the fisherman in our family, stood in his backyard of afternoon light. My grandfather waited for me in the light off whitewashed clapboards of fence and barn. From the back porch, I could see him the way I knew him best, wearing the soft clothes he wore, holding his hat. My grandfather Caron was the stander at the stove, the sweeper and card player those summer afternoons with Grandma Rose and the other women with their shoes slipped off in the grass under the card table in my grandfather's backyard. Grandmother Caron, my mother too, all those other women, had something in them different from my grandfather and from me–they were different quiet with different secrets, but that is a different story. For this story, my Grandmother Caron was the one snapping the teeth of my suspenders into biting up my pants. She was the one who had my baseball cap on me.

Out in the heat and light, my grandfather put on his hat. His hand held my hand. His strength and his tallness had us walking on the grass. Our walking shadow was a fisherman, who had pulled up a boy on the hook of the fisherman's hand. Our shadow disappeared into the bigger shadow of my grandfather's barn. His ladders and lawnmower, his Ford, seemed to me to wait for him from the deeper shadows. Climbing–with my grandfather helping me, boosting up my backside–inside the Ford, the seat sank under me as if I was crawling, or swimming, in the belly of a giant fish that we were letting swallow us. From before, my grandfather's Ford fish had swallowed his cob pipe and his fold of tobacco, a penny become underwater green I found between the seats, a pistachio nut. I stood myself against my grandfather starting the Ford. From that springy height, I could see into the back seat, see his fishing pole and reel, his blanket.

Light came from everywhere onto and off the shiny metal and glass of his car while grandfather drove us. His Ford finned us through the deep water of familiar streets. The salty red from the shelled nut was sucked out. The shell too hard for me to crack was spit into my hand and wiped on my pants while I looked at my grandfather under his hat. He was my mother's blue eyes and her nose on a man. His eyes and the rest of him steered us through a rattling of light, the tunneling of shadow from trees taller than he was. I rested my small arm over his suspenders, which were bit with tiny metal fish teeth wider than my suspenders. My small fingers felt the way over the hills of him until my hand was out the window. Air blowing cooler, heavy as water, pushed at my hand. I felt where we were.

At the bottom of the hill was MacSheen's Store where Grandmother Caron bought me red sodas. The store was carried off behind us. The world itself was water sliding around us. The house where my mother was born went by. The place where grandfather got gas for his Ford came gliding up and by. I knew the Dairy Bar was coming up. With my hand, I could feel the wind as if from the Dairy Bar sweeping around the bend. The Dairy Bar had nearly floated by us when grandfather slowed the car, air whistling to a flutter in the window vent. He turned the steering wheel with his hands that tied knots for fishing. The car popped, pinged over gravel. We quieted to a stop. Through the glass of the windshield, through the sunlight on the Ford's green hood, through the big windows of the Dairy Bar, I saw people sitting at the counter on swivel stools. I saw a man with too much potato in his mouth putting some potato back on his spoon.

"When you eat pistachios," my grandfather said to me, "try not to wipe your fingers on your pants."

I felt for the penny in my pocket. Grandfather held open the car door for me stepping down. The heat was like heat from an oven, as if Grandmother Caron's stove was held open huge on the summer afternoon. Grandfather guided us between the sides of cars too hot to touch.

Inside, in the cool of the Dairy Bar, I touched, pulled and let go the metal knobs of the cigarette machine holding my father's Lucky Strikes. A woman sitting in a booth laughed a croaky laugh with cigarette smoke wisping out from between her teeth. Dirty dishes and cups, a spoon, clacked under the counter wiped clean for my grandfather and for me. Grandfather helped me up, lifted me to sitting at the counter. Grandfather sat, put his hat on the counter. He ran a hand on the gleam of his head. Light chopped from off the blades of the ceiling fan at the sweating metal of the milkers, at more knives and forks and spoons set out for us, at the coffee pot, at my grandfather's head. The ceiling fan cooled the sweaty band of hair around my head where I had taken off my baseball cap.

"Hello, Leo," the woman wearing all blue on the other side of the counter said to my grandfather. "Hot enough for you?"

"Hello, Adelle," my grandfather said to the woman. "Hot enough to keep me and my boy sitting with you a while."

"Lucky for the brookies," the woman said and smiled in such a way that her smile seemed to include all of us.

My grandfather laughed and said, "Lucky for us."

When the woman asked my grandfather what we wanted to have, my grandfather told her, "My boy likes to fish for himself."

I told the woman what I wanted. My grandfather told her he wanted a slice of apple pie with a scoop of vanilla ice cream.

While waiting, I smelled cooking egg and coffee smells. I turned around and around on my swivel seat. I turned all the way around. I saw my grandfather in the light striking him again and again.

The woman brought my grandfather's pie and ice cream first. He waited for her to bring me mine before he would eat. His vanilla ice cream ran melting while he waited. My grandfather was the one who watched over me. He was the one who waited for me to take the first bite.

A man no longer the father he was drove us fast. A flock of birds in their little lives flew faster trying to keep ahead of us. From where I sat by the window, I saw that the man had my father's face. His smoke and his Ballantine beer smells were my father's smells. His hair, his glasses, his teeth had some secret I was afraid of, a secret I knew was different from the secrets of women or what was known between my grandfather and me. The man drove us in my father's car by broken cornfields. My grandfather was in the same ground of another field. His fishing pole and reel were cobwebbed in the shadows of his barn. I looked at the man wearing my father's face and hands. When he turned his head and saw me looking at him, I looked out the car window. Sunlight came through the clouds the same as in the painted picture of Jesus above my Grandma Roses' bed. In that picture, Jesus was a fisherman held upon the water by the giant sunlit hands of his father.

More little birds burst up over a cornfield. The birds headed for some woods. I looked at the man turning the steering wheel with the hand with the ring on the finger that showed he was married to my mother. I drew lines on the fogging window with one of my fingers.

The window had fogged up again by the time the man stopped the car under trees by the side of the road. Outside the car, I stood in leaves lifting in the wind. The light coming through the leaves was such it seemed that I could look and not miss looking at any thing in the world. The man smoked a Lucky Strike while walking in the wet leaves up ahead. The leaves scuffed up dry from underneath smelled of summer afternoons. I looked back between branches blown clean of their leaves. Ahead, the man was walking by a pond with ghostly old stumps.

Things came to this: leaves of red and gold on a pond. Between and on the leaves, on the water mirrored with light, a boy with his father's eyes, his teeth, looked up at me looking down. Trees with a few leaves seemed to float upside down. Clouds crossed quietly as if in some other wind. Through and under this other world, mossy twigs and leaves rested rotting. The boy touched at the bones of his face.

I looked up and saw the man weeping, touching at the water with a stick.

Fish, tiny fish, sprayed from the water into the air.

"Did you see that?" he said to me.

I once saw my father naked, crawling on the floor, eating what was left in ashtrays, hitting his head on the wall over and over leaving hair and blood on the wallpaper until my mother called the doctor, who came and took him away for a long time.

I sat in my dead father's canoe out in the cold in a field. Shadows darkened the snow where the field ended, where the woods began. The hills and sky were losing light. What was colder, the sky or the snow? When I moved, the canoe my father never got to go fishing in creaked on snow so cold and hard the crust could cut me. The cold had crawled up from the metal of the canoe into my father's boots that I wore, into the three pairs of socks.

Wind and colder came with the going of the light. The few leaves left curling on branches chittered. My lips tried to warm my teeth. My coat sleeves were tubes where I tried to work warm air. I remember thinking that if I died then, out in the field or down by the river, maybe no one would find me until spring. Cattails with calling blackbirds would grow out of me, up through my soggy old coat. Someone would call my mother and she would have to come fetch what was left of me–a twig, some hair, a sock–from out of the cattail thicket. I heard branches skinned in ice clicking against other icy branches. A dog howled somewhere down the hill through the woods. Some old tracks, the hollowed of the canoe's run again and again, crusted from the field and down through the hard snow in the woods. I poked at the crust with the poling stick. I chipped ice chunks while the cold held in the metal of the canoe burned at my backside through my grandfather's rotting old blanket.

The fire whistle set the dog to howling some more. The dog seemed to howl the news that it was time for my Grandma Rose and the others to get out of work. I could see down the hill through the woods to the road, to the roofs of row houses along the river frozen over, to the mill where Grandma Rose worked. Getting to work, shoving off, I pushpoled from on my knees. The canoe, taken, scraped faster along the crust. The windy cold in my mouth was a fishhook. The cold on my teeth was the sound of the push pole ticking on icy crust. I closed my mouth, warmed my teeth with my tongue, while the canoe scraped down through the woods closing in on me faster. I pushed, again, harder, dodging trees.

At the bottom of the hill, it seemed as if something was waiting in the woods to get me. Something, it seemed, was getting ready to jump me taking aim at a hump of snow with my poling stick become a spear.

I dragged the canoe behind a log by the side of the road. I crossed the road trying to stamp feeling into my feet. I clunked along on the ice blocks that had been my father's boots, making my way behind the row houses and past a dog chained to a barrel. I was in the car wrecks river-banked before the dog let loose with a howl. On the other side of the river, the mill windowed down light. Women were walking through that light on the snow. I could see her coat, Grandma Rose in her coat with her own say-so and secrets walking with the other women and men to cars snow covered in the parking lots. The night's coming on was helped, I believed, by the lights of the mill.

With that coming-on feeling on my shoulders and on my neck, I started across the icy river. The colder was colder than before. The ice groaned, moved, under me. I kept going, slower, tapping at the splintering ice with my spear as I went. A bubble as big as I was moved under the ice under his boots. I did not call to my grandmother, who I could see so clearly. I did not yell to her or to the other women waiting while the men brushed snow from the cars. The boy I was, my father's son—and not some drowned dog, not a fisherman caught in the long weeds in the cold dark under the ice—would not and did not call for help from those soon shouldered snug into cars heading for home.

More than halfway across the broad slide of the river, in what little light was left from the sky, I saw a glint.

Again, under the dark ice, there was a flash, a metal glint. The metal moved and I saw it was a fish.

On my knees, I looked through the ice. I could see the eyes, the gills and fins, the tiny teeth of a fish. I tocked the ice with my stick. A bubble billowed long. I tocked again. The fish stayed caught.

From where I sit writing this, I can see out the window. I can see the house across the street. The house is rotting clapboards and flaking paint in the afternoon light. A woman and a boy come out of the house, the boy shading his face with a hand while looking up at the woman. Holding hands, talking, the woman and the boy go out the gate and along the sidewalk. I cannot see them any more.

I look down at what I have written, and I know that I am caught. I know that I am not getting away from any of it.

THE LIVING

I lived. Because of the rain and the cold and where I was, I walked and ran. The blowing rain rattled storefront gates, poured into the darkened buildings where hardly anybody lived. Neon now and then was the only light sunk into all that darkness. Neon was slicked on the black street in the shapes of puddles. I hurried. I ran for as long as I could and there was no one around. No junkies drifted in the darkness with the rise and fall of smack in their veins. No men were standing around a trash barrel with flames leaping out. There was no one for a long time, and then there was.

A man was up ahead, staggering at me in the rain as if he was drunk, or hurt in some way. He was wearing a suit coat under a long overcoat, both open to the roaring night. As he made his way closer to me, I could see his necktie blowing loose. He tripped up to me and stopped. I looked into his wet face and he looked into mine. I pushed past him, splashed past him. His blond hair whipping about his face in the wind and the rain was the same as I had remembered, his face was the same. His eyes and his mouth were what it was about him that looked so different to me.

The rain turned to snow in the little time it took for me to cross the street. Flakes as big as baby fists struck at me from out of the darkness. Snowflakes held wet on my eyelashes. The snow brought a new light to the darkness, and that light was the same as the dying flesh of Christ. Something like that, or something else. I was tired. I was afraid.

It was him.

I knew it was him, or his ghost.

I turned and looked. He was down the street, already farther along than I thought he would be, or could be, in the little time I had taken to pass him. Farther down than a dead man should be is what I thought. I really didn't know. I stopped and watched as he slipped and fell to his hands and knees in a puddle that seemed to have filled up around him. His necktie hung down as if hanging him, drowning him. I watched as the snow covered him and the raw blackness of the street. I watched as he pulled himself up and stumbled on in the blinding night.

The last time I saw him alive was in the hospital. The red-headed nurse behind the counter was doing three or four things at once: talking on the phone, giving directions to an orderly wearing a big diamond stud in his nose while pushing a gurney loaded with a mutilated birthday cake and balloons of various bright colors, reading a patient's chart pulled part way from a manila folder, those kind of things, when the nurse said into the phone, "That's all very well and good for you to say, Mrs. Vitello, but as far as I'm concerned, we're doing the best we can. Now, hold on," and then the nurse said to me, "Okay, officer, I know who you're here for. Just do what you have to do and keep out of my hair."

Not too long ago on the subway train, a skinny guy wearing a hospital name bracelet and slippers made of green tissue paper shuffled over to me minding my own business. He pointed to a scar puckering fat from his ear to his throat. I don't know why, but I thought that the wisdom of a whole life would come corkscrewing up out of his scar, as it might out of another mouth, in time to help me live or die. Instead, he said to me more or less what they always say to me.

"Hey, I know you, man," he said. "I can smell you out, and you either cop or con just let loose of the joint."

This sort of thing happens to me often, and almost always with somebody I have never seen before, some big dark guy or another one of the trembling lost or hunted coming up to me, falling into step alongside, and telling me about how he has gone straight, clean, etc. The way I look with my Boston Blackie moustache is one reason why. My hanging around cop shops for more than ten years while working for newspapers is also probably why. All the murdered and the murderers, the jumpers, the cutters, the torch jobs, the drive-bys, the drownings, the motorcycle wrecks and the car wrecks that I saw and wrote about are the biggest reasons why I guess so many of these slaughtered souls must think I am the law.

The nurse in charge that night, when she first looked up at me from all that she was doing, had the kind of face that promised me what everybody wants–I could still remember then what everybody wants–before that face–beautiful, powerful–composed itself back to dealing with the dull terror of working in a hospital. Before I could plead for an explanation from her of absolutely everything, the nurse said to me what she said–wrongly believing, I guess, that I looked like a cop, or like someone who had a clue.

I went down the dirty corridor from room to room in that place of no more pretending.

In the first room, a woman, I could not tell you her age, somewhere in her middle twenties, moaned from a bed. Her legs were covered with scabs, with clots of dried blood and pus under a shroud of sheet, which I went over to and lifted. The smell from under the sheet was the same as rotting meat found furry black on the kitchen counter after coming home from a long vacation. She moaned even more when I lowered the sheet.

In another room where the tile floor was one big drain, there was a boy with a bluish head, a massive head and a body shrunken to the size of a baby's body. The boy was wired to a machine that beeped. The boy's head could have been another balloon getting bluer and bluer, a balloon the orderly had somehow forgotten to wheel off on the gurney with the cake wreck and the other balloons. The boy looked back at me with what I wanted to believe was a kind of blaming hatred.

The one I had come for, other than for myself, was in the last room I looked in. I can tell you his name now. He was my friend, and he was the one behind the cloth partition I pulled aside. He was not dead, not yet. The back of his head was held together with gauze pads. A respirator mask was taped over his nose and mouth. The sound was of his breathing amplified as Bret's lungs billowed open with oxygen, the respirator machine loudly clicking on and off with every breath. His rising and falling chest was narrow and white.

As I said, I had worked for newspapers for a long time. I had educated myself by studying the daily police blotter. One lesson I still remember was of the jumper pulled from an iced-up river. The hook had snagged deep in the dead man's mouth, yanking up half a grin along with the heavy rest of him. His hair swung icy, throwing droplets of melting river water. His long hair swung the same way his frozen-hard body swung from the chain and the shining grappling hook. He was dragged up hand over hand by three cursing, gasping cops standing on a bridge. The cops hauled him up clunking hard, smacking things, and dumped him on the steel girders of the bridge: a human person about to become part of the grainy landscape, a photograph for the daily newspaper that almost no one reads anymore. I had taken several photographs before I realized he was someone I knew. He was the owner of the gas station on the corner near where I was living at the time. He had been a big, backslapping kind of a guy who a month before had changed the oil, the points and plugs in my four-hundred dollar Buick, and had told me that a coffee black, and a ten were enough to cover the job. I found out later that what he'd done to himself was over his woman. He sure was something to see. His eyes were gone, eaten by something. Most of one cheek and the muscle underneath flapped to show bone laid back bare and white by the hook. His hands were swollen a purpling-blue darker than the skin of the big-headed boy in the hospital, closer to the color of ice water in my grandmother's heavy glass tumblers kept wrapped in old newspapers. Ice water flowed off him. Water trickled from out of his mouth and out of his socks the color of river weeds. A minnow gilled its last after flipping onto the bridge from some where inside his coveralls. I flinched when something twisted itself from out of the dead man's mouth in a way I had thought was his tongue, or more water, something twisting and moving in such a way that I thought more hook was somehow ripping free before I understood that what was wriggling out of the dead man's mouth and down his chest, trailing long wisps of flesh, was an eel whose head a cop crunched off with a boot.

"Shit, we could eat that," one of the cops had said. Another cop blew a fart of laughter. Everybody on the bridge laughed.

Doing that kind of work, I learned a thing or two and I saw some of the dead. There was no doubt about it, their faces were very different from any living person I have ever seen: their eyes open, their mouths open, the weight of them. But they were all empty. When you are with the dead, there is the forgotten knowledge that you soon remember, the little flurry of discovery you might laugh about, that nothing much matters except that *you* are breathing and alive.

My friend Bret was alive from the pure oxygen pumping into his brain. I was about to put my hand against the whiteness of his chest when I looked up and saw the orderly watching me from the shadows of the corridor. I saw his diamond nose stud gleaming, catching and throwing light from some hidden source whose origin I could not find in the very real darkness of that place. Before I could ask the orderly anything about the light his diamond had captured and lost, he walked away singing, softly, gloriously. The darkness closed up around us again while I heard the orderly's voice going softer and softer until I heard only the whooshing and clicking of the respirator. It was then that I remembered what it was we all want that the nurse's face had for an instant both asked for and promised me: the hope of perfect understanding and acceptance. I wondered what this scene must look like to someone else, how we must have looked like a photograph of people you don't want to have anything to do with. As if from the corridor, I could see myself as maybe the orderly had seen me, sitting on the bed with my hand outstretched and shaking over Bret's chest. I saw myself wanting Bret to rise and look at me from wherever it was he had gone. After a while, after I had once more lost faith in myself, I pretended Bret was no farther away from me than the other side of the jagged line you sometimes see drawn through a comic strip panel in a newspaper.

I don't know much about this night and the next early morning, other than that we were both alive when I sat on his bed in the hospital in the darkness. I know the memory–the weight within me of what was, and what no longer is–and I wonder how so far, after everything, I have remained among the living and not among the dead.

For a while, all of us lived together at 107th Street. Both the street, 107th at Amsterdam, and the building we lived in, were the kinds of places you either came to at the very beginning or at the very end of something. I think all of us–Bill, J.D., Bret and myself–believed something big was going to happen to us. We were either at the start of some wonderful opportunity or of some terrible injury; like someone down to his last dollar in change finding a twenty in the ripped lining of an old coat, or someone who has lost all control of a fast moving car just as he enters the dreamy understanding of oh, no, my head is smashing through the windshield. I think I knew even then that we were already casualties helping each other as I waited for the end.

In those days, the street was owned by drug dealers and their boys, who, I know for a fact, have murdered people the same as you or me for a night's beer money. My first week living on that street I saw three people get shot. I don't mean just hearing gunshots, which was something we heard all night every night, with the pops, booms, the crackling of automatic gunfire louder and more frequent near dawn. What I mean is, I saw murder on a hot afternoon two days after I had moved to 107th Street when the sidewalk on Amsterdam Avenue was crowded with sweaty people on their way home from work. A tricked-out car squealed smoking tires along the avenue while four or five handguns and shotguns jutted out of the car's windows. Rap music pounded from the car with the bass rumbling so loudly that I could feel the vibrations in my teeth and bones. To the sound of that mauling music, I saw one of the dealer boys, sitting lookout on a crate across from where I was walking, get jacked right out of his sneakers by the slapping slugs. Another boy, shot and bleeding from his mouth, crawled along the sidewalk. I ran without looking back. Flowers, hand-written notes, Virgin Mary prayer cards, were underfoot on that short stretch of Amsterdam Avenue for a week or two after I saw this happen, as they were after other things happened too, none of which appeared in any of the newspapers.

The night after I saw the drive-by, I was looking out the dirty windows of the tenement where we lived when I saw three men chasing another man. One of the chasers pointed a handgun and shot the first man, who tripped wounded and fell between the sidewalk and a parked car. The shooter walked up to the fallen man, rested the handgun on the man's chest with an easy, almost negligent grace, and fired two more shots. From where I was crouching by the window, I could see the man's shirt burning in circles of blue fire. His killers laughed and acted out for one another their roles in putting him down while they strolled back to the corner bodega and to the line of buyers trapped in their own burning circles–the blue glowing bowls of their crack pipes wrapped in tin foil, wraiths not yet released from their bodies clapping and whistling for the celebrating, high-fiving killers.

The tenement we lived in was about the same as most of the tenement buildings on the block. The only way in or out, other than to go out a window and down a fire escape or up to the roof, was the broken, hard-banging front door. Once inside the building, you noticed how the doors to most of the apartments were covered with steel plating to protect the dealers, the Dominicans and Cubans and Puerto Ricans, the young and rarely innocent and the very old, the old getting older fast and young getting stronger, the few ancient Irish left behind who would dodder, blinded, onto the streets only around noon for the little cans of cat food they survived on. Even at noon, the stairwell in our building was dark, the light bulbs on every landing broken so you could not see the bodies brushing wet against you in the darkness until their skin was against your skin. You could not at first see the faces of the men, and the women on their knees in front of the men, and then you could. You could see the men gaping, their tongues out and their eyes rolling as if they were being hanged, or drowned. Their faces would bob under into deeper shadow, twist back up so I could again see their faces, their mouths grunting and gasping and calling out. From the darkness of another landing, hidden, or not, I watched and breathed in the sweat and cat piss smells, the cooling crack smell the same as incense used at funerals.

I would watch their resurrection to the seeming impossibility of this human life.

The apartment we lived in was long and narrow as if an old subway car had run off the nearby IRT Broadway tracks and was buried in a collapsing building in Spanish Harlem. Cast iron pipes ran under the ceiling and down the walls. The pipes, the walls, the floor, were covered with six or seven layers of flaking paint. Every stick of furniture was broken. The carpet was napped-up where bullets had traveled through the ceiling of the apartment below, bullets splintering through the floorboards before whapping, caught, in the rotting carpet. Cigarette smoke had been blown over everything for years and years.

There were other things too, things that I have never told anyone before now, a sense of something, others, I could somehow feel, really feel, and sometimes see, as if these others were the afterimage burning on the tube of an old black and white television. There was what remained of a boy studying a leather-bound book in the wavering circle of a sputtering oil lamp, pimps wearing bowler hats and fur-collared coats while snapping down cards, drunks huddled together over a bucket of sudsy bathtub beer: all dead for many years by the time we lived there, and yet something of each of them remained in those rooms, their ghosts, or whatever you want to call them, that I felt as suffocation, a slipping under into the layers and layers of lives long ago and yet somehow present.

Every moment I was there, I knew my life was the same as the smoke and the dust settled thick over the lampshades, over everything in the apartment. The dust of years somehow lost sifted through my veins.

As for the others during our time together at that place, I can only say what happened to them. Bill soon married and got out. J.D. left to travel around. Bret turned twenty-two or twenty-three, something like that. I waited, and ate rotting fruit. I was at the end of what I had had with a woman. I had run around on her and when she caught me she tried to claw my eyes out, which I could take. Her being near forty and desperate for a baby is what got to me. Her desperation, along with two or three other things—my not having much money, and little chance of getting any, my fear, were what brought me to 107th Street.

Before he was ash and bone scattered by his family over

a grassy hill in the park, before the light from that diamond, Bret was someone who lived in the bigger back room of our tenement apartment. Why there at 107th Street? I would like to ask him that now, and why then, as if somehow knowing those answers could tell me anything. I am not sure why Bret was living there. His youth, and his wanting some sort of adventure maybe, his not knowing what he wanted and trying to find his way. I know he was someone I was not necessarily looking to find, with his silliness—a cheese doodle in his shorts as if he had a tiny hard on—with his stories and laughter and his Alissa girl. Together, holding hands, Bret and Alissa would stroll to the corner bodega for ice cream at one o'clock in the morning. We would tell them not to go. They held hands as if they were children who believed what they had read in some book of fairy tales and they skipped over those bloody sidewalks past dealer boys in hooded sweatshirts who waited there to hunt them down and eat them, who wanted to turn their small-town goodness, their innocence, into predatory flesh and bones.

Even during the day, when the Irish old timers, starving without a sound, would venture fearfully from their seven-dollar rooms into the blazing sunlight of the world, Bret stood out as if he was a gleaming, blond stalk of Indiana corn suddenly poking up through a crack in the street. He was a boy from a music video version of the world. When we walked those streets and sidewalks together, I could see how the dealers and their younger runners, the junkies, the ranting panhandler who would sometimes hang by his legs from a telephone pole on the corner, naked and drunk, would all watch Bret, trying to figure out what he was doing and why he was with a cop. They would wait for an opening before coming up to us, try bumming coin or cigs, and say things to me like, "Chief, I got friends, I got *real* friends, who know I'm okay."

Another time, we were walking back to where we lived when a junkie, bleeding all over as if he'd been the loser in an ice-pick fight, stumbled up to us. The bleeder went toe to toe with

Bret and laid this out, "If you don't eat me right now, you're meat, dead meat."

I would tell them once, just once, as I told the bleeder that time, and they would startle away from us before taking a sudden interest in a tied shoelace, or their fingernails, or a mailbox. Who can honestly, truly blame any of them for trying? What I guess they saw in Bret was his yearning, his belief that things would somehow work out and everything in life that he wanted to do was still very much possible. The truth is, I no longer know what they saw in him. Maybe they saw in Bret what I saw in Bret. The drug market on 107th Street at Amsterdam Avenue is like any other place–life eating life. What is different there is how fast the whole thing happens. Kill one dealer and three more take over.

Sometimes, when I was alone in that place where we lived and wondering where the people who knew me when I was know-able were, I would go into Bret's room and look at his things. His neckties, his shirts and pants, were all cleaned and pressed and hanging on a clothes rack. On the desk were photographs, snap-shots of Alissa, a pack of bubble gum, a tin ray gun that whirred and lit up when you pulled the trigger, an Indiana University pen and pencil set, stamps and coins and picture postcards, Star Trek action figures, a plastic snow globe, things a boy would have who had a whole life to dream into.

I would shake the globe and watch what were supposed to be snowflakes, glitter flakes, blurring around what were supposed to be the famous buildings of New York. Fake snow settled over the fake, tiny city. I would shake the globe again and watch the silvery flakes swirl around what I wanted to believe was the mag-nitude of God's love where God sees everything and sees the good despite everything.

Outside our tenement apartment, the forests were far away and I was no longer any good with a gun. On the side-walks and on the streets, the summer heat and everything else were murderous.

There was the time we met at La Bella China, or Casa China, one of the three or four places near where we lived where we could have two eggs any way we wanted, also rice and beans, a basket of the hot bread that they make the delicious Sandwich Cubanos with, a soda and a couple of coffees or a cafe con leche with caramel when somebody else was buying, all brought to our table by lovely Latina-China girls, who smiled at us–the whole amazing thing for four or five dollars. We had already eaten, Bill and I had already eaten, with Bret finding us after Bill had picked-up the check. Bret was wearing some kind of overhauls or bibbed shorts that afternoon, the kind of sunsuit you might see on a tod-dler, on my two-year-old nephew Aaron standing at his and his sister's toy box, and not on a man, not on a white man, and not on streets where school girls slashed you with razor blades. I saw this happen to an old man early one evening after I had gotten my rotting oranges. I stepped around his spraying blood. From what I could tell, the four girls cut the old man, razored him some bleeding lines through his thin windbreaker because he had the audacity to wear his white skin while carrying home a carton of milk and the Sunday newspapers after the sun had gone down. Everybody in La Rosita or Flora De Mayo or wherever it was we were eating that afternoon, was looking at Bret, the Latina-China girls gawking at him in his outfit before they turned away while holding their long hair over their mouths to hide their laughter.

I said to Bret something like, "Bret, all you need to com-plete your little get-up is a big bonnet, and then we can call you Baby Huey."

The way he looked, his blonding height, his little bibbed shorts, and the meanness I had said to him, broke up everybody in the place. He really did look like a big baby needing only a rat-tle and a nippled bottle to finish the joke. Everybody, all the kill-ers, and hustlers, the waitresses, the down-and-outers, the insane, were laughing at him. Bret was laughing too and his laughter was as real as the smell of pork chops frying and the cafe con leche hot on our tongues, or as the loveliness of those Latina-China girls talking to me with my not understanding a word they said, and not caring, just feeling less like a poor leper in their presence, in the grace they gave us.

There was also the time not long after the time we had all laughed at Bret. I had been eating little more than fruit for over two weeks, losing pounds fast. I was down from 197 pounds to 162, losing more than I wanted or needed to lose. Fresh fruit is good for what I have, the doctors tell me, and the rotting fruit I was eating went as far as anything went on the twenty-dollar bill my grandmother had sent me from the change she would find in the washing machines and dryers while working her three, ten-hour days a week at the Thrifty-Bundle Laundromat.

I have no doubt my grandmother can whip your grand-mother.

She could then and she can now.

She was eighty-four then, slopping piles of laundry in scalding water and bleach, lifting bags of stinking clothes weigh-ing almost as much as she weighed so she could send me that twenty. I was down to the change sliding along the top of my tilting-broken chest of drawers. When the Koreans running the fruit stands would quit trying to smell me out for a cop and turn their backs, I would gouge down a banana peel, dig a thumb deep into an already over-ripe peach or plum, so they might sell the damaged fruit to me cheaper, which is what they usually did for my not stealing from them outright. One night, when they did not want to put up with my clumsiness and I did not have the guts to steal their fruit, and when the change from the last twenty my grandmother had earned the hard way and had sent me was about all gone, I dragged myself hungry back to where we lived. I let myself in, felt along the walls to the room where I slept with a hunting knife under my pillow. I sneaked a little light on. On the bed, on my tattered blanket, and under Bret's snow globe, was the miracle of a hundred dollars as if given to me by the god inside that little plastic world.

There was also the time we were sitting in our apartment in the darkness. We had been watching the street below from one of the windows in the front room. We were watching the dealers selling their three-dollar vials of Black Top crack cocaine they kept in the frame of a stripped car under a shot-out streetlight. Many of the buyers were bent nearly double in their agony, little more than shadows pushing bodies before them until they could hide somewhere and take a smokey hit. We sat watching, doing nothing, dredging up brief dreams. We were voices floating in the darkness once in a while.

"Do you feel it too?" Bret asked.

"Feel what?" I said.

Bret didn't say anything. I could see him–his face and his hands in the dark. A light was coming from him, out of him, so that I could see him even in the full darkness of that place where so much was and was not hidden to me.

"Feel what?" I said, knowing of the boy under the light of that oil lamp I told you about, and about the others in their time and ours, and not telling him, and not telling Bret how as a newspaperman I would sometimes sneak into the darkroom after the day's paper had been put to bed. I would print up some of the day's photographs on special paper I would hold to diffused light. I would watch the silver halide crystals cluster into the darkening ghosts of Rotarians at their weekly luncheon, a young fisherman holding high his prize-winning fish, two girls sitting headless in their father's car the older girl had failed to drive under a tractor trailer.

"It's the crazy feeling that I'm being called, but I'm not answering," Bret said.

"Called to what, by what?" I asked, looking at him, his flesh luminous in the darkness.

"I don't know," Bret said. "I told you, I'm not answering."

As I told you, I moved to 107th Street after my girlfriend went wild wanting a baby–something to keep herself less alone for a little longer, something I know would have had me closing in even faster on more cowardice. When she got even wilder, angrier, after finding what I had written to another woman, Eva told me, "I hope your cancer kills you."

What I have not told you is that despite her scars, her beauty was such that before I left I smashed around at my Charlie Parker and Puccini music with a hammer. I ate a big pot of black beans and garlic and then cleared out for good.

At the newspapers I worked for, death was something poked at from the safe distance of words that meant very little, words such as, "died unexpectedly," or "passed away suddenly." My editors told me this was done out of respect for the family. Most newspaperman I knew tried to do the best they could on the obits they worked on, getting all the so-called facts in, a summary of somebody's whole life in six or ten inches of column space in the fifteen or thirty or forty-five minutes we had before deadline.

Most of us try to stay away from the hard knowledge of what really happens when we die as if we are innocent bystanders to even our own lives. We try to carry on as if nothing as bad as death will ever happen to us. If we are lucky, just more dates and names and other messy print will come off on our hands from the back page of the newspaper's second section, after the weather and before sports. We will continue reading of wars done, loves done, lives done.

I have tried to come up with words that might show you how he died. The words used by his doctor are like the sun in winter, something I can see, but not feel.

His brain quit, closed down, could no longer do anything

more with the oxygen pumping into his lungs from the respirator, and he died.

A cop was the one who told me much later, after everything, what happened.

"Yeah, we pinched the fucks, but we couldn't get nothing to stick," the cop told me in return for something I once did for him so way-back-when that neither of us could remember what the something was. The cop told me this some time after I had gotten away from 107th Street and I was living in an office I had to leave during the day and come back to at night after business hours were over. This was after Bret had moved with Alissa to one of the better neighborhoods where he should have been safe, where he should have made it. Another something that I have forgotten to tell you is how Bret was also looking for work at the time he gave me the hundred dollars he left under the snow globe on my bed, and how I am sure he could have more than used the money. He never said anything to me about paying him back, paying him for what he had given me that had kept me from joining the ranks of the dead with their faces looking the same as ice painted yellow while they knocked on the walls of that place where we had all lived together.

The cop told me Bret and Alissa had returned from running in the park. They had gone for a run on a day that I believe I really do remember, that I want to remember, as one of those days at the end of summer when sunlight and shadows are large and all around you, the light and shadows larger than the high rise buildings, the falling light and shadows so seemingly absolute, with those shadows moving slowly, absolutely, while there is the dry leaf smell, the lazy quiet, the almost Paradisal heat. The cop told me that following their late afternoon run in the park, Bret and Alissa had stopped at a grocery store. Bret was seen by witnesses as he stood outside the store in the shade of the building, eating a popsicle, plastic grocery bags at his feet. Witnesses also later told the cops how Bret was seen minding his own business when two young men walking by went out of their way to kick the grocery bags, sending apples and oranges rolling along the sidewalk and into the gutter. Bret said something to them. The bigger one hit Bret. The bigger one walked up to Bret and sucker punched him. Bret fell and struck the back of his head on the sidewalk. Alissa was coming out of the store when she saw Bret go down, saw the two young men running from what they had done to her toy collector, her laugher, cheese doodler, who was already twitching colder by the time she held him.

They got his killer, the cop told me. The cops got the guy and locked him up and saw he had no record, no warrants, nothing, and a grand jury agreed the killer did not have intent to murder, so the courts and the cops sent him home. The killer went home to work behind the counter in his old man's delicatessen a few blocks from his victory over a popsicle eater. Bret became blowing ash, little shards and knobs of bone scattered under trees in Central Park, his soul leaking away into sunlight.

The doors to the subway car closed behind me. I had pushed my way on in a hurry yesterday morning and I was the last one in the car before the doors closed. I held on, late for work, and watched a cop leaning up against a door at the other end of the subway car. There was something about the cop, who was most likely half my age, which made him look older than his years. I could see what they see in me in him, but I am not a cop. I am not a newspaperman anymore and I have not worked for newspapers for a long time. I am an office boy closing in on forty, who, once in a while, will get up the courage to steal books from where I work to sell for train fare or to eat a little better. What I could see in the cop was that we had both seen a lot of things and we had both come to understand how most things do not work. Most things do not come close to working as they should and none of them can be saved.

The train car we were in whammed along and I watched the cop and some others: paperback readers, a man working a pencil at a crossword puzzle, briefcase carriers, sleepers, a young woman hiding behind sunglasses, all of them looking a lot braver than I feel. Not one of them was letting on how they were tiny nerve-ending bundles of terror, stunned hearts and minds, neither loved nor loving. None of us, whatever we were or were not, had the imagination to scream. I watched a woman with three sleeping kids and a gigantic bag of laundry.

I could be making up what I am about to say, but I seem to remember this as true. The name of the laundromat where my grandmother worked was changed and named after her. The Thrifty-Bundle Laundromat was changed to the Rose Maroni Laundromat and Car Wash, or it was just the car wash they named after her, or they named the day the car wash opened Rose Maroni Day. Whatever happened for her should have. All of whatever happened and more should be true for her. She is the same as Bret was, somebody who is not afraid to love straight on through.

The train clattered underground and came out again quieter. The girl with sun-glasses was watching me, I could tell she was. I stared back at her until she took off her sunglasses. Alissa, appearing a lot different from just having her dark hair cut wavy short, different from the photographs and snapshots of her that had been on Bret's desk, looked at me and did not say anything. When she did, she said, "I know you."

I talked, talked, talked from my small mouth while the train hurtled on. I talked and the last tiny words I remember saying to her were, "You know, I've been thinking about him."

She smiled at me, at my meagerness, and she put her sunglasses back on. The braking wheels screamed the subway train to a stop. The train doors opened and we got off together. I kissed her hair before she walked away into what was left of her young life, already old with sadness. Seeing her like this, her dignity, her very real bravery, was better to me than eating steak. I watched her walk away until I could not see her anymore, and I was again reminded how there is never any answer good enough, never any consolation.

Last night, I dreamed I was walking in darkness. I woke in the coldness of my empty room and from where I lay in bed looking out the window, I could see there was little light from the sky. In my dream, I was walking in a place of absolutely no light and I was afraid. Snow was beginning to fall. Snow filled the darkness with a pale light as if the faintest kind of blessing. I looked closer, and instead of snow-flakes, fetuses no larger than snow-flakes were falling all around me. I held out my hand. Tiny fetuses floated into my hand. I looked down and I could see their tiny feet, their tiny hands and heads. But in my dream, I knew they were fetuses and I knew they were alive. I could see their blind eyes, their chests rising as they drew breath, the beating of their tiny, bulging hearts through the milky skin of their nakedness. I could see their mouths opening greedily for the sweet, hot milk of life, and I was no longer afraid.

THE YEAR OF

THE PURCHASE

"Is this your good shirt with the frayed collar and cuffs?" my mother says to me. Before I can answer her, my mother answers herself, "Let's go for a new good shirt."

Goldberg's is where we go. Behind these windows is the same display of faded mackinaws and plaid shirts I believe I remember from nearly twenty years ago. The door opens to the same clack of bell and clapper. The smell is the same smell of new shoes, belt leather, moth balls.

"Come in, come in," says Mrs. Goldberg from the dark at the back of the store. "Red, put the lights on for these customer people."

Fluorescent tubing hums light on the glass case holding clasp knives and buck knives, compasses, belt buckles. Stacked boxes of dress shirts are on top of the case near the shirts for this season—hunting shirts and sweat shirts. Shelves from floor to ceiling support the weight of new-jean stiffness—straight legs, bell bottoms, boot cuts. Near the cash register is the cardboard cowgirl that as a boy I had wanted as my girl. The cowgirl, young as ever, advertises her jean brand while sitting on a fence, admiring the bronc riding of a cowboy I had wished was me. Mrs. Goldberg, who was old when I was a toddler young, sits old as ever in the shadows at the back of the store.

"Red, come tell these customer people of ours about the sales we are having," says Mrs. Goldberg.

Radio tuned in to high-school football comes from the back room. Cheerleaders clap up a cheer. Dickie Dassatti makes the tackle. The home team has the ball on their twenty. Red has them all in the back room as if somehow in miniature.

In this room, my mother looks at shirts in boxes as if she is looking down into the lives of boys and men. I look at my reflection off the glass of the case. A man all the ages I am looks back. A man thirty-seven-years old whose mother is still buying his clothes for him looks back.

"This one might fit you," my mother says to me. My mother puts a shirt into my hand. The shirt is an Oxford blend, button-down, white. The price, written in ink on the sticker, is twenty-four dollars.

Before I can say what I should say to my mother–who wears my old army jacket, sweat pants, sneakers with the heel backs broken in as if she is wearing slippers–my mother says to me, "You should have at least one good shirt."

"Listen to your mother," says Mrs. Goldberg, and then says, "Red, listen to me and turn off that radio. Come take care of these customer people of ours. Keep in mind the sales bargain we will give them on a good shirt."

My mother snaps open the breast pocket of a long-sleeve cowboy shirt with pearl snaps for buttons.

I lay the white shirt on the glass case safekeeping the shiny desires of boys.

The home team has driven to the Chicopee ten.

Red opens the curtain that closes away the back room.

Red comes to see what he can do for us not from folding pants in the back room so much as if from the bleachers below the press box at Noel Field. My God, Red, what little that is left of your namesake has turned white. Why is it I thought of you, Red, as young as ever, the same as the cowgirl?

Red takes a look at me.

"I remember you," says Red. "You're the one who broke a long one in the last minute against Hoosac Valley and fumbled down near the five."

"Yes, that's me," I say.

"How are you doing?" says Red.

"Still fumbling," I say.

Fluorescent light flickers over all of us.

The home team goes in for the winning score.

True to Mrs. Goldberg's word, my mother pays thirty-two dollars for both the white shirt and the cowboy shirt.

On our way home through the great light failing is when I say to her, "Mother, please forgive me, please."

HUNGER

Some say you are what you do. Cooking in the slam is what I do. Cooking three squares six days a week. Cooking for those on row alone with themselves and what they have done. Some say to me doing such work is as low as it gets. I say that standing for years running to one long day back of wire mesh that can take the heat of the blow torch has had me a look at things. Rib sticking with grits and fat meat. Dealing white bread marked by thumb prints. Spooning rice pudding for those taking the trip up the pipe, I say, has heard me things. Take Richard Lee Hooker with his hands and arms hot-wire tattooed with crosses burning. I heard it said how Richard Lee clawhammered an old neighbor woman's teeth from her living head. How he tried swapping silver fillings for nickel crack. He was caught preaching on a street corner with four stub teeth in his shirt pocket.

Take Bubbus Duhon, who told his story to a boss on the killing floor with the old boss later telling me. Bubbus and his hunchbacked wife had another drunk going to get through another night. Drunk turned to yelling turned to throwing hands with furniture snapping, dishes smashing, the smacking over and over of heavy meat hitting meat. Bubbus was said to have said the fracas quit when there was no more chairs, or cups, or whelping of breath left to beat loose from his broken-backed wife. Old boss told me how Bubbus said he knew he'd got himself a seat in the gas house when he took on the cops the downstairs neighbors called. Bubbus did both cops with a flashlight. Bubbus kept at it, wanting his full ticket's worth he said, long after the flashlight busted and all had gone dark.

Raymond Lester is another. He was said to have found his youngest stepdaughter crying among the shoes in a closet of their trailer house. His stepdaughter, five years old, tried to get away from him come again to pecker her bloody from her mouth and privates. I also heard told how he later burned and buried what little was found of her and her two missing sisters out by the trailer's tool shed.

Before gasping cyanide gas for what they did, Raymond Lester and those others had me behind my wire mesh cooking what I could for them. I fed them their last the best I could. My list I keep of what they wanted runs short:

Ned BIG DADDY Kane: T-bone steak gristly fat (well done), two corn on the cob, two butter pats, lettuce and tomato with creamy Russian dressing, French vanilla ice cream with Boston cream pie, raspberry Kool-aid.

Deejohn Dragus: One slat of saltine crackers, peanut butter, marshmallow fluff, ice water.

Rufus Riles: Pork loin, chicken livers, mustard greens, grits, beets, honey-topped corn bread, butter-milk biscuit, watermelon, ice tea with real lemons.

Rudy Childress: Salisbury steak, tater tots, snap beans,

chilled green jello "with just enough wobble to let me know it is chilled good before I taste it," grape Kool aid.

Carlos Roberto Santiago Ramirez: Dirty rice, refried beans, flour tortillas, three slices of white bread, lemon ices, Tecate beer in a can room warm, coffee black.

Charles A. Gaspardi: Trout skillet-fried light with red onions and baby potatoes, sweet sausage with fried onions and peppers on a hard roll, strawberry Pop Tarts, Lone Star Beer.

Richard Lee Hooker: Two boxes of sugar frosted flakes, one pint of skim milk, two Snicker candy bars.

Alexander L. Daugherty: Smokey-grilled chicken leg and wings done up "Florida traveling style," Dorito corn chips, peach schnapps.

Raymond Lester: White bread sandwich with tomato and heavy mayonnaise and heavy black pepper, raisin and rice pudding, ice tea.

Bubbus Duhon: T-bone steak (rare), twin lobster tails served along side a little paper cup of drawn butter, six hot dogs with the works (mustard, catsup, chili made with meat and beans and jalapeno peppers, Velveeta cheese melt, sauerkraut, onions), chicken ka-bob on a stick, french fries, potato chips, chocolate birthday cake with a candle, Twizzlers, pounder sack of bite-size Kit-Kat bars, six pack of beer any brand, six pack of diet 7-Up.

I carry my list folded in my wallet. The very same ones that say what I do is as low as it gets are the first to ask me to see it. They are not the only ones. Others ask. A lot of people ask. I take out my list folded so many times it is falling apart at the creases and I let them read it. One name is not on it. What T.J. Mettler had as his last meal is easy to remember. What T.J. wanted was wrote to me as follows word for word:

Mister Roy, I know it is most likely than not you have heard and read this kind of thing many times before and since, but here I go anyway. . . I want the BEST of what I have all ready had with more of it. I write that and I look around now and there it is not. I know now when you come to understand THINGS, it is mostly too late, and, Mister Roy, I know there is nothing worse than "too late." Knowing that, I want back morning and the feeling I had when I first rode time down.

I was up before my old man from bed I had wet again and I knew I would catch hell for again. I slicked my hair in a hurry trying to flatten it down from looking the same as hair around Aunt Gert's poodle's asshole. I palmed on some of old man's foo-foo water he would holler hell more how he would break my ass over if he ever caught me at it again. I gulped cola gone flat left on kitchen counter overnight. I snuck cigs, chewing gum stick torn in half, meal change, all found on floor under old man's pants tossed pockets-out over his chair. "Doublemint" gum for cig breath and my teeth cola-coated for when I would lay a "HEY" first thing I could on Lucille, and later, after, big lick on Bob Blay. A little gum is good, a BIG GUN is better. Old man's .38 with its long barrel fit the bill nice enough and besides I'd already gotten it from his sock drawer. I had pulled it loose from sock tangle and loaded it heavier with the most fearsome of beauty–I want to say it now as I saw it–the clean beauty of those BIG golden slugs. I wrapped it all up in one of the old man's snot rags. I put it easy does it in wire basket hooked on handlebars of his Chink bike. Barrel pointed through wire with me feeling as if .38 was somehow something ALIVE, something POWERFUL and pointing at what was to come. . .

Now set your mind, Mister Roy, on colding fall morning. Leaves scurried around in wind as if some little animals. Crows croaked. Misty mountain hop. Great noise when you got some-place to go. Now see if you can let loose of your mess hall mashed taters and meat loaf long enough, Mister Roy, to imagine how this boy flew on that morning. Time, as in got to get to her, get my glimpse at Lucille, was running hurried layed out in the road potholed, tarred, graveyarded in the cool of night with snakes having crawled to what heat was left from the day held in road tar's blackness with them snakes run over killed. I finished the JOB, what was left of IT, skull-popping them snakes good with fat tires wheelied. I flew my skinny little nothing against chill, wind messing up my hair more, blowing my old man's aftershave off me for what must have been miles and miles behind. I was a kid who had rode way hell out on a bike my old man stole from Chinks bringing around slippery noodles and won-tonned cat. Can you imagine being so "skeezy fucking low mein as to steal from Chinks?" my old man would snort out, heaving and crying with laughter, later, after, having a couple tall boy sixes in him. He stole it and I rode it. I rode past some raggedy woman leaning on supermarket shopping cart, listening to transistor radio sounding tinny loud to me as I came up on her fast. I whooped and pooped her for the sheer shit of it, for the feeling of how it made me feel better than somebody, something more than a wedgie waiting to happen, somebody bigger and better for a moment lasting maybe half too long as one of Aunt Gert's shorter beer farts. I flew past laughing from seeing her leap all afraidy at my whoop! The best of a bed wetting full time nothing boy I was wobbled bike under old oak ghost-peopled tall with shoes tied together and thrown to dangling in branches that held onto leaves cold burnt red.

Front bike tire wob-bled, wob-bled, wob-bled.

I steady huffed up Lucille's hill and skid gravel spray against her daddy's car barn where I leaned my old man's bike. Grass frosted dewy wet piddled some through my Hush Puppies, set them to SQUISHY-SQUEAKY FARTING with every step. I can really remember now. I can remember how it was a feeling of everything around me and coming out of me.

It was like MUSIC!!!

Mister Roy, those wet shoe farts could have been ragpicker's transistor radio playing top-forty countdown for all I knew, or cared. Truly, and all I know or care now is how early morning time hung for me then as a throbbing thing.

I was ALIVE!!!

Most mornings that I got away the same as I did that morning, I would do what I told you I did, minus old man's .38 gun jumping and rattling around in bike basket. That morning, I stood myself on plastic milk crate pulled from weeds. I climbed crate and looked in Lucille's window until I could see some in her dark room. Past curtain float, dark was throbbing dots on my eyes about same as the molecule lesson shown from slide projector in our fifth grade science class. I looked on until I could see her hair lighter than jumping dark, her long, soft hair blonding EVERY-WHERE in place, even when she slept, and looking more, I saw what LITTLE I could see of her FACE. I stood on my tiptoes on rocking milk crate, rested myself on my elbows on her windowsill long enough for ache in my arms to turn to numb, that is, long enough for me to ready myself to say "HEY" when it was Lucille too soon saying sleepy to me, "T J, you give off a big stink for such a little dinky dog."

I thought nobody else could smell me and my old man's Old Spice, or see me then, from what I could tell, or had crossed my line of sight such that they would likely see me at her window. Somebody's neighbor somewhere drove by in a car. Sprinkler threw beads of water sunlit at grass already drowned pretty good. By then, it was as if Lucille was passed out, maybe from my smell, or most likely had forgotten me, or had lost INTEREST altogether.

"Hey," I said soft to her, as if I was way far off while right there too.

I heard her brother Glen let clap the screen door to ride his paper route. I heard a faraway train's whistle. I heard other sounds and I knew time hanging all around me, blowing inside and around me.

I knew lover boy Bob Blay was coming. . .

"Hey, what?" I heard her say kind of sleepy pissed off, which made me think she might be saying it to me.

"Another hey coming right back at you," said I, not knowing what more to say.

By then, Mister Roy, whether it was me or not, my eyes were about as ready to see in her dark as they would get. I watched as she stretched and groaned herself awaker, as she legged herself out of her sheets to standing in her T-shirt nighty too long for me to get a good look at what it was I really came for and wanted to see most. Seeing what I could of her, her face, it was as if time rolled uphill for me in a way that is like the hanging glide on bike before you have to pedal. I tell you this, Mister Roy, because she had a face as ALIVE as it gets coming from out of that darkness, a face that gathered light and others to itself. She also had a hard-on woody way about her that might let her get away before it was too late. She knew it too. She knew it and used it. She knew some other things too, things about me same way as my old man did and just about everybody else who knew me did, without any of them having to say a word on how I would never get away from anything. They all knew I was somehow already zeroed-out with all sorts of laws and averages and plain piss-poor luck against me.

I have always thought I must be week-old newspaper

blown caught in the spokes of some crummy Chink bike with the headline wheeling around that read, T.J. METTLER FUCKED FOR LIFE. Either some of that, or GOD, or somebody, or just about everybody who knew me, or had met me, was shining light through my head. A big old flashlight, or light from a slide projector shining through my head onto clouds and trees and wherever it was I passed, or stood, showing everybody and ALL THE WORLD what I thought, every dopey, dumb-ass thing I never said, every sneaky or weepy or fake feeling I almost had, or could have had, or did.

Knowing what little I knew then, I knew to keep on looking at Lucille. She turned her back to me while she bunched her T-shirt over her head. I looked at her wearing nothing but panties, her secret hair hidden under them polka-dotted panties with my knowing it, and like I already wrote to you, Mister Roy, it was as if time both rushed and stilled down for me. That time then was ice-hard store-bought ice cream eaten and eaten past the headache cold. It was United States Marine Corps marching band boys snapped to at full dress attention and ready swelled. Lucille stood swelled big as life with her butt backed to me, holding herself in her arms. She lifted arm enough to let slip a little bitty titty, a puppy nose of pick nippled tit!

The USMC boys struck up, "From the Halls of Montezuma to the Shores of Tripoli. . ." while my woodward tapped on her daddy's aluminum house siding with Lucille saying at the very last, "TJ, you little prevert you, put that teensy thing away before you hurt yourself."

We are all such broken creatures.

We are, and the beautifully fearsome thing about it is how we all come to know it, usually too late, and how knowing either saves us, if anything can save us, or kills us.

I stood up within myself. I did and the whole thang slipped down to time, rolling away. I got back to bike and pedaled downhill at breakneck fuckhead speed. Woody and .38 pointed and I pedalled faster. Fuck my fucked-up hair. Forget smell blowing off me of old man's aftershave. Skip anything other than getting to that oak before she did, before he did, before they did and got themselves together to drive on to school. I did ALL THAT with time getting there in me. I got under talling oak tree with me sweating in chill, buzzing inside from the MUSIC that was her.

I got there before them.

I left bike on middle road line, front tire wobbly spinning, and I got .38 from out of snot rag and layed it down. I lay down on road too among acorns. Looking up, I could see clouds doing their flying floating thing. Shoes too, up in tree branches, doing their air walking, moving in the wind. I counted seven shoes up there, felt tar and twigs sticking in my back, and knew what them snakes knew before they knew nothing more forever. I lay ALIVE in the road, Mister Roy, looking, smelling tar sun-warming, feeling winter closing in, listening up for his fifth-hand, five-hundred dollar Ford.

When I heard it, he was on me quick. His flat-header Ford rumbled-up LOUD at me lying in the road, roared louder up closer, while he hollered, "YOU ARE ONE LUCKY LITTLE NOTHING THAT I DON'T RIDE OVER YOUR HEAD WITHOUT SO MUCH AS LOOKING BACK!

I was lucky for once and he was not.

Doing my broken back snake thing, I was both lucky and good.

Bob Blay rolled his big fucking Ford so right up closer to me that I could feel heat blasting out of its grill, could suck deep its oil and coolant breath, could see underneath at his leaky gunked lube job while he sat his killer that close, ready to eat me as if I was some nothing motor meat soon to be forgotten as a old burp.

More clouds, I remember, I do. I remember the kind they was too, billowy as comic book clouds, and more shoes swinging from branches, more busted road and the long barrel of old man's .38 digging into my back as I lay there steady does it dog boy, steadier, chewing my "Doublemint," laying steady-still inside listening to the SCREAMING HOT HUNGER of his motor that seemed to me to be his want and hold on Lucille.

"Hey, dipshit, what you doing?" I heard him call out over the roar of his big four-barrel carburetor.

He gunned it bigger a few times, blasting redding leaves and dirt around me. Crow I thought was shoe flew from out of oak. Shoes that were shoes kicked wind.

"Yo, dog breath, get out of the road before I run your funny looking head flatter," he called to me.

I chewed slower.

"Yo, white trash motherhumper, if you had one," he called even louder to me.

I knew only time.

When he himself got out, slow, I could see his pointy grown-up shoes and drooping thin ankle socks. I watched them come around, slow. I looked up at him dressed in his tweeding jacket and strung cowboy tie, and NOT ONE, NOT A SINGLE ONE vaselined slick hair of his was out of place. He dressed as if he had aftershave of his own. He decked himself out as if he had candy kisses up his ass. He put it together as if he was twenty-one while I did not know on which side yet to part my hair. I did not know how to sleep a night without soaking myself through, a wetter boy still.

"You all right, or what?" he said.

It almost saved him—Bobby, Bob, Bob Blay—with his asking me like that, and his thin white socks, but then he did IT. He ran a hand with a little pinky ring over his hair while he watched at himself, looking himself over good in his windshield. His looking at himself hollered at me louder than his big fucking road hog. Bob looking at himself without saying one word more yelled at me,

"FUCK YOU, JACK, FOR I AM BURIED IN MY OWN LIFE IN A WAY YOU ARE NOT AND WILL NEVER BE BEING BECAUSE YOU ARE ALWAYS GOING TO BE YOU–SOME PUNY NOTHING CREATURE WOUNDED HURT!"

That is when I got up swinging old man's .38. I let one go. It went tearing up somewhere through topmost branches of olden tall oak tree. It stopped him from looking at himself, I can tell you that. So I let off another just to feel BIG POWER in doing a thing so small. I could hear pop taken by wind. Old man's .38 seemed so light then, flying upward on its own, and me letting it go where it wanted to while Bob looked at me, almost as if looking through me, and it made me wonder, the gun and its POWER not every-thing yet, if he could see what I was thinking. Could be he knew what I would do before I did it. I looked around to see if my words were somewhere behind me, drooling, or pissing, or scratching at themselves hard on the roadside. When I looked back at him, he was looking at me more, so I started tossing my old man's gun from hand to hand, not thinking so much as feeling weight of .38 gun, showing Bob I was feeling it, and whatever came next would be "ONE BIG SURPRISE" to both of us, wouldn't it? Dog breath? Dipshit? I guess Bob saw what I was thinking and feeling because his face went soft afraid and he said what he said in a way as if them candy kisses up his ass had of a sudden gone melted sticky. He said croaky whispering, "This ain't fooling around is it?"

"You're right," I said back to him. "You're right about that, now get the keys out and open the trunk."

He did, older and better haired and for once more afraid than me that he was, so I told him some more.

"Now get in," I told him.

He looked at me more until I pointed the .38 straight off into his mouth with both my hands.

We stood around some like that.

I wanted to mess with his hair bad, but held back.

We hung around with .38 pointed until he did what I had told him to do. The trunk closed gentle with a click. Chink bike, clunky big wire basket, knobby fat tires, the whole deal was wheeled up into his back seat Bob had covered with fake pussy hair feeling almost as soft and as good, I bet, as Lucille's hair did.

Later, after, I looked at my kid hands on steering wheel. When I was a young twelver, I first drove on back roads muddy with night. I would drive all the way to Fire Lake where I was afraid to get out of the car into dark and night. I would sit awhile before I would drive them roads all the way back. I drove to Fire Lake then, with Bob, not knowing why I did, thinking how with summer gone and all, I would not have to brave those browning girls sunning themselves. I drove thinking why not just drive forever? The reason, best as I can make out, Mister Roy, and it is not a good one or nothing, is how I was thinking like I was not really a part of IT any longer. More as though I was watching a movie or lip reading, sounding out a story, and I needed to see what was going to happen. This is true, Mister Roy, but I also knew it was all longshot gamble, how every thang was already all to hell and gone.

I drove trying to miss dead things in the road. I did pretty good, I guess, and it was quiet. Sure, sun was rolling up and radio was on low, and it was somehow all too bright and quiet. I stopped once, along the roadside, at a place good for a family picnic if you had family not yet killed dead, or farting drunk, or driven off. I got out of the Ford at that family place and listened to see if he was still in the trunk. All I could hear was his ride throating its rumble in quiet. After I got back in again, and after I was driving again, it was as if I somehow fell asleep and had a DREAM I do not remember. Time was that way too, Mister Roy. Time has been that way for a long time for me now. I do not know any other way to say it or write it. That, Mister Roy, and how I looked and there I was not.

Out at Fire Lake was awfully BRIGHT and QUIET with nobody or nothing around, no girls, no nothing other than water and a old raft dragged to shore. Mr. Powell once told us in science class how the lake was left by glaciers before time itself. Funny how all that ice did what it did, dragging and carving everything up while crawling back north, mountains of ice, Mr. Powell said, and now the lake and its water is all that is left and is somehow known as Fire Lake. Thinking about it, feeling it now, I guess it makes as much sense as most things, as anything really, as how in that nothing light and quiet I tapped on car trunk with barrel of old man's gun, heard nothing inside, so I tapped again.

There is, I know, loneliness in this world so great that you can see IT and hear IT in the ticking hand of a watch. ALL THAT, then how it was again when our time together got almost too good.

First slug got Bob Blay screaming, begging, screaming. Slugs that were left banged big right into trunk, fucked over his loverly paint job good. Things got quieter. The nothing around before that, hiding fish and birds and shit, really got gone. I got him gone. I got him and the quieter gone by gunning his old Ford, holding the gas pedal down with some heavy burnt log dragged from some open fire pit, by driving Bob Blay and his old flathead-er right into Fire Lake in little swirls of water that sucked soft into bullet holes, pouring faster and bigger and louder into all the windows I had rolled down. The radio, still on, I heard long after the motor had cut out and I saw nothing other than water.

Hours later, I swear, I could still hear Buck Owens gurgling, "Tiger by the Tail" from the deep waters of Fire Lake.

The old man got his with his own .38 after he hollered about me piss-sopping my sheets again, hollered more about my smelling like a "French whore house," kept hollering louder and longer after he broke my arm of mine in two places. Aunt Gert and Aunt Gert's poodle got popped a little later, Aunt Gert for farting her **MILLER HIGH LIFE** beer farts, her pooch, just for reminding me of me, looking like I felt–hairwise, that is. Lucille herself got away! Not that I would of hurt her other than loving her the best I could. She got away as much as anybody gets away. Her life would most likely have caught up with her too. She could be right now bursting preggers with her fourth or fifth "linoleum lizard" (as my old man would say if he was around to say anything) while sitting under a hot blast of hair dryer and reading blah-blah-blah in a week-old newspaper about how after all this time they are finally going to "take me out for good."

The rest of this story, **MY STORY**, Mister Roy, is about bored-to-death lawyers pointing pencils and waving sheets of paper at one another, lockdowns peeling grey paint and smelling of piss, too much murdered time no different than the water at Fire Lake closing over me for all time.

And who cares?

Not me.

I am not one least bit sorry for what I did. I am sorry for what I **DID NOT** do a lot more of! For that, and for the bigger truth of why I am writing this now.

What I want, Mister Roy, is for the day to shine once more as if something is really happening.

What T. J. got at the end is not carried around in my wallet. What he wanted most and what he got is not something I have ever said to anybody before. I say to you one look at the gas house is all that you want. It looks like a big pressure cooker with gauges and pipes. Inside sits the chair high backed and heavy on blocks set on a cast-iron crate. Leather straps stained dark from sweat hang loose to the floor where there is an old copper pan the same as you might have for dirty dishes. I was told the pellets drop through the crate holes into the pan of acid, go to gas sizzling and smoking the same as a dirty griddle too hot.

I have also heard told he took it the way he wanted.

A stick of gum is what I got to him. At the end, he turned to Doc Rivers and said to thank Mister Roy for him.

For a time, I say, maybe I fed something in him until what he wanted most came greasy real and forever.

FLIGHT

From the darkness, a bird's whistle rouses him. He kneels in the mud and the leaves where he has slept. He lurches up alert, not bothering to brush the leaves from his prison coveralls. The weight of the pruning shears in a back pocket tugs down his coveralls.

He keeps to the woods until the light is enough that he sees he must make his break. He moves under the trees with young leaves turned yellow from the way the low reach of light shines through their leaf skin. He watches the leaves flutter. Birds hop from branch to branch. The birds are small, as fleeting as thoughts. Between branches, as if he has imagined it, he sees a house. The house, surrounded by plowed fields, stands starkly lit.

His work boots are muddled more. He walks as if in a dream he has already had, knowing again the weight of his boots, the quality of the light that is on him. Soon, he is walking up to a window at the side of the house.

A woman moves about the kitchen. He watches her sip from a glass. She talks to a child sitting at the table. She wipes the girl child's lips.

Voices move him away from the window. He hears music, a cartoon gunshot, comic talk. He listens for other voices, for a man's voice. He looks in the window to see if the woman and child have changed from the way they were, changed shapes, changed the words the woman speaks to the child in a language he does not understand. She speaks the language of the birds flitting in the trees, nesting words, soft, so soft.

When the voices change to a man's voice saying there is the possibility of rain, he kneels and snips the telephone line. He pockets the pruning shears and quickly, angrily, walks around to the back of the house. He opens the screen door without knocking and walks into the kitchen.

"Who else is here?"

The woman and child look up at him.

"Look, I'm not kidding, who else is around?"

A voice from the television in the other room does the talking. He grabs her and feels how small she is under the loose flannel. She is little more than a child. Her bones feel hollow. She is another bird, who will flit away if he is not careful.

He shoves her ahead of himself into the other room. There is the television on the floor, cardboard boxes, a wooden chair. As if further proof of what she is, on a wall is a fan with painted, blood-red peacocks.

He pushes her upstairs.

In the first room there are toys scattered on the floor, on a child's bed. He shoves her through this room and into the other bedroom. On top of a chest of drawers is a mirror. A mud man–his hair standing straight up–looks back. He looks from his reflection to the wooden boxes, the brush, the comb, lined up on the chest. The bed has a white bedspread. A man's cloth slipper almost hides where the bedspread hangs to the floor.

"There is only you and the girl?"

She stares.

"I'm talking to *you*, Chinawoman, or whatever you are! Don't act like you're seeing your things for the first time! All this shit layed out, as if you was ready for somebody to come and take you and your's off somewheres!"

"My husband will come," she says without bird talk, wind words.

She looks out the window. He looks too. Far down the road, like another toy thrown at their feet, is a school.

"When's he coming?"

Her eyes come back to his. He holds the shears at her eye as black as a marble a boy would put in his mouth to clean. The shears snip so easily.

"Mama!" the child calls from downstairs.

She is almost past him when he has her arm, holds his face near her face. Her eyelids flitter.

When he does let go, he follows her downstairs and through the living room where he shuts off the television.

"I'm hungry," he says to her and the child. "I'm hungry for a lot of things."

He stands at the open refrigerator, eating what he comes to as he comes to it: a black beet, a bunch of long onions, something yellow he drinks, a quartered head of lettuce, a bag of cough drops, a little seedy orange, milk he drinks from the carton. He goes through the cabinets and eats a box of crackers. When he is done swallowing, he puts the shears down. He pushes her so her back is against the counter. He lifts her nightgown, throws it over her head so she stands shrouded, a little orange tree covered against the cold. Maybe the orange came from her small breasts, her slight branches, the tree she is that she will change back into as in the old stories.

She trembles as if against the cold. Less of her is hidden from him now, not her golden skin, not her downy hair.

The child watches him when he puts a hand on the soft skin of the woman's belly. He holds his hand there, draws his face closer to her warm breath blowing out the flannel softness. He feels the heat from her belly walk up his arm and into his shoulder, fill his chest, fill him until he too breathes out.

He pulls the nightgown down from over her head. He picks up the child, tugs her up, her legs hanging limp, like he is pulling something green and rooted from the ground. The child turns her face away from his muddy beard. Her hair is like the woman's hair, cut straight all around so that her hair moves like the fringe of a silk dress, or grass in the wind.

Carrying the child over his shoulder, he is out the back door. The woman hurries after them. When she catches up, they walk the dirt road. A crow, flying high above, caws, as if to kin. From that height, they appear as paper dolls scissored from a book of cutouts, a child's dream of walking.

When they come to the school with the windows boarded over, they walk in the shade of trees, the first shade since leaving the house that now looks no bigger than when he first saw the house through the branches of other trees.

Behind the school, past the rusting tall swings, they cross the ball field. Fading signs on the outfield fence tell them how NOTHING RUNS LIKE A DEERE, MILK DOES A BODY GOOD, WILLIS HOME INSURANCE IS ALWAYS A HIT! The grass of the ball field is so new, so green, he could sit and eat it, slowly, himself a deer, with the two quiet ones watching him crop the tender grass giving him what he needs.

He brings them to the rusting batting cage. Inside the cage, among the weeds, are rotting rags. Netting, ripped and tangled, loops down. He lowers the child to standing, helps her and the woman through a hole in the wire into the cage.

Birds flush up from the weeds in the cage. The birds flap close to the woman and child, fly out where the wire opens. One bird snags a wing, hangs. What was once a bird, now a curve of wing bone, a claw, hangs in the netting.

The woman and child watch the living bird twitch, tangle itself more. He goes to the bird, puts his face close, blows. Feathers furrow, darker feathers show underneath. The bird stills, blinks. The bird's eyes are rings within golden rings the color of the woman's skin.

He pulls the bird from the snarl of netting. He smooths the feathers, puts the wing back into place. The bird heats his hand. He feels the bird's heart–the small beating, like what was at the throat of the woman when she stood in the kitchen with her nightgown over her head–and he throws the bird up into flight.

The bird whirs about his head, then flies to the trees along the road.

The sky looks empty.

He pulls the woman and child from the cage, hurries them to the playground. Seating the child in a swing, making sure her little hands are holding the chains, he pushes the child from behind. Her hair lifts, falls.

He gets on a swing. He toes off where the clay is gouged hollow, points his feet. He gains height. His arms work as he pulls harder. He moves faster, higher. The old swing shrieks him higher and higher, his feet now over his head, kicking at the sun.

From that height, he can see the woman and the child walking together under the far trees--their slipping away from him as his own life has--and that is the moment he lets go, throwing himself higher, farther, into the light that will burn him clean.

SON OF MAN

Prayer, that hope of conspiracy with God in the guise of thanks or worry or want sent heavenward, demands getting down on one's knees. The change in elevation, Bass notices, position his head in a downward tilt, lifts his hands holding the saxophone, helps clarify what is about to come out.

Held, low, his hum carries out an open window into this night of fenced backyards: wires overgrown with strangler fig and ivy, brick soot-blackened, shacks peeling tar paper and shedding tin, a pipe dripping fecal mire, weeds standing in sidewalk cracks. A cat striped by moonlight and fence pickets hears what at first seems the long call of an owl or some other hunter. A rat sits still in rusting mattress springs. A man smokes a cigar on a fire escape. Those rows of windows are dark, but for a lowered light in the bedroom of a child speaking in dreams. A woman spectral in the flutter of pale silk comes to her window to hear the hymn.

Tendons cricking in his bent knees keep time. His moving fingers on sax parts help throw rods of reflecting moonlight. Beyond, rise trestles and spires that is the city lighting the sky.

The cat disappears into full darkness; a squeak. Fired leaf curls to ash, a last smoke ring, cigar smell. Hearing the music, the child sits up without knowing whether he is dreaming or awake.

The woman cracks her knuckles. The cat, quartered by moon-light, has the rat by the neck.

Want is what Bass hears coming back from the weath-ered brick and board that is this place, this hour; a boy wanting to make himself new: a fresh start, a different soul to rise to. He wants a style never heard yet right away known from buzz and folly and hope that is all Bass. From way down low, Bass flares an upward riff. An echo mocks softer as if someone is doubling him breath for breath, note for note.

The subway cavern is a carnival of performers: rag heaps animated by men and women. This one man, Hillbilly, is naked other than for a Hawaiian sport shirt yellow with hula dancers and jump boots worn sockless and with the laces loose. He wields a dented horn both drawing and scattering those about him–these toothless crystal-hitters jittery high, these homeboys fronting gold medallions while carrying rusting razor blades tucked cutting edge down between gum and cheek–"Careful with those smiles, boys," says a chick with a dick, McAmon, old Button Down out running young game, Vet-Air-Cav-No-Fucking-Way-Sir-Private-First-Class still rolling point by arm-poling his legless torso along on a chopped supermarket cart, Tillie, Meat Puppet run away from pappy stomp, Orrin, Rangoon with chin hair long and sparse as hair on the pizzle of a water buffalo: all carnied over by Hillbilly, hula-girled, Hibernian-grogged, armed with a horn. His horn's sound, his Lila Lee's speech, is a fit of tenderness turning to threat above the other's howls, groans, an empty bottle of Ye Old Mother Sod's Murkiest Blend *ponking* off something hard–from off Button Down's brilliantined head.

Trash fires waver shadows about these tiles. King Hill-billy's shadow reigns over these clammy walls. His hair awry is a shadow crown. His Lila Lee of a horn is a shadow scepter spiked and fluted as if a monster sea shell scooped from the nether depths, as if a giant conch bringing forth regal song. His vintage jump boots are his mark of the martial. His rule and sway are manifest in a final mighty blat.

The shadow of less-than-half-a-man creakily wheels itself before Hillbilly.

"Says the fuck who?" says the pint vet.

Hillbilly gazes about as if he has not heard. Water sluices somewhere hidden. Wind comes down corridor. Flame flutters, sifts through plastic, over wadding newspaper and rotting fruit rind. Hillbilly wipes Lila Lee's mouthpiece in a luaed armpit before launching a roundhouse heel kick that catches Vet-Air-Cav-No-Go-On-This-One-Private-First-Class in the wishbone, lifts the less-than-halfer off his cart in a *harumph* of breath, dumps him in a sprawl in a puddle between cross ties between rails. Rats horde around, set to eating.

Hillbilly hiccups breath of liquery charcoal.

The cart rolls creaking over and over in the dark.

Celebratory din ensues in Cloaca Maxima Carnevalesca: crystal hitters gibbering for more and windmill slugging each other, homeboys doing the dap, chick with a dick softly-clapping so as not to loosen her fingernail sequins. Meat Puppet moves easily from Tango Solitario to Hullabaloo to Watusi. Rangoon zealously plucks his chin hair while laughing and yowling. Button Down produces a spiteful fart. Hillbilly falls to his knees with bone *crack* echoing softer and softer down subway passageways. The *clatter* of Lila Lee does the same when Lila Lee drops from his hands gone numb, *hiccup* even softer, *chock* that is barely heard by those who are crowding about him when Hillbilly collapses forward and his nose cartilage, lips, gums, incisors and canines, hide already puffy about his eyes, hair arrangement, skull—all encounter concrete.

Rain leans past a streetlight. Bass hurries in from the rain, down the stairs of the station. A drop dripped from his nose trembles a puddle oily as bathtub gin; a show of spectra. A puddle ripple carrying nearly the length of the train station tides out an over-turned porkpie hat steadied by money. The ripple laps once at the boots of the hat owner: a wet man in a wet season: a man with a bruisey swelling at his temple that gives his face half a twist: a man hugging a tenor saxophone and smoky pint of Hibernian swill to a sodden shirt with a print of dancing girls wearing grass skirts: a man with his knee-caps boning out the dingy-damp knees of his khakis.

Hillbilly pooches from the pint, he spits.

Bass splashes past the fare booth supplying tokens, nickels, dimes, quarters, singles not necessarily meant for pocketing.

"You, yes, you, my good lad," says an old man wearing a suit raveling much nylonic thread. "Could you, I know it is on short notice, see fit to lend me, oh, a grand?"

Bass continues past those selling keffiyas, frankincense, paperback books with the covers up curling from the damp.

Up close, Hillbilly is smell: moldy feet, cloth rotting from piss, sweat, smoke. Bass sniffs, looks down at Hillbilly's skull rounding beneath its hair and flesh, at the horn engraved LILA LEE dulling brassy black around hole sockets, at the drifting porkpie boater. Not in the pocket he searches, nor that one, nor. . . there, a quarter, that Bass, stooping, places in the porkpie hat.

Hillbilly says mumbling, "What was it you was saying?"

"Not me," Bass says. "I didn't say anything."

Static rackets from a speaker overhead: "Delays due to track flooding will prevent. . ." More static. A rat swims near a rail sided by wooden planking, noses about without touching either metal or wood, swims a tad more, grazes its longish tail between the planks. Electricity arcs blue-ribbony from rail to rat: sizzle, churning water, smell of hairy steam. Station lights dim; darkness overtakes all.

Bass listens to dripping, electric sputter, a cough, a prayer whispered to Allah. Hillbilly blows through his saxophone, lets loose with what Bass hears as calling-the-dog squeals of a redbone bitch and her brood under a cabin poled-up rickety from sliding down a hill of slag into holes man-dug and hazing off smoke from fires burning the hills from inside out. Fire ashes the bones of men and boys buried lost but for the nightly prayers of their remaining family few above. He hears a boy Hillbilly twang a wire twisted tight from nail to bent nail in a bed slat after having returned from those seams furnace hot to help his granny pressing her hands age and work riven to the browning pages of her Good Book while rocking cane chair on the cabin porch. Boy and old woman watch coal smoke roll from in the hollow to coming up the hill to darkening over wire pluck, runner creak, redbone whine.

Station lights jitter on, stay on.

"You was going to say?" Hillbilly says.

"I was?" Bass says.

"Well, whether you say it or not, there no ways ain't enough room for both of us," Hillbilly says.

He, Hillbilly, hits a few licks Bass conjures as waiting at dusk in a wooded hollow, whippoorwill harmonics, saplings poking up through rotted floorboards, brogans on the rusting fender of a junker once the speedy wherewithal of some hooch hawker's livelihood. Bass hears Hillbilly's saxophone song as a prayer for some young sweetness to come from hurried chores, a racheting of springs when she mounts what is left of the Ford with her laughter and her red hair all around, her freckled arms skinning out of the dress lifting over her head: as a mortally too short ride ridden in this wreck going nowhere: as Hillbilly finishing his run.

"Somewhere to start," Bass says.

"Not here you don't," Hillbilly says.

Upstairs, outside, the rain has quit. Angled sunlight strikes Bass as if proof, mostly to Bass, that he is someone newly enchanted with possibility, someone with a good idea.

"Yes, ma'am, that is a composition of my own I have titled, *A WANDERING PILGRIM, I*," Bass says.

The woman—tassel loafers, stockings coiling down her legs, a ring of green brassing around a pudgy finger—drops a nickel into his saxophone case. The nickel tinks into a till consisting of pennies, several other nickels, a bent Show Palace token, a Seven-Up bottle cap.

"Thank-you, ma'am," Bass says.

"And, yes, ma'am, I will keep that in mind," Bass says.

"Yes, ma'am, all suggestions are appreciated, and yes, I will remember, *A WANDERING PILGRIM, ME*," Bass says.

The damp, cold, wicks from the concrete through a cardboard box broken flat by his knees up into an ache that settles behind his kidneys. Wheezing is his music making. His take after more than half a day is four nickels, four quarters, a book of bent matches advertising how YOU TOO CAN GET A COLLEGE DEGREE IN NO TIME AT ALL, a spiney French tickler rubber, a dollar and thirty cents worth of dimes, a pacifier with tiny teeth marks.

Sunlight is more than halfway up the brick wall of the building across the street with that sunlight, with the shadow below, serving Bass as a reminder of how fast the whole thing goes.

Mostly scattered quarters shine from out of the fraying emerald felt. Bass blows something old and soft. A quarter is tossed into his case by a woman licking ice cream from a cone leaking milky about her wrist; a couple, a she and she holding hands, pause; a man with a briefcase nods as he passes, comes back—strangers all, giving Bass quarters, one-dollar bills, a fiver.

Sunlight has shifted to shadow on the top row of bricks in the wall of that same building across the street; purpling shadow deepens to darkness.

A water drop the size of a dime splats to the size of a half dollar on his cardboard after leaking from a pipe fitting in the shadows up near the high roof of this station, then another drop, another. Bass moves his case with its *chinking* contents, his saxophone, his cardboard. A drop splats on the concrete.

Bass resumes stroking it out, raising and lowering his eyebrows to the beat, eyes closed, face beatific, rocking as though in a rowboat. From the distance of his playing, Bass sees those gathering around him as swimmers. An old woman is dog-paddling in an attempt to keep her head above water. A wearer of a three-piece suit pauses to listen at the end of a lap before churning away in an Australian crawl. Two schoolgirls link arms in a synchronized underwater ballet about what they know best–youth. A train conductor done with his day's work does a lazy back crawl. An older fellow with a bump in his carmelized hair treads water. Less-than-half of a man on a cart arm-oars his way to the front of those standing around Bass as if it, he, this less-than-whole man, is what is left of a swimmer or a surfer after a shark attack.

A drop streaks filth on the cheek of this cart man peering upward, agog, his tongue catching a drop as coppery tasting as an old coin, as blood.

The train slows fast, yanking sleepers: a Chinese woman with a super-market bag scuffing along the floor, a young jack stretching seven seats long sliding the length of two more seats, a drooler flinging drool end over end to hang wattled above Bass going with the pulling weight of his coin-and-saxophone-heavy case before bracing himself awake.

Sleepers still, Bass sees of the others.

Yawning, Bass opens his case and examines this day's receipts: a withering carnation, a mostly silvery-fat slinky of change, forty-two dollar bills, a card encouraging him to DIET BY PHONE–LOSE TWENTY POUNDS IN TWO DAYS–CALL 788-0058, four Abraham Lincolns, a pair of ten dollar bills, another flower curling brown that upon closer inspection is a human ear–crusty with dry blood, gnawed.

Something wet, droolie–Bass shivers–drips down his

neck.

Hillbilly, with a style no one would mistake as belonging to anyone other than Hillbilly, has a boss attitude of I'm-doing-this-one-for-me-motherfucker. A slew of cash money—easily a hundred in bills alone—stuffs his porkpie hat.

This money-making ability of Hillbilly is particularly impressive to Bass when every several yards of this subway station is populated by those beseeching easy money: dobro players, dancing poodles and their masters clacking spoons, three-card monte dealers, jugglers, evangelists jabbering in forgotten or never-known tongues while rolling about in their shiny suits, a poet or two lying in couplets, tumblers, a turbaned fortune teller, gangs of stick-up artists with sawed-off shotguns strapped in swivel-holsters under the sweep of long leather coats, a girl of about seven or eight years of age proffering her naked buttocks and a paper coffee cup containing several pennies, Hillbilly catching his breath while gathering his spill-over spoils.

"Hey," Bass says to the Hillbilly man.

"Do I stutter?" Hillbilly says.

"What?" Bass says.

"Do I stutter was what I said," says Hillbilly.

"No, sir," Bass says.

"Then there is no reason to make me repeat what it was I've already told you," Hillbilly says. "And son, don't sass me, don't even think about sassing me."

"I'm not your son," Bass says. "And I don't want to sass you, you clodhopper you."

"Candy ass," Hillbilly says.

"Bohunk," Bass says.

"Pisswillie," Hillbilly says.

"Pennsyltuckian," Bass says.

"Youngblood who doesn't know any better than to think the sun shines up the same dog's ass everyday," Hillbilly says.

"Jethro-Fucking-Bodeen," Bass says.

"Opie-Left-A-Load-In-His-Diaper-Fuckwad-Taylor. Run right back home to Mayberry to your oldish Aunt Bee and tell her after she changes you to get herself ready for me because I'm a going do her up hot and crusty," Hillbilly says, laughing. "And don't laugh so fast."

"Yes, sir," Bass says.

"That's better," Hillbilly says, "because I'm asking you. . . What did you call me?. . . Jethro?. . . You shitbird you. . . I'm asking you man-to-man, shitbird-to-shitbird, don't make me do what I don't want to do. I'm asking you, and now I'm telling you one more time, there ain't room at this dance for both of us."

"But. . ." Bass says, "there are all these. . ."

"Hear me," Hillbilly says, "because I'm done asking."

His knees, bearing much of his one-hundred-and-forty-three pounds, indent cardboard advertising Andy Boy broccoli. A pang, a tingle, an ache shoots up a leg, winds up and around his spine to sprout again and again into a lung with every saxophone grok, tweet, erk echoing from these tunnel tiles. Water pours some where sourceless to his eyes. That creaking is from somewhere else. Urine smell pervades all. A poster for a circus having many years come and gone tatter flutters. No one is in sight.

His case holds barely enough walking-around change, thirty cents in silver, a torn dollar bill, a brass token needed for the ride home, his horn.

That creaking–the same measure over and over, louder and louder–is that less-than-half-a-man on patrol rolling toward Bass from the darkened far end of the tunnel. This specimen of half a man, thinks Bass, is as if the result gone wrong of a boy hob-byist dabbling after dinner in the basement with his little brother and a do-it-yourself-mail-order-taxidermy kit–creak! Tethered from around this half-of-a-man's neck is a scrap of cardboard with a crayon script reading: KEEP YOUR WORDS OF GOOD

WILL, THIS VET WANTS A FIVE-DOLLAR BILL–creak! The legs of the man's rotting fatigues are folded-up empty on the plywood seat of his supermarket cart–creak! This man's knuckles and finger nubs are righteously calloused from striding concrete, jabbing back swinging doors, clawing up his sack of weight–creak! Ribbon molders from a Purple Heart, a Silver Star, four Bronze Stars for meritorious service to his country–creak! This man's face is blackened with smut and is pitted bleeding as if from many tiny teeth bites–creak! This man's wisping longish beard and hair are matted with dried blood trickled from a spiraling hole where there was once a ear–creak!

Bass, attempting to stand, standing, trying to limp away with legs fallen to circulatory sleep during the slow advance–creak–of this cart man, totters, falls to one knee. The Andy Boy face, Bass sees, stares back sideways from the cardboard.

"I heard you playing the way you were the other day, not playing so much as swimming, as floating, as flying far off high and away from the rest of us," says Vet-Air-Cav-I-Just-Want-To-Tell-You-Private-First-Class.

"I heard you, like, you know, free, lifted up and above it all in a way I never heard or felt anything in a long time and I had to turn over something of myself, sort of, well, give you something, my ear, what was left of my good ear, in return for all, you know, you gave me. Hope you liked it."

No sound is heard from those city streets high above this subway side chamber. Little is heard other than the spatter of water in this domed grotto of crumbling brick and mud spit hanging down, of flow stone bearing the skeletal prints of trilobites, sea ferns, and mollusks.

Hillbilly's skull rests against damp flagstone, his lungs exhale the peat smell of Hibernian Short. Hillbilly rears up, fending-off phantoms seen only by Hillbilly. Button Down's face bends shadowed between Hillbilly and a track worker's stolen lantern suffusing the grotto chamber with a red glow as if both Button Down and Hillbilly are buried alive in a burning seam of coal. His voice whispers to Hillbilly, "Rest easy, it is all right."

Groaning, making little fluttering shapes and gestures with his fingers, Hillbilly again presses a cheek to damp stone; Hillbilly again sleeps.

Hillbilly awakens to a smell similar to that of burning coal oil that is his breath. A beard of dry puke is stuck in the polyester hair of a hula girl. His lips are parched and split. His tongue is swollen. A silhouette of Button Down rimmed in red, hands over a screw-top bottle. A long pull roils clots and flakes of sediment from the bottom of the bottle.

"Great God Almighty!" shouts Hillbilly rising up on his boney knees, shivering, twisting his face away from the bottle.

"God Almighty. . . Almighty. . . mighty. . . ."

Water taps on stone; claws scrabble; dirt sifts down.

"You should hear that cute thing playing his brains out with everyone *simply* loving it," Button Down says.

Hillbilly jiggles earwax with a pinky finger.

"I thought you admonished him to take his–forgive me, but I must say it–considerable talent elsewhere?" Button Down says.

Hillbilly holds the pint bottle up to the light, examines the liquor curling flame red.

"Why, cute cheeks is right now probably holding musical court in Grand Central surrounded by adoring commuters tossing him kisses and cash," gushes Button Down.

Hillbilly swigs from the bottle, eyes closed, gullet jerking, until the whiskey is bubbled gone.

"Now let me tell you something," Hillbilly whispers, touching, gently, a hand heel to his broken lips. "I like that boy, and he's a good boy, and not half bad with that horn seeing how he stole most, if not more, of what he knows off me, so don't be croaking around like some dressed-up-froggy-goes-a-courting-in-a-cloud-of-fruit-flies telling me what I already know and what I have to do."

"Well, that boy. . . ."

"GODDAMN IT, HEAR ME!" Hillbilly yells.

"Hear me. . . hear me. . . hear. . . ."

Button Down looks at the brick and the twisted iron rods, fiddles a finger over limestone seahorse ribs, sniffles creamy green snot in and out of one nostril.

Hillbilly whispers, "Now that, you old bunghole biter, is about the first anything of sense I've heard out of you."

Blue, smoking columns of sunlight tilt through the shadowed high vaultings of this terminal as if through the great nave of a cathedral, as if down through the sea of some coral reef where finned and clawed inhabitants shift and scuttle. In the hurried schooling and scattering, a tidal coming and going, more than a few of these carnivores, these omnivores, pause, pay heed, give applause and whistle and coin to the call of the kneeling boy praying himself through a horn. His song runnels up grooved pillars, among the higher reaches of plaster frieze and foliate scroll work, in the dusty joists of light traversing ceiling to floor to reverberate in the ears of those assembled about him: these shoppers stalked by pickpockets working in pairs, McAmon fondling himself under a mantle of rotting rags and newspapers, pushers alert for police while peddling–"Nice Ice! Rocky Road! Mister Softee!"–pimps in studded leather and plumes on the prowl for fresh quail, Blind David shifting eyes cataract-white behind his sunglasses, Rangoon nattering to himself, Hillbilly–his Lila Lee agleam on his shoulder–strolling through these partitions of light and shadow toward Bass.

Hillbilly's face, Bass sees, is as grime-blackened as the face of a miner first surfaced into the light. Bulging a fist into the pocket of his khakis, Hillbilly pulls out and throws down a balled ten-dollar bill. Hillbilly jumps in at the end of the refrain, improvising on the old familiar with a way of phrasing that Bass perceives as two skinny hounds followed by a skinny boy trotting down a wooded ridge on a frosty morning. Those hounds pad to a stop, smell the air, click teeth, bristle, give cry and chase.

Bass comes back with a doubling and tripling of the time, staccato notching high and low, a glide followed by ditty bop, swing, a Delta blues continuum, boogie woogie, a snatch of *Why Don't You Eat Where You Slept Last Night*, jook-joint jive, pentatonic scales, Coleman Hawkins encounters Ben Webster, whammer-jammer, harmonicat.

Hillbilly steps in with what Bass discerns as a Saturday night at an old-timey roadhouse filled with harmonica cry and smoke, couples dragging one another around. A boy shambling up to the door of the roadhouse followed by two panting hounds is how Bass hears it. A pop from inside the roadhouse results in shrieks, the music picking up, a woman holding her side stumbling out the door past the boy and his scattering hounds to fall to her knees, that boy running into the night.

Bass responds with a measure of *Walking After Midnight* followed by Dixieland, shout from Chicago's West Side, gut bucket, Generique, appoggiatura and escape tones, zydeco, a reel, a polka, heebie jeebies, rocking dopsie, three bars of *Corrine Corrina*, strut, hymn.

Hillbilly falls by with Lila Lee throating low and soft in a way Bass hears as a boy and his hounds out on a ledge watching cloud streaks cross the moon, the stars coursing in their tracks, a train looking small clicking across a trestle down in the valley until the small rows upon rows of lit windows in the passenger cars and caboose draw off into the darkness, that boy weeping.

Tears stripe the filth on his cheeks as Hillbilly listens to Bass—sunlight striking off his horn—play Bass.

"Beautiful," Hillbilly says, sucking up a sob. "Really fucking beautiful."

The subway at this late hour is a rivulet from a broken pipe, rats thrashing in a pile of cardboard boxes and plastic garbage bags, on top of which lies a hidden sack of less-than-half-a-man-on-the-scout asking himself whether he is sleeping on duty even as he sleeps. He asks whether he is dreaming this vision of Bass blowing his horn while Hillbilly watches from across the tracks. He asks himself if he is hearing the burble of water and rats tussling in that high note held by Bass.

From the height of that note, from where he rests down on his knees, Bass sees Hillbilly–porkpie, hula girls beckoning, jump boots–on the platform across the tracks. Hillbilly crosses the tracks, hops up on this platform in the time it takes Bass to rise to his feet. The first blow–Lila Lee flashing high over the porkpie's crown–chops Bass back to his knees. Hillbilly chopping, grunting over and over, stands above Bass sagging in a spew of blood. An ear hangs half off. An eye starts from its socket. Lila Lee, twisted, is flung aside and replaced with a found length of pipe Hillbilly uses until the boy's skull smatters and brains spurt, until the weight of the pipe is such that Hillbilly can no longer lift his arm.

"I. . ." Hillbilly says, breathing with difficulty, ". . . I call that tune. . ." lowering himself slowly and with effort near his handiwork no longer recognizable as Bass, "I call that tune *Whistle Up The Dogs And Piss On The Fire.*"

Awake, knowing he is now awake, the less-than-half-a-man slides himself down from his heaped perch under the cover of a train rumble-rushing through the station; he mounts his cart and arm strokes over to the prone pair. Vet-Air-Cav-What-Do-We-Have-Here-First-Class–after first looking about for onlookers, after looking for signs that Hillbilly is faking exhausted sleep–pulls a length of wire from a legless pant leg, loops the wire around Hillbilly's neck as daintily as a little girl looping a ribbon around the neck of a kitten, and yanks, nearly yanking himself off his cart. Hillbilly grunts awake, kicks, tries to get fingers between the gouging wire and his neck. Hillbilly dances his jump boots over concrete, kicks with his boot tongues flapping. Hillbilly horn man browns his khakis with piss and shit, curls his tongue in a face turning dark as the face of a drowned man, grins a crazy grin, lets it go, goes limp in the widening pool of his own piss.

Vet-Air-Cav-In-The-Valley-Of-The-Shadow-Of-Death-First-Class collects the horn once belonging to Bass. He lays the horn across his cart, then rolls down track tunnel concealing another sinner in darkness but for his song–that diminishing creak!

MARISA, YOU WERE RIGHT
ABOUT HEARING WE
MADE THE PAPER AND SO I
THOUGHT I WOULD SEND
YOU THIS FOR OLD TIMES
AND ALSO TO SAY PLEASE,
PLEASE, PLEASE, DO NOT
BURN UP ANY THING
MORE OF MINE IF YOU
HAPPEN TO COME ACROSS
MY SILK BOXER SHORTS
AND DISCHARGE PAPERS
AND A BOOK BY HARRY
CREWS WITH CREWS ON
THE COVER SHOWING OFF
HIS BEAUTIFUL TATTOO
THAT READS, HOW DO YOU
LIKE YOUR BLUE-EYED
BOY NOW, MR. DEATH?

POLICE NEWS

T wo Brooklyn men were arrested Tuesday afternoon after ramming a police car with the vehicle they were driving at a high rate of speed.

Virgilio Diaz, 17, of 116 Havemeyer Street and Fernando Vasquez, 18, of 112 Fifth street, were arrested following a car chase that at times exceeded 90 miles per hour along a lunchtime-crowded Metropolitan Avenue, police said.

Officers reported observing the pair weaving through traffic and driving up on the sidewalk at about 12:15 p.m. Police entered into pursuit, which ended forty minutes later when Diaz drove the new 2003 BMW sedan into a patrol car driven by Det. Phil Ciccola.

Ciccola was taken to the hospital where he was treated and released. Diaz and Vasquez sustained facial cuts and bruises, but refused medical attention, police said. Both were charged with resisting arrest, reckless driving, driving without a license, and driving while intoxicated.

A 57-year-old Brooklyn man was arrested after threatening his neighbors with a gun, police said.

Alexander Ibor of 446 12th Street was taken into custody Tuesday afternoon after approaching five members of the Minardi family and pointing a World War II vintage, German machine pistol at them.

The Minardi family was sitting in lawn chairs on the sidewalk in front of their 12th Street residence when Ibor came out of his garage and threatened to put an end to the family's talking about him, police said.

This was a normal occurrence for the last several years, police added.

Officers and firefighters responding to a report of a fire early Tuesday night discovered a heated domestic dispute.

Police said they arrived at 115 Lorimer Street at about 5:30 p.m. when they observed Ms. Marisa Martinez Rivas, 39, cursing and throwing burning clothes, books, and papers from a second-story window.

Rivas told police the blaze started after she took numerous items belonging to Peter Christopher, 31, of the same address, and put them in the bathtub.

Police said Rivas told officers she did not know how the items caught fire.

Christopher said he returned home from work to find smoke billowing from the windows of the apartment and the front door locked. He yelled at Rivas that their apartment was on fire when she appeared at a window, started cursing him in Spanish, and threw a burning shoe at him.

Firefighters extinguished numerous blazes, police said.

DROPPING YOU ANOTHER
LINE, MARISA, TO LET
YOU KNOW THAT YOU ARE
TERRIFIC AT KILLING A
DREAM WITH X-RATED
POETRY AS REAL AS THE
REPO MAN KICKING IN
THE DOOR AT 7:43 THIS
A.M. BEFORE HE TOOK
THE CLOCK, TV, COUCH,
ETC., BUT HE LEFT ME,
TRYING TO MAKE THE
PRICE OF A SIX-PACK AND
WONDERING OVER MY
LUCK AT HOW MY MISSING
CREDIT CARD HAPPENED
NOT TO BURN UP TOO

YOUR LIFEPLUS CREDIT CARD ACCOUNT 4312 221 446

New Balance	Total Credit Line	Total Available Credit
$1517.88	$1500.00	$0000.000

Transaction Details

Date	Trans. Description	Amount
07/13	Hung Yung Chinese Rest Brklyn NY	66.44
07/13	Lady Luv Shoes Brklyn NY	232.70
07/13	Lil's Bed & Bath Brklyn NY	88.48
07/13	Appliance City Brklyn NY	273.19
07/13	Clown Drugs Brklyn NY	47.64
07/13	Tony's Market Brklyn NY	123.18
07/13	Estelles Brklyn NY	51.13
07/13	La Mancha School of Dance Brklyn NY	70.68
07/13	Shoprite Value Savings Mart Brklyn NY	344.14
07/13	Easy Strider Brklyn NY	91.99
07/13	Los Tres Mexicano Cochina Brklyn NY	33.23
07/13	XXX Video Brklyn NY	77.09
09/15	Finance Charge	17.99

SINCE YOU SKIPPED LAST MONTH'S PAYMENT, PLEASE MAKE A PAYMENT THIS MONTH. QUESTIONS? FOR HELPFUL INFORMATION, LOST OR STOLEN CARDS, CALL: 800-441-2753

MARISA, IT'S ME AGAIN,
ASKING IF YOU COULD
FIND IT IN YOUR HEART
TO STOP BY THE LIBRARY
ON YOUR WAY TO
WHEREVER YOU WANT
TO GO NOW THAT I HAVE
CUT-UP MY CREDIT CARD
WITH YOUR SKID MARKS
FROM WHEN YOU BOMBED
YOUR SKANKY FAT ANGER
ALL OVER TOWN WHILE
SOMEHOW MISSING A
CHARGE-UP AT DELPHINA'S
DIET AND WEIGHT LOSS
CENTER

THE BRANCH LIBRARIES
Tel: 2122390908
Ninety-Sixth Street Regional Branch
112 East 96th Street
New York, NY 10128

LAST NOTICE

Library records show the following item(s) are overdue. It you have returned them, please excuse this notice. If not, please return them as soon as possible.

LC 91-53201 William Tester: **Darling** (Knopf) ISBN 0-394-56872-9

At notice printing you owe: $273.75. Return immediately to avoid $0.25 per day additional overdue fine.

REGULATIONS GOVERNING THE USE OF THE LI-BRARY ARE AVAILABLE AT INFORMATION AND CIR-CULATION DESKS IN THE LIBRARY.

The New York Public Library
Celebrating Its Second Century

HEY, MARISA, THIS IS ME
FINALLY GETTING MY LIFE
TOGETHER AND I WANTED
TO TELL YOU HOW AFTER
CHEWING OVER YOUR
ADVICE ABOUT DOING
SOMETHING DECENT
WITH MYSELF I DECIDED
THAT EXCEPT FOR THE
DRIPPING POISON YOU
WERE RIGHT AGAIN SO
NOW I'M TRYING TO
LAY OFF THE POTATO
CRISPS, THE BEEF JERKY,
EVEN THE SCHLITZ,
WHILE GOING FULL
BLAST ON THE ERNEST
& JULIO GALLO HEARTY
BURGUNDY, REALLY, NO
SHIT

WELCOME TO TONY'S MARKET

Pringles Potato Crisps	1.69	F
All-Fruit Jam	1.99	B
Celery	2.44	F
King-Size Twix Cookie Bar	.99	F
Pabst 6pk Btl Beer	4.69	T
Pabst 6pk Btl Beer	4.69	T
Pringles Potato Crisps *******	VOID	
Wheat Muffin	1.86	F
Pabst 6pk Btl Beer	4.69	T
Carrots	1.49	F
Sardines	.98	T
Irish Spring Soap	3.29	F
Vaseline Petro Jelly	1.39	F
Pabst 6pk Btl Beer *******	VOID	
Tony's Beef Jerky	1.29	F
Pabst 6pk Btl Beer *******	VOID	
Q-Tips Swabs	1.49	T
Pabst 6pk Btl Beer	4.69	T
Pabst 6pk Btl Beer *******	VOID	
King-Size Twix Cookie Bar *******	VOID	
Cheez Wiz	2.29	F
Apples	1.49	F
Pabst 6pk Btl Beer *******	VOID	
Schlitz 6pk Cn Beer	3.39	T
Bologna	2.98	F
Tony's Beef Jerky *******	VOID	
Schlitz 6pk Cn Beer *******	VOID	
King-Size Twix Cookie Bar	.99	
Gallo Burgundy Wine	7.99	
**** Tax 5.94 TOT	36.61	
Credit	40.00	
Change	3.39	

THANKS FOR SHOPPING TONY'S MARKET

THAT HEAVY RIDER

Who would imagine that such a life as mine–a life lived with valorous deeds against the ill will of bullies and fiends, midnight raids and hold-ups, chub whores three at a time at two dollars a throw, the failed plottings of triggermen law bought and boys addlepated, sparks striking from the ringing hooves of my huge striding getaway horse–could somehow come to this?

I tup up my twist of neckerchief. I hook what remain of my fingers in the cyclone fence cornering off the broken macadam of the Chatsworth School playground. I watch the children from behind these sunglasses with one mirrored lens punched out and lost.

Stella stands smallest among those jockeying for place, the pushing and pulling that passes as play. Her small face, pale, appears solemn, sealed. Stella is right, now is not the time to reveal ourselves. I feign nonchalance, hobble along the fence to behind this towering butternut tree imprisoned by sidewalk and street and block; another holdout among these cars and buses. Seen from around the peeling-back bark of this tree, in the wire air-diamonds of the fence, Stella's smallness of four diamonds big.

With her face rounding up into hair elastic-banded back into a pony-tail, Stella looks up at Miss Ashkenazy. Together they turn, join the others jostling toward school. Miss Ashkenazy takes up Stella's ponytail, flaps Stella's ponytail as if she is flapping reins. Both break into a skip.

Regard, if you will, the bouncing shadow of horse and rider, foxtail weed, sand blown into macadam cracks, the fading paint of a foul line under their hippity-hop strides.

In that instant when Stella and Miss Ashkenazy slow to a walk, before Stella and Miss Ashkenazy pass through the school's open doors, Stella turns, and this is the instant–and this is how we know what we must know–when Stella sees me. In the dark of this one lens, Stella sucks a finger, stares. Miss Ashkenazy turns, making me, hugely famous for my boldness, duck into hiding behind this tree.

Ants traffic along the bark.

Truck gears grind from the nearby street.

A runner wheezes carbon dioxide, lead, oxygen enough to continue on.

Peeking again around this reaching shade tree, I see a pile of jacket used as home plate perhaps forgotten in the sweat brought on from broomstick-swatting a tennis ball high over the basketball court. I see, I hear, the creaking sway of empty swings. I see Miss Ashkenazy hugging herself as if having seen something: a haint perhaps, a ghost not yet weaned from the living, the sight of which has chilled her cold.

"Jesse," she calls. "Is that you, Jesse?"

My mind is a thing clomping around in the dark.

My mind is the roan stolen from the prosperous railpack attorney James Tillman Ryan. That roan–some years later run off and found skinnied to eye sockets, knee knobs, tufted clumps of mangy winter hair–is wandering through a wealthy grain dealer's long abandoned house with the once chandeliered rooms and hallways now latticed high with wisteria, spiral tendrils of trumpet creeper, golden groundsel, zinnia, bougainvillaea. The roan's red-horse wanting to find a way out of the place, to restore itself to what it was, has dwindled to nibbling at what woody vines and blooming flowers a weary stretch of neck can reach. The roan twitches an ear free from bluebottle flies while gazing now and again through the glassy shards of a second-story window at a moonlit world.

I have gone to ground too long.

Stella is the one who whispers me over, halters my wandering mind and leads it chocking loudly down the overgrown curve of cherry wood stairs, around where the thick planking of the dining room's floorboards have fallen into the fruit cellar sighing up onion and potato rot, leads it from out of the old house altogether.

Lightning bugs go green-gold, green-gold out in the dark. Squeak of saddle and scabbard. Glint of moonlight on this one-mirrored lens.

Again, I am mounted.

Water currents around her fingertips, about her and buttocks, tiny twisters down the drain. She haunches goose bumped, hands palm to palm between legs, dangle of big breasts humping together bigger. One breast with the long stretch grooves, the green vein that branches into the pegged nipple, this breast is so much bigger than the other breast.

"Brrr," says she.

With a spread towel beckoning her, Miss Ashkenazy stands up in tub slosh and squeaks. She gathers her sleeking hair in both hands, hand over hand squeezes down the dripping length of her hair. She takes and covers her face with the towel.

I look at the hair stringing between her legs.

She towels off the breasted big front of herself: the freckles and moles on shoulders and arms, her waggle of breasts, hip jut, her pimply buttside. She lifts a leg lean with the curve of calf. God Almighty, what a great leg this woman has, the slim ankle, the cocked foot laced in the arch with tiny veins, the toenails lacquered baby pink: all lifted gracefully to the rim of the tub.

In a kind of preening, Miss Ashkenazy towel pats at herself while one hand holding onto the shower curtain: a cartoon scene bright with hothouse big orchids and hibiscus, the plastic scrape of fringed palm fronds, sawgrass hiding speckled salamanders and horny toads, a shy peccary or two with now is not the time to look closely for more, the tree- top- high flocking of parrots, macaws, fruit bats, a troop of spider monkeys chatter-picking through the choicest avocados, casabas, mangoes; all the meloned fruit and flower and flora dripping from the recent downpour, hotting up the place, chasing that brrr.

It is hard, I say, not to want to love a woman who loves herself.

Her grimace, somewhat equine, morewhat equestrienne, is somewhere between she does and does not like this as in this is a little too herky-jerky for her, easy, slower, there, better, much better, keep it going while working some on her tremolo, no, hang still, keep it going more while getting a better grip in the mildew slippery branches of the shower curtain, shifts her footing along to where the porcelain is chipping off for the upcoming whinny and warp.

Woman is God's greatest work; how the sinews tine into bone, hide back under flesh, tie in, hide back; this flapping of big breasts, the huff of breath blown toothpaste minty, the flutter of eyelids.

Tremors later, her teeth and vertebrae clicking, she slips, sits, pulls down a rain of plastic tropics, hollow rod, plaster dust. A shower of shower curtain rings roll loose as pocket change around and around on the tile floor.

Laughter now, and her saying, "What can I say?" from

under this canopy of colorful jungle life.

After laughing too, I say, "Stella–tell me about Stella."

Listen for yourself, look: the bell, the voices echoing in the stairwells, lockers clanging, those doors with the bars for handles clunking all the way open. The sound and sight is that of humanity in small running forth into a slanting rain in a kind of cattle drive, a kid drive: a question now of getting this very herd, the stragglers, not to Abilene so much as on the bus.

Carrying a crayoned sheaf of paper, wearing a backpack drooping four or five books heavy for her bones bundled small, Stella plods with her patient goodness in this circle of dark lens. I see her as if through a dusty viewfinder too long up on a shelf, as if Stella is one of those scratched stereoscopic photographs: an ambrotype doubling, a blurring of a little pioneer woman in too big plow boots toting a slop bucket back from the pigsty. Stella is one of those women worn down young wearing a brother's or a husband's too big muley hat, standing surrendered out in front of the homestead, it's sod roof buckled from a three week rain and no let up, other than the one old as birth, anywhere in sight.

Stella wakes through a puddle knowing better than to get her feet wet, I know, perhaps not so patient, perchance proving Miss Ashkenazy right.

If the stallion Stonewall Jackson was now cropping these rain-lank weeds drooping through this wire fence, I would collect his head up, ki-yi his muscle and heart on to hoof-holing puddles in pursuit of Stella. The clatter of more than half a ton of iron-shod horse and arsenaled rider on this macadam, the cries of those others scattering, the splashing, a snort, the slap of wet stirrup and billets, the flop of my open slicker, the chink of rowels, oat farts, the clicking of the great beast's teeth on a slavered chunk of greening copper bit would surely twist Stella around to have a look at me.

The tallness is what I miss, the wonder writ bold on the

face of this child.

Crouching through a hold bent back in this fence, careful not to catch my slicker-length on these dove tailings of wire–fuck! not careful enough–revealing myself as the someone I am in this life of mine not yet completely slipped away. I say to you I am someone whose time has not yet wriggled free with still more than a twitch of rage in this rag of a man flapping rainblown on a fence, in this ignorant farm boy caught out in our bottomland behind the handles of a sod buster; that boy Dingus whupped good by bored bullies in blue each lugging two pounds of pistol in the name of civil conflict, in the shared beliefs proven again and again that voracity is a virtue, that might is right. This boy was quick to catch on; the shots fired blood-drunk for revenge, the righteous butchery, the education gotten from a Minie ball nubbing off a middle finger, a lead slug splatting open a lung, another lodging less than an inch under this straddle of breastbone, a fourth slug puckering hot in the meat of my leg, a ticking bum knee that tells the weather, an ankle breaking in the stirrup of a clay bank gelding whoaed-up short by an ounce of lead heavy in his heart. So too you learn from the hands of a loving woman, the peaceful sleeping sounds of our child. You learn from the catechism lessons found in wanting to spread the word of our Lord, doing His work Sundays and nights while filling the other six days with once again swallowing dust behind a middle buster and a mule under a sun harnessing my head and shoulders along wavering hot furrows of king cotton parched princeling puny until I know the ache of a different want in every part of me. Either move on or die, I say, with my moving on to hammering up more than my share of outsheds, selling coal, stomping fence, swapping saddle stock, pointing armament, stealing stock outright, hurrahing whole towns and trains, bickering with the wife, spoiling the child, knowing civil warfare of a different kind, going all to the way with that feeling of what at the time seems like a good idea until night hawking full time. All of which sums up to one morning surprising yourself, feeling the fat thickening about your waist, around my heart; seeing the squint wrinkles, the gray gleaming on my head while catching myself tugging this tearing slicker sleeve free from this cyclone fence.

Stella still channels behind the other children.

The smaller ones wait to giant-step up the bus steps, the bigger ones have already shoved their way on: shadow children now shading along behind the window glass. One boy stretches his gum string long to lasso a sweetheart or a mama's boy or leave it strung from seat to seat. Another boy is lost in finger-fishing for boogers. A girl with ribbons in her hair rubbers her face into a monster mask against the bus window glass at Miss Taylor, who is Remedial Social Studies, I think, or Math. That girl scowls at the ones smallest not yet on the bus, at Stella now waiting last.

"Stella, over here!"

He calls from the opening door of an idling car. A shotgun barrel, no, an umbrella tip points at me as he limbers out suited with a tie blowing out of his suit coat. Tall, he stands himself taller. The umbrella flaps up while the open car door lets the rain soak leather the color of aerating blood: a lung shot, a heart shot.

Stella stands bedraggled wet.

Take a look for yourself, I say to you, and see how quickly you are alone.

Stella looks at him, looks back at Miss Taylor motioning Stella to hurry get on the bus with Miss Taylor now also looking at him, a suited attorney, a tall one, with Miss Taylor changing her waving motion from let's get along little doggie to, okay, Stella, I see him, and I know it's okay, your mama told me it's okay, so sure, you can go with him if you want to, well, go on.

Stella looks back at him, starts walking toward him.

Make no mistake, this is how it is without etiquette, without influence other than the brief history of what has gone before, my own marred body, this mind galloping apace with my fear and desire, the ferocity that so long ago already became a friend.

Stella, her face looking up at his face, hands him the soaked-through, runny-colored sheaf of crayoned paper.

He says something to Stella I cannot hear.

Her lips move.

I see his lips move.

I am the one who sees how he holds the colored paper in the hand holding open the car door.

Stella is the one high stepping up into the car, wobbly stepping onto the driver's seat, onto the passenger seat; Stella bounces to a sit, sits. His getting in, his pulling shut the car door with the tinted window glass that hides what I see of her, that opens the way for that which is not always hidden in me.

Greetings, old friend.

I say to you, "And there went out another horse that was red: and power was given to me that sat thereon to take peace from the earth; and that they should kill one another: and there was given unto me a great sword."

Stonewall Jackson twitches his ears at the scratching of crickets, of peepers peeping in the cattails around Surprise Creek. This steady old bay Stonewall Jackson bestirs himself with the thud and clank and murmur of horses and men, with this wind whispering through the copse of sandy pine. In the butternut tree hangs a blade of rising moon. I whisper mostly to myself, "His terrible *swift sword*."

I swing down to the reminder of that clay bank gelding shot out from under me, peg leg it up through shale slide and dust, through pant ripping nettle and bracken to the boot-crunch of cinder. I bend to the smell of creosoted tie, to the burnished rails ribboned silver. A hand to the still warm rail finds hum.

An "Okay, Frank" has Frank "Yea-ha" riders–Tucker and Liddil and one or both of those Ford sons-of-bitches–up the bank, high-stepping their horses over the tracks above the cross ties taken up, up the rockbed side of the cut and into the shadowed cover of a pine stand and lone butternut tree. Frank opens the lantern to hissing. Frank fires a match. Lighting the lantern, he hoods a red flap of raggy long john leg around the glass so the flame shows red.

"Frank," says I, "have Woodson come up with Long Boy."

Frank calls down to that Cracker Neck to do as I bid. The cinder bed starts its dance. The ties and rails join in. Sparks blow crown-high in the dark of the trees below the cut. Piston chuff pumps within earshot. Woodson scrabbles up the shale bank with Long Boy, hands Long Boy over by the barrel.

"Remember," says I, "no molesting now of preacher daddies, nor widows, nor old Rebs."

Woodson nods. Woodson dust-tail slides down the bank to steady Stonewall Jackson and Gypsy Dog, Bell and Black Gold.

The locomotive–sparks and smoke and smokestack and lamp and cowcatcher–sways around the curve of track to head on with the lamplight sweeping, sliding fast as spirit folk along the worn smooth of the rails toward Frank. Swinging the lantern low, Frank commences the wail of steel on steel, sparks scattering up from the rails as if the cowcatcher is plowing fire up from this night. I can hear the clank of couplings, creaking, hissing, almost feel the gut-felt lurch and sling. Cummins or Ed or a Ford runs through the dusty funneling of locomotive lamplight with a neckerchief pulled up over his nose, a hammer-cocked pistol held at the ready.

Frank points his foot-long patented Colt revolver at the slow coming-on locomotive. Frank is a declaiming Shakespearean actor, the champion in a penny dreadful, a latter-day hero of the silver screen with the locomotive's lamp showing the feature film of his life. This is a talkie, five-D, sense-o-surround with the sound of a shot *kaponging* off boiler steel, whizzling close, the doing no doubt of a Ford, trigger eager, with both those Ford boys ever ready to ventilate something.

The metal smell of grinding brake blocks, the piss-squirting of hot oil, the hiss of boiler steam stinks past me. Cummins, it was Cummins yellowed out earlier in the swing of the locomotive's lamplight, catches hold on the ladder of the crummy, hops up, while Frank casually steps aside for the locomotive creep. Faces peer from the gas-lit windows of the carriage cars; a portly man sporting a bowler hat and the waxy upsweep of a handlebar moustache, a woman loosely braiding a child's hair in readiness for rocking sleep, a man paused in creasing over the page of a newspaper. The light from inside the cars falls bent on steam rolling and sucking away, on weeds and cinder bed. The engineer and stoker lean out of the cab for a look at Frank clicking back the hammer of his Colt.

"Go ahead now, just say what it is you want us to do and we'll do it," says the engineer as if he is used to this sort of thing and bored by it.

"Much obliged," says Frank, just as easy and bored as the registered voter, as the raiser of bristly hogs, Frank is. Frank hikes one foot up on the cab step, reaches in, yanks up a long throttle lever so the locomotive sighs out once, then again.

Tucker, Liddil, and a few of the rest scramble and slide down through the brambly side of the cut to brandish their artillery every which way and that as if they are thespians from a bankrupt stage company.

Long Boy hinges quiet from an arm crook. My neckerchief remains loose around my neck. Woodson, now masked by a flour sack with eye and nose holes cut askew, holds a Whitneyville upright near an ear while another pistol, this one mismatched shorter and heavier to the Whitneyville, snugs down his pants to pointing at his nads.

I grab the top rung of the ladder of the second carriage

car and swing up. Woodson does likewise. Frank and the rest of the boys should by now have begun hurrahing this train with our routine tried-and-true of gruffly ordering the grimy stoker or brakeman to toss the fire ax or a coal pick into the scorched weeds along the track bed. Frank will oversee Cummins or one of the Fords sideways-swing the weight of that same ax or coal pick through the complaining wood of the mail car's sliding side door double-bolted from within by a messenger faithful to, among other things, the ideal of a ten-dollar pocket watch with nickel plating bearing his curliqued initials and the roman numerals of his dedicated years of employment. The wood breaks out in groaning great blonde splinters with steady-as-he-goes Frank producing a burlap feed sack from his bellied-open shirt-front while consoling the messenger blubbering snot and blood. Frank will help the weeping messenger fill the burlap bulging of that sack to almost-too-heavy for Frank to carry with waybills and bonds and bundles of gold dust tied tight and silver bars and pieces of eight scattering loose over the floorboards and packs of crisp loot from the squat Wells Fargo safe the combination for which the messenger has had a momentary lapse of memory until Frank offered up encouragement by chopping the messenger across the nose with the chamber part of his percussion Colt. The others, Tucker, Liddil and the other Ford, should already have sauntered down the aisles of the dining car and the sleeper car and the other carriage car upholstered in red. One of those rovers will most likely poke a dirty thumb into a cowering dandy's fat cheek looking suspiciously swollen from a-what-do-we-have-here wad of one-hundred dollar bills. Another one of those bad boys will spot out how this peacock plume of a bejewelled woman stands two or so inches taller than she normally would because of the urge to suddenly insole her rhinestone slippers with greenback stacks, or how a daddy pony rides his daughter on one nervous knee, the daughter sending a wheeze of mirth through our marauding deputation with her whining whether it is all right now to take that shiver-cold tickle of Daddy's silver money from out of her under drawers. A Mennonite farmer hands over his savings saved from day-after-choking-day of breathing in bitter tobacco dust in the now-strangled hope of starting anew some where other than the hot and dark of the curing sheds to which he will most likely return. The lawyer wears a stovepipe hat Tucker will slap off because Tucker would later say the hat reminded him of that gawk of a man they call the Great Emancipator. That sour priss of a Princeton College boy on holiday out to the Territories to drop himself a sickly buffalo or bushwack an old Pawnee scout has to meanwhile show God and himself how brave he is by offering up several stut-stut-stuttering words of reluctance about pulling off and giving over a ruby pinkie ring until convinced otherwise by the triple hammer click of a .44 caliber Smith & Wesson. The soiled dove whose wages of sin are secreted in her corset scented with lilac strong as garlic is sniffed out by that pawing hound of a drooling pup that is no other than the younger Ford. Lastly, and certainly not least, we, I, come to this suited tall man with an umbrella carried across his knees as if a shotgun, or a sword, in a worn scabbard and whose living presence on this great globe earth is affront enough and reason sufficient for my stopping this locomotive.

I sit next to him in the blood-red seat.

I close the car door.

His suit is Italian-tailored. His hair is the smell of rose water. His breath is the long tobacco smell of good cigars.

"With your final breath now before I let loose your brains and skull bone bits and sissy-scented strands of hair around the leather and glass inside of this fine automobile, you will tell me what I want to hear concerning Stella," says I.

He keeps both hands on the steering wheel while looking straight ahead. His hands and fingers, knuckled-large for an ambulance chaser, resting on and over the steering wheel, are larger than my hands: his hands with all of his fingers, a thumb with the quarter moon at the base of the nail showing no glint, no great sword. The whole of this man is revealed in small to any who are willing to see, with our hands almost always revealing more than our faces, with his face cast into hollows and planes from the hooded lights of the dashboard; a face that is already more death mask than living face with the eyes pissing fear straight ahead.

"Look at me, motherfucker!"

He does not look at me. He sits as if driving us on although we are parked.

Know, says I to you, dear reader, my coming to that place in myself beyond the welcome-home handshake of an old friend named ferocity, a place that surprises you even when it is the very place you have set out to reach, an old place in ourselves once reached that allows a man to kill another man.

Long Boy's mouth nuzzles his ear, kisses down along his neck and along the line of jaw bone, feels for the right place for that one big fucking hickey.

Long Boy's tongue clicks back.

What is heard is outside, on the other side of this tinted glass reflecting the lights from the dashboard as if a Milky Way wash of constellations: the flashing moons of his watch crystal, my one lens. Hear the jangle sound of bridle and bit. Hear the licking sound of a horse's tongue and lips on and over this car door, the black gums and tongue and lips lipping the chrome door handle for the salt of my sweat. The sound is that of another known man-killer-this one by the name of Stonewall Jackson–too long left standing faithful in his trace, or Black Gold, or one of the other mounts gotten loose after skying and stepping back, rearing and running from down below the cut where the fuck-up Fords were ordered to picket them steady.

His eyes meet mine.

"Prepare to meet thy maker," says I to James Tillman Ryan.

The car door opens surrounding us in a nimbus of light; him with the fear of my vengeance beading sweat on his forehead, on the sweat, on the tears streaking his cheeks. The light glances along Long Boy swooning as a lover on his shoulder. The rounded mouth mark of Long Boy's love bites have already nibbled red into the flesh just below the line of his jaw. I sit spraddle-legged, pointing Long Boy's length, and look out the window at Stella fleeing over the basketball court into the dark.

Her breath breathing-in lifts her back, swells her lungs, filters into her bloodstream as bubbled gases heading for the tidal pull giving her this life of hers: chemical, electrical, molecular. I feel the weight of where her leg touches my leg. I feel the wetness evaporating from the game of connect-the-dots using the moles on her lifting-back that I was playing with my tongue, that sleeping sense she must have of me hotting up against her breathing-in in this dark.

Watch now for that moment when this woman becomes a thing, meat, a housing of gristle and hair with no one at home. Think of her, it, with the heart in your chest the same as my heart, which is mostly a forgetter and a liar and a rapacious thug. Try to think of her, says I, for all of her singularity, with all of her beauty and loyalty to me now, as no more to me than another favored whore soon to grow as practiced and tiresome as those other chubs in what she says and does. Or more precisely, consider her as no more than an operative of mine spying on the day-to-day doings at the Chatsworth School playground. Or perhaps, and this is not as far off the mark as you might at first think, she is another would-be murderer out for the notoriety, or greedy for the reward put up by the railroad gangs and Governor Thomas T. Crittenden of twenty-five thousand dollars in silver currency for my arrest and delivery living or dead. Or maybe she is someone able to imagine the salary and bookings and travel from the nightly performance of THE LAST MOMENTS AND MOST COWARDLY ASSASSINATION OF THE FAMOUS OUT-LAW JESSE WOODSON JAMES acted out first at the Theatre Comique in Kansas City, then, in short time, the playing to the shabby seats of the having–seen-better days that are the Richmond and Paramount and Mohawk theatres in towns that give rise to our loneliest knowing of what it is to grow up and labor and die anonymous to history other than to the history we invent for ourselves. Watch her in her last performance down a darkened hall in front of the streaked glass of a mirror showing shadow to light to shadow that is a bare light bulb and cord swinging shadow and light across a pipe leaking onto broken bathroom tiles. Hers is the face of someone others call by her name. Her latest invention is the curve of a razor slash leaking her life. Or more likely, her last moments will come at the hands and traitorous heart of a cohort or a friend or one that is loved.

Ah, Miss Ashkenazy, I pray I charge you falsely.

My face is what is seen reflecting in the glass of this picture of the stallion Stonewall Jackson: my face, the way my face is for now, mirroring down double, smaller, in the silvery twin lenses of my sunglasses. See for yourself the bigger reflection of my wife, those looming bigger Ford boys slouching at my back watching me up on this chair straightening this picture.

"Straight enough?" says I without turning around, seeing Bob's reflection straighten itself taller, fist and shake out the fingers of his shooting hand. I see Bob glance at his mouth-breather of an older brother thumb-tapping the hammer of the .44 caliber pistol holstered down the front of his bagging pants.

The cane chair I stand on creaks.

Heat from the approach of noon has already risen hot up near these rafters.

The voices of children playing out in the heat and dust of

the road drift in through the sitting room's open windows with one child's voice calling above the other voices, "Coward, coward, pants on fire!"

Bob snickers the handled pearl and blued iron of his revolver from its leather, straightens his shooting arm, sights up the barrel at the curling clump of hair at the back of my head. His brother slides slack against the flowered wallpaper, leaving smear of hair oil over a chrysanthemum blooming big. His brother's limp wrist shakes his pistol at my back.

"I'm ready," says I, turning to face my murderers, knowing all along as we all know. "It's what I deserve."

My wife gives it to me.

Smacking the picture of Stonewall Jackson with the back of my head splinters the glass, swings my sunglasses loose from one ear, pops one lens to plinking and rolling along the hardwood floor. The cap-and-ball blast of my wife's whispered words topples me with my falling weight thundering under and through this wooden house, tinking the China fine tea cups and saucers, setting the framed picture of that steed to rocking.

Blood speckles my shirt front, spots a cuff as if a ruby cuff link, streaks fingers already feeling separate from myself, drips, pools seeps into a crack between floorboards.

The rafters shadow over darker in this one remaining lens.

Breath rips up short, catches, stays caught.

She breathes out, that chemical tide washing back, the blood flushing back into branching capillaries, alveoli, lobes of lung collapsing, wrinkling, shrunken. Feel the twitch electric of her foot and fingers, her tail bone tip, the skin of her back cooling loose from my cheek, the breath rushing out of this woman's body she sleeps in into the dark.

Seem in this light potshotting through the leaves of the butternut tree, Stella bobs her head, bounces her curlicue to the jumps of a bigger girl rope-thwapping the macadam. Seeing Stella this close, watching her from this car with the waiting getaway horses under the hood, is a reminder. Her leaping horsetail of hair shines about with sunlight: hair–I want to believe I remember–that is fragrant a day or two or more after having missed hair washing day, her hair with its crooked line ending at the nape of her so slender neck. This face of hers reveals itself as a child's face, this child's face, and her sunlit hair, and the almost too much for me to take in all at once of her that is the flapping long sleeves of an over big jean jacket, her puffing shorts too baggy for her too thin legs marked darker about with scabs. No, I see her legs are marked with tattoos, with one tattoo that I cannot quite make out half hidden into a sock rolled at the ankle. Her sneakers sparkle suns, moons, planets she gooed on with glitter. She does a dip as the bigger girl jumps. The bigger girl slaps the rope over to a stop. The bigger girl loops the rope up, hands the rope to Stella. With her face, the set of her mouth, going to the serious Stella she too often is, Stella shakes out the loop. Stella hops on one foot.

Opening the shyster's car door, I foot the flutter of leaf shadow. Stella hops. I get out of the car leaving Long Boy resting in the dark of the back seat. I straighten myself up in this light to showing what is left of myself wearing bloody hands. I reveal this face flashing a circle of lens at children teeming around teachers paired-off talking, on Miss Ashkenazy on the basketball court bouncing a ball with some of the smaller boys, at this resurrection for me that is Stella.

Stella dips, hesitates, trips on the rope. The bigger girl laughs. The bigger girl takes back the rope, skips over to gabby other girls. Stella leans lit to darker against the fence in the deeper shadows of this playground world.

An airplane buzzes overhead hidden by branches, burrs of butternut clustered, leaves wavering in the wind.

The wind lifts the side hair of someone else's girl moving

her lips as she reads.

A ball bounces against the fence, rolls to a stop.

Miss Ashkenazy becomes shadow fetching the ball. Miss Shadowkenazy says something to darker Stella, puts an arm around darker Stella.

"Bless the heart within this woman," says I.

Stella hears me. Stella turns, sees me. I know this is when Stella sees me, knows me for what I am coming around the car with Miss Ashkenazy now looking over, seeing me. Holding Stella, Miss Ashkenazy says another something into Stella's ear, kisses into the smell and the feel that is Stella's hair, holds the kiss. Miss Ashkenazy lets Stella loose to run to the lighter and brighter side of where the hole is bent back in the fence with Stella easing her way sideway through, careful not to catch herself on that wire. Stella stops when she is all the way through and looks back at Miss Ashkenazy walking fast toward school.

Stella walks fast, skips, runs to where I have the car door open for her Stella face, her sway of hair, the small hands smaller looking in the big sleeve holes of her jean jacket. Her legs knobby kneed are patched over with having run tattoos of Popeye the Sailor, Donald Duck, Chevrolet, the Stars and Bars of the Confederacy waving away from me closing the door on this child sucking two fingers. This golden child watches out at me limping around the car in this full light, mouthing these words, saying to her, "The wolf also shall dwell with the lamb, and the leopard shall lie down with the kid; and the calf and the young lion and the fatling together; and a little child shall lead them.

Away and away through this rain-swept night on the striving of tendon and muscle and flesh; in the pulmonary-deep heaving of breath snorting bloody. Run until the life blood brims free from your lungs, froths in your mouth, whistles, flies. Stride away long over the going ground felt in the here and here and here of horse vertebrae, up through these blankets, up through the saddle into back, neck, head. Chew the hair, grassy-whipping, of the roan horse's mane. Smell this rainfall hissing. Count the tumble of heartbeats between lightning and thunder shout.

This night brings fire. Trees burn. Rocks lie cloven, smoking. Balls of blue flame follow close, closer, crackle, string wispy, ghostly from the glowing metal of the harness, rivets, buckles of brass; smoke rises from these human parts tattered and rancid: lifts from hair and heads, tongues shriveled, crooked fingers and toes.

This night brings hail. Ice stones crack, snap forests down to kindling. Chunks of ice, boulder big, crater this landscape, glitter up huge with lightning, glacier in small, recede, pool to flooded plain reflecting up horse and riders.

This night brings plague. Locusts chitter, rattle. Swarm after swarm clatter, deafen, devour all stick and leaf and stem. Rats river the flood. Snakes swim after. Toads rain, torrent.

This night brings wind. The sound is wail, voices calling, an under rumble; the flooded hardpan groans, slants sunders wide, spills up waterspouts, twisters, this swirl of wind-borne dust, rags, a shoe, a hat stove in, blooded clots of hair and flesh, bones high piping past end over end. Blow on. Heave us home. Run us away with new tallness upon this earth. Ride the stars down and the sun up. Ride that long last pull of a bursting heart.

We walk with her walking ahead among the rows of parked cars, between the young mothers pushing strollers past the old timers loogeying between their shoes. These old liars knuckle at their lips, recalling, perhaps, the smell of ignited gunpowder in the folds of their clothing. Perhaps they remember the flight of tired men and horses through canebrake thickets, the dark of haunted Missouri barns while they now await that one great mystery more on bench slats in front of a store selling discount creams and shampoos, the card shop, a deli, this super-market.

Stella has us in this thicket of wire carts. Carts ding other carts. A cart chimes to a halt against the chicken vending plastic eggs yoked with watches from Hong Kong, loops of bracelets that glow in the dark, decoder rings. On tiptoe, Stella fingers chrome flaps for forgotten jaw breakers, the smaller gum balls, gummy bears, auto decals, lick and stick tattoos most of which she already wears. Not finding anything to chew or stick or wear, she shies past a bench rider sliding up a sleeve to show her a heart home-made gouged in green ink.

Her heart stands hidden within her.

Stella runs to the *kerchunking* of horse: a fiberglass filly whose hide spray painted midnight dark is scratched, chipped down to the rough glass shell. This creature is a study in fear and pain, metal grating meant as whinny, the bare blocks for gum and teeth, eyes narrow set and blinded white without the pupils, ears back flat, neck crosstreed by handles, belly impaled by threaded pipe leaving fetlocked legs kicking the air as if in a fall or awkward flight. The wind of fall or flight has blown both mane and tail into grooves still blowing after a last *kerchunk*. A nappy-headed boy slides off the saddle.

Stella weeps, waits.

"I know you're going to keep me and never let me go," Stella says in sobbing breath. She sobs with her narrow back to me, her head bowed.

I lift her from behind, hold her up under her arms, feel her bones so light weight. This grievous angel sucks phlegm, coughs, dangles limp, while I look through this one lens at her hair gone golden at the tips from the sun arcing over the playground. The baby downy fineness of her hair is spaced so that I can see the pitted crescent of her scalp. I smell her head there, her fragrance, the smell of summer sun and sweat I knew I remembered. I take her ponytail into my mouth as bit and bridle, no, as hair.

Her horse waits. I sit her on, foot her small feet into the

stirrups, wait for her to wipe her eyes, then slot a quarter–the horse *kerchunks*. There is, I see, I know, no horse fast enough for her, for us, for anyone.

I answer, "No, my true life, no."

My child flies on–on the molded glass and iron that is this horse.

LEGS

When the cab stops, he sees what looks like two bullet holes in the door to the back seat. Around the holes, the yellow paint is gone and rust has taken over. He opens the door and slings in his duffle bag.

"Airport, right?" she says.

"Yeah, right."

She gets them going. They pass a girl chasing a boy the girl whacks on the head, a dog opening and closing its mouth in barks they don't hear from behind the cab's tinted windows, a shoeless old man sitting on the curb with his head in his hands.

He catches her watching him in the rearview mirror. From what he can see of her, she is older, a sister wearing a leather cap that looks good on her.

"Running?" she says.

The cab stops at a red light. Not far from where he sits is a cinder block shack with bars in the window. Three men are out on the front patch of dirt. One raises a quart beer bottle to his lips.

Looking at her in the mirror, he sees that she is doing something with her mouth that he might take as a smile.

"What are my choices?" he says.

"Working, playing, running," she says, driving on.

"Yeah, running."

He sees how the bigger of the two holes comes in above the armrest. If the slug didn't bounce, or break up, or drill somebody–where it came out is as big around as his pointer finger and curls back the metal and plastic–it would have passed into the other back door. There is a hole in the other door. Looking down through the hole, he sees the road.

"Running from what?" she says.

"What do you think?" he says.

The other hole comes in behind and below the armrest so that he has to turn to see it. This one is cleaner, as if left by a target arrow in cardboard. The slug must have gone into the driver's seat. Down near the bottom of the bucket seat, yellow foam fluffs out.

"I don't mean much by it other than trying to stay awake, but I would bet your fare you is running from a woman," she says.

The meter reads $6.75. At $1.65 for a quarter mile, he figures she is betting $25 dollars or more.

"Well, is this ride on the boss, or am I going to get a jump-up tip?"

"Yeah, you're right," he says.

"I know I'm right. It took Queenie long and hard to get to know what I know, but I got it now. Queenie will tell you what to do after you tell me what the woman's side of. . ."

"Tell me about these bullet holes," he says.

She watches the road. She pumps the brakes for a girl running a bike through traffic. The girl makes it to the curb.

"My used to live-in said I was messing around," she says. "I'd be on back-to-back doubles, sleeping in this cab, barely keeping it together for both of us since I was the only one paying the everyday dues and that mother had the nerve to tell me I was messing around."

"Were you?"

"Course I was," she says, and laughs. "But not enough so it counted."

"I count two holes," he says.

"There's trey."

She steers the cab down the main street where most of the stores are boarded over. The ones hanging on are a travel agency, a pool hall with a couple of motorcycles in front, a pawn shop.

"She's young and beautiful," he tells her.

"I hear you," she says, checking him in the mirror. "You and me are the oldest we ever been and we both know old and broke ain't nobody's friend. My most recent, my baby face man, was beautiful too. He was younger, about fourteen years younger, and everybody knew he was crack crazy from when he was eleven on. He had a voice though could make Marvin mad. When he was alive, and off the rock, he sang to me. When he started taking all my fares I had to let him go. It about killed me. Last time I saw him he couldn't talk a word, only look at me, wanting nothing more from me other than the ten dollars I give him."

"He was the one who shot up the cab?" he asks.

"No, he wasn't the one, that was my live-in I first started telling you about who moved in after my marriage busted up. Live-in one night caught me on break and emptied a gun on me. I'm still paying off those holes."

"You said three?" he says.

Trey times I was shot at," she says, working the radio. "The first one was the one who got me. That was my husband. I don't know what it is with me and men and guns. You got a gun?"

"No, but I used to shoot a bow and arrows."

"That's not too bad, as long as you ain't shooting cars or people sitting in them cars trying to eat a Chinese egg roll or nothing," she says. "At least not four-hundred-and forty-seven dollars bad anyway."

"When I was a kid I shot a cow. The arrow stuck out of

both sides of the cow's neck. The cow looked around and went back to eating grass. I threw up my breakfast, three or four chocolate Ring Dings, and ran home.

"You sick alright," she says.

They roll through town and head onto the highway. Fields, burned brown by the sun, stretch away on either side.

"I keep thinking about her hands and hair, how I once saw her riding her bike with the light all through her hair."

"No wonder it didn't work, she twelve or what?"

"No, she's twenty-six, a teacher," he says.

"That's good, because you don't at first look like no podiatrist. You a little white cat running, trying to get away from your hurting, and that's alright, that's okay."

"Thanks."

"No need to thank me, Queenie knows now. Queenie would have been better off if my husband had been a podiatrist, or whatever, but he was a cop. He shot me in the face one afternoon. He was watching football on the television and said I wasn't feeling bad enough about the calls going against his team. He reached under the couch, found his cop gun, and shot me."

"You're looking good now. I like your cap."

"Thanks, but no need to sweeten Queenie up other than my tip. I sure wasn't looking so good that afternoon. Lucky for me I was talking when he shot me. I was telling him not to do it. The bullet went in my open mouth and out my cheek. See?"

She turns her head, opens her mouth, and points inside. He sees what looks like a little hole sewed-up hard. When she turns back to look at the road he sees the scabbed wad of flesh above her jawbone where the bullet went on its way.

"He shot me and it shut me up. He sat back down and watched the rest of the game. When I could, I crawled to the phone and called for the ambulance. Live-in was better than my husband, my babyface was better than both for a while, and right now none is better than any."

She finds something else on the radio.

"Knowing that," she says, "I can tell you that nothing ever goes the way it should."

"How does it go?" he says.

"It goes the way it must go."

"Anything else?"

"We almost to the airport," she says.

"Yeah, I know, I mean is there anything else you want to tell me before we get there?"

"I know the end is getting close enough by itself. I don't need any help from a man."

"What else?"

"She still winning. Teacher is winning large because you is talking about her and she not even thinking about you. She twenty-six and then thirty-six and then fifty-six and by all those thens who got time for men and their foolishness. Queenie knows it's hard learning, but we is all we got, that's it, and the little else that's left, and keeping on."

He puts a finger in the bigger of the two bullet holes. The metal around the hole is jagged. He puts his finger in deeper, feels where it goes smooth and hollow.

"You quiet on me now," she says. "You thinking of stiffing Queenie because I told it to you straight?"

"No."

"What you thinking?"

"What it would be like to feel the hole in your cheek."

She laughs. He can see her laughing, her open mouth in the mirror.

"You fingering my bullet holes now?"

"Yes, I am."

"Keep doing it," she says, "I'm almost there. We both almost there."

He laughs.

"It's about time I saw you laugh," she says. "You even most likely got decent legs, for a white cat, at least when you is laughing you might. Besides, you got Queenie working too hard for her money."

"Anything else?"

"Keep going."

LET IT LOOSE

Trying not to wrinkle it more, sweat it up too much more than it already is licked damp and carried stuck against my skin, I slide the card up from against my belly to the hollow above my heart. I hide the bike in the high weeds. I walk the road in until coming to the stone wall rumored to have cost him nearly half a million to put up. About four heart beats is what it takes Mister Werewolf Special-Ops to pull myself up and over into the tangle of prickers and pines. I stand bleeding in the sap smell. Time to slow down, breathe through my eyelids. I smell water, the air rich with its scent.

Soft stepping through the pine straw, I come to a pond full of not-yet night. Closer to the bank, the water shows back first stars, the cut-off jagged tops of the darkening pines, lights from the house. Hear it? Hear it above the throbbing of the little tree frogs? Hear how the wind chimes are in these trees too, the high chimes, or is it ghost voices following me to their house?

I go around the fringe of floodlit grass. I shadow past the **Protected by Armor Security** sign bracketed by lighting bolt zig zags, as if that is what is going to happen to me, and it might could, out of a clear night sky, my hand on the door knob, when CRACK, Doc becomes bacon served up cinder black. I freak peek into the windows at the long sofa, the television taking up one whole wall, the lamp down low. I take my time bleeding around to the four-car cavern. Every thing is much too neat, picked up, with no toys--her tricycle waits cobwebbed in the corner--left out to get run over flattened by mom and dad flying off late with the overhead doors wide open and the Benz missing, both cars missing.

Inside, in through the garage and the unlocked side door to standing in the air-conditioned cool of the kitchen, it is as quiet as a house. The hooded stove light throws down on the sink filled with soaking empty jars and jar lids. Some things never change, as in save the world, the downtrodden and dispossessed in Portugal, Latvia, Senegal, as well as every jam, coffee, peanut butter jar you happen to come across until all the closets, shelves, cupboards are filled, while the smallest kindness, such as the outside light left on so you can see to get out your house key after twelve hours of soul-suck brought on by staring at a computer screen in order to put tofu and peas on the table, is not considered important.

"Try taking it easy," I say, as if the head docs were there to say it for me.

The music playing in my head is Monk, something Thelonius, as in piano keys plinking solitary notes, mostly all the right notes.

Looking in the refrigerator, I see Cecilia's usual: the soy cheese, the soy salami slices, the rows of special vitamins, including soy tablets, the soy milk, the pulpy style orange juice in the easy-to-pour-no-spill carton. Raising the carton to my mouth, I laugh a little before sputtering some up my nose, before grabbing a glass from the cupboard. Boy, oh boy, wouldn't that piss off everybody good?

The living room, huge, is filled with expensive antique shit, the golden sofa that could sleep a nine-foot tiger, the golden thick carpet leaving tracks as if I am wading through a savannah having that just vacuumed smell and look. I look in the too-clean fireplace, no hissing Duraflame logs for this showroom hearth, uh-uh, nope, no fire whatsoever. I heft a two-handed heavy poker, point it at the wall-to-wall television screen, prop it back with a clank. I am not even going to mention the matching of the god-damned carpet, sofa, drapes with brocaded velvet sashes, or the floor-to-ceiling bookcase jammed with books, that are. . . hey, they are not even books. They are cardboard, fake books with fake titles and fake authors on the fake spines of what look like books that you cannot pull out to read. I try, but the fake library is all glued solid and not going anywhere fast.

All too easy, right, as in go ahead and check out my place with the Winn Dixie plastic grocery bags hanging heavy off a counter drawer handle while overflowing with oil oozing sardine cans and rotting fruit rinds, the widening ring of black mold around the bathtub gone to climbing the shower curtain, the socks worn three days in a row in the interest of saving on laundry left standing stanking stiff by the bed.

I head upstairs to her bedroom.

On the way, I pass the photographs of his twins in front of a massive Christmas tree, taken, I bet, out at the Galleria Mall. On the landing, is the photograph of three-year-old Angelene looking out from under her beret.

Their bedroom is first and has his super-king-size, round, I'm-a-rich-cockmaster-of-a-bed: the his and her dressers against different walls: the his and her walk-in closets. On top of her dresser is her perfume in the bottle size costing a week's salary, a brush bristle thick with her wavy dark hair. There is also the photograph of Angelene gappy toothed happy astride her tricycle with the once festive colored streamers charging from the handle grips. There is no photograph of him to turn over, or hide, when she becomes ticked the way she did with me so all I had to do was look at her dresser to know whether I was in the doghouse that day. I do observe, however, uh-huh, uh-huh, that she still keeps her silky panties, her seamed black stockings and garter belts all twisted together as if in haste, or hate, or, oh yeah, passion, in the top drawer. His dresser has Hugo Boss baggies, gold-toed socks, and, dumb fuck, numb nuts, shit for brains, a magazine with eight hollow points, which most likely means one is in the chamber. His closet door folds open to the faint smell of rose water, of suit-after-shiny-Italian-silk suit. New white shirts, half a dozen still in the Paul Stewart tissue paper, stack up on a shelf over the suits. I slide my hand around underneath the shirts until feeling its check-ered-wood stock, the density, if not the full weight. It is a nine-mil-limeter Smith & Wesson with one golden fang in the chamber. I slide it mag fed and fattened underneath my shirt, make myself a real bulge in my khaki shorts, stretch the rotting waist band of my tattered, dingy gray, grandmotherly big skivvies from Family Dollar store, a dozen to a pack.

I leave the empty orange juice glass on dumb fuck's dress-er, make sure to leave double sweat rings on the dust-free mahog-any finish.

The twins have their boy bunks, metal Hot Wheels and countless Lego parts underfoot, clothes piles both clean and dirty, a model aircraft carrier with much dried glue over the landing deck, Creature Feature collector cards.

Her room, drawn blinds, sealed from the winter night, is painted pink. I want to say ventricle pink. A baby blue night light shades the pink darker, makes the room and every thing in the room the color of living blood. And it smells of her, a titty milk smell, her pajama top sleeping smell. Polar, good old Polar, waits for her belly-flopped on the bedspread. I sit on the floor, my back against her wooden bedframe, the same one she had as a baby that I called the corral because of the high slatted sides she used to kick in her sleep. The sides are down now, all the way down, and put away for good. My legs stretch along the carpet with my boots almost reaching her seashell night light burning baby blue day and night. There is her little girl dresser with the framed photographs I cannot make out from down where I am sitting, her Gator ball cap hung on the closet doorknob, her poster of Stewart Little--and every where else, all the evidence of the life she has lived without me, so that I close my eyes, wait in my head.

A downstair's door sucking back, boys' voices, bring me out.

I can hear Cecilia's bangle bracelets chiming as I imagine her putting down groceries on the counter, pushing back her hair. He is there with his lawyerly voice on saying something about no, no dessert, and it is getting late, and no way, there is school tomorrow.

Its hammer bites gut. I elbow up, gut suck and shove it more to the side, get myself to standing hunched in her closet. A stuffed puppy with ears floppy long as its body, a strap shoe, Barbie's pink convertible car with only three wheels, a plastic cash register with the drawer open, jumble underfoot. The register soft rings another no sale as I shift from foot to foot.

To kill, you must either be young, or not care all that much, or pushed to your very limit, or able to enter into the mind of the thing you wish to kill: the wood dove startled up to flying above the broken stalks of the cornfield, a deer grazing in the dusk, a man, so you know in your bones what that thing, the man, will do before he knows, and then you surprise him at it.

The boys stampede up the carpeted stairs. I move from the closet to standing behind the door, look out through the hinged crack as they run by. They throw elbows at one another on the way to the bathroom where there is much slamming on and off of a water faucet, teeth brushing, spitting, "Cut it out or I'll spit on you!" more faucet work, long peeing and flushing, laughter, a wet towel slapping to the floor. They return on the run to stomping down the stairs. The television roars on.

I crouch back into the pinkish dark of the seashell illuminating the great depths, such a little light to keep back so many monsters, all our fears. I sit on her pink bedspread and hug Polar. His bear eyes are beady and do not reveal much. Pulling it out, I slide the pistol down the knuckle bones of my spine, flip my shirt back over it. Commercial after commercial, much canned laughter and music later, I hear someone coming up the stairs, her bangle bracelets taken off now, or quieted.

"Doc," she whispers, standing in the doorway. "Doc, my loose is tooth, I mean, my tooth is loose."

"Let me see," I say, and suddenly my body fits in the air of this world.

She wiggles one, lower and to the side. She still has her chubby baby fingers and hands.

"See?"

"Oh, yeah, but it is not going to come right away, work it with your tongue every once in a while, but not too much."

"You hugging up Polar, Doc?"

"Yeah, giving him some until you got here."

Her arms squeeze around my neck. Her smell is even better than I remember. Her living smell is every thing.

She lets go, looks into my eye close up.

"I can see it, Doc, does it hurt?"

"No, baby, not now it doesn't, but thanks for asking."

"I have to brush my teeth now and be careful not to wiggle it too much," she says, skipping to the bathroom.

I am someone hunting his happiness. I am someone from the past somehow allowed to come back.

"Angelene!" her mother calls from the foot of the stairs. "Are you in your soft clothes yet?"

"I am careful brushing, Mama!"

"Alright, but it is getting late."

She comes back cinnamon smelling, toothpaste dabbed

white at the corner of her mouth, the same side as the wiggly one. She tears back the velcro on her sneakers. She tugs up her long-sleeved shirt over her face, gets stuck. I help pull--"Watch out for the wiggly one, Doc!"--until fine baby hair falls back into place and her head comes free. She puts on the pajama top all by herself, the red one with the Disney Dalmatians, and the bottoms too.

"Okay, Mama, got my soft clothes on!" she calls down over the bannister. "I'm going to look at a book for a little while."

And we do, with her in the light of the bedside lamp. She and Polar snuggle up in our heart cave under the sheet, blanket up warm with my arm around her and Polar, her head resting on the bent card under my shirt. Her hair moves with the words I read. The little horse runs so fast that the horse flies. The little horse flies through a velvet-soft-night sky tossed with stars. The little horse visits the stars. She cinnamon breathes shmoogily--one of her made-up first words for when her stuffed animal babies were sleeping--by the time the little horse flies past the moon on the way back home.

You have to have something snapped off sharp in you not to feel wonder when watching a child's face as she sleeps, her baby face returned, the mouth sucking the memory of tit, of life itself, and the way she reminds herself over and over.

I am reminded how there is still so much about love that I need to know.

And the music in my head? None, no music now, there only is.

The television laughter and voices turn to something sports, a basketball game with the announcers giving the first half stats. The twins thump tired up the stairs followed by Cecilia's lighter step, by her bracelet jingle as they come closer.

Clicking out the light, I lay Angelene's head on the pillow, kiss her hair.

When the boys sleepy shuffle by followed by Cecilia, I am watching from behind the door. How can they not know that I am here? How can they not feel the black hole of my being in their home? The air is different. The night is different. The texture, the complexity, the simplicity of where the breaks occur and where the breaks do not occur are different. And I am different, the deepest me until I am all will and want. Maybe that intent, desire, the very last that is left us, is what others call a ghost, a real ghost, a ghost both dead and alive in my own living.

Cecilia pushes at the door, enters the bedroom. She leans over Angelene, soft strokes the hair from Angelene's face. Nothing distracts her, not even the breathing of her own body as she looks.

She is so close I can breath the Chanel underneath the sway of her hair at the back of her neck. I could touch her cheek, see the skin whiten under my fingers, whisper how I miss the love we never had.

Her face is burnished by the seashell light at the bottom of the ocean of our own making, not that that is an explanation, or an excuse for anything, not a single fucking thing, okay?-- but to me she is beautiful, and it is all exactly there in her face: her enormous brown eyes shining as she watches Angelene, her cheekbones, her lips parted as if in answer. I try to look at her now without the devotion, remember her hiding away our photograph taken at the old Spanish fort in St. Augustine, see her at the sink slamming broken bottle glass under the suds. I look and see how she is still girlish: her slim, bracelet-adorned arms coming from an oversized T-shirt tucked in, her braided belt holding up the tan shorts, her slender legs and delicate sandals.

As a ghost, I could haunt her forever.

She turns, hesitates. I can hear her held breath in the hesitation. Perhaps she feels me, senses me, after all we have known and been and done with each other. We have slept belly to ass, ankle bone to ankle bone, waded together into that intimacy night after night for years. And yet there are the places in her of quiet and fear and longing that I will never know, all the connections, the costs of things living under things.

She breathes out. I hear her breathe all the way out as she passes, pushing back the door along the carpet with a shhhhhh sound until the door is a pointer finger's length from my face. She pulls the door almost closed behind her, snatching the air from my chest as she does, almost, but not all the way closed so she can listen for her baby girl waking and wanting her.

I listen to water splashing in the bathroom sink, Cecilia brushing her teeth. When she is done, she goes to their bedroom and closes the door. Downstairs, the announcers count down the clock, offer up the game's post mortem.

Angelene sleeps and I watch her sleep. There is nothing like a child to put you in the present. Feel a child's belly skin, or the skin on the inside of their arms, the little neck hairs. Feel that softness, the smoothness, and watch as she sleeps, a part of yourself, and yet a mystery complete in herself, and me left with all my fierce wonder.

A moment, or hour, or lifetime later, he cuts off the television, makes his way heavily, noisily, for fuck sake, step by steady step full of courtroom menace, up the stairs. I could grab him by the hair as he dick swings past and put the hidden and yet-so-convenient Smith & Wesson in his mouth, jam it hard all the way to the trigger guard while looking into his eyes, let him read and understand my stipulations and power of subpoena and habeas corpus, motherfucker, keeping a loaded pistol in the house with his boys, my one, numb nuts, fuckhead.

I could, because it all becomes simple, and the way to simplify is to get rid of things.

He pisses, flushes. He opens and hard claps shut--I almost jerk around to see if the pistol went off--their bedroom door as if he is the only one in the house, and I come close, the gunshot report of the door echoing throughout the house, that close, so help me God.

I close my eyes, steady it down to breath, one breath, and then another breath, and another.

When I look again, there is the seashell light and the world held in that light. The house has again become the breathing of the living, her with her books and bear, the two of us. I lay what is left of myself near her warmth, the solace of her soft skin.

In the longer part of the night, drifting through the underwater quiet, I almost know, almost believe, that I will never lose her.

Morning is the change in light between blind slats. I kiss at her eyes, smell her milky self, unbutton my shirt.

I pull out the valentine card run streaky pinker and leave it on the pillow next to her fingers curled as if wanting to hold onto something.

My daughter is as magnificent as the sun.

Outside, the light already silts down through the tops of the pines, the pine cones, the needles themselves. The breathing warm wind barely moves the chimes to sound, the weakened music of those beyond, the ghost voices, diminishing for now with the coming of the light.

And the other music? Something by Bill Evans, easy as flowing water.

At the pond misting up its own ghosts, I take the pistol from underneath my shirt. I palm its weight. It is balanced, single action, concentrated enough to put a hole in you so your life sprays out and out and out. I underhand toss it out to where it becomes splash becomes ripple becomes soft slapping where water meets the roots naked at my feet.

THE VISITOR

How the yard has grown over. Blackberry bushes bend with leaf and berry about the rotting pew on which I sit. The wall once fitted stone by stone by father and grandfather from fieldstone wrestled from the cellar hole for the house is nearly hidden by blackberry bushes. Thorned stalks thick as the fingers of working men trail over a wall fallen mostly into a scattering of stones. Father and grandfather fired-up that stone with cleared brush cracking and popping. The men of my family fired stone to glowing hot before using water and sledge hammers to split that stone. The boy left in me remembers firelight on the shed. Fire was in the shape of leaves. Sparks were firefly flitting. Smoke was rising pale against the night. The men, I remember, splashed cold water on hot stone showing hell to a boy. Water was bucket carried from the mossy wet of a neighbor's spring house, sloshed on hell hissing, and then the men–shadows of men on shed side sagging into the bigger shadow of night, and the men themselves, father and grandfather, with their faces and their hands the colors of that lasting fire, with their skin colored as if lit by fire burning inside them–grunting, having at the smoking stone with the hefted weight of sledge hammers.

Blackberry bushes grow where the shed was, become

thicket between the house and old Mrs. Dufresne's house. Mother lives alone in the house surrounded by thorn and berry and saw-toothed leaf, by ivy, by milkweed, by wild aster, by chickadee and jay, by sumac, by lilac. The lilacs, I am told, I do not remember, were planted by father for mother so mother could have, if she so chose, her favorite flowering smell without leaving the house. Her wind chimes make little bells sounds from the branches of a sumac rising high as the roof of the house. Her blackberries gone wild are picked and eaten from this old pew. The berries not taken by birds and other beasts, the ones hidden or hard to get at, are the ones I want. These berries, even the blackest, most seasoned berries, are more tart than I remember. Berry juice darkens my fingers. Berry juice, or is it blood? The color is the same ripe blood color I see when I look in a mirror at my eye eaten by cancer. These thorns held up are seen as the catching and cutting edges that they are. More than thirty years later, and Sammy still has scars from when we blackberried all day along the power lines. Nights we slept on grandfather's porch in his sleeping bags blanket-lined for hunting. We slept in the healing smell dabbed on red of Mercurochrome.

Wild aster flowering among blackberry sprawl is now the smell. Aster and ivy root in the shadows where smaller wall stone shims bigger stone. Ivy nets capstone, reaches for this pew father saved from the old French church and set out for mother. Ten-drils curl about this wood soft with rot. Tendrils lift to light and wind, coil down to the dirt to again root their way in the dark beneath stone and blackberry briar. A trap door under the table in grandfather's kitchen let out the dirt smell and dark of the root cellar. Hands along cobwebbed stone got us down the stairs to reaching in the dark above my head for string that could almost also be cobweb. Light tugged on from a light bulb showed roots fingered long between the huge fieldstones holding grandfather's house. Roots tangled sought the damp and dark and whatever else roots seek behind the empty bins for potatoes, behind the shelf holding dusty jars of blackberry jam, behind the dusty, BB-dented tin of maple syrup from sugaring time how many years ago? Roots clung to a locked plank door with a peg hole plugged with cork. Digging at the cork with a bent spoon left on the dirt floor, I pushed the cork back into the peg hole until air poured out damp as the inside of the neighbor's spring house, air drafty damp and smelling of apple rot. I remember putting an eye to the peg hole and never seeing a thing.

Sam remembers. I know my sister Sam remembers the peg hole and some of the other things we did. I have heard Sammy tell her little girl how two skinny scratched braggart kids were awakened on grandfather's porch by the licking, by the lowing of cows gotten loose from grandfather's pasture. Sammy tells how two kids went in skivvies and sneakers night-wet to find out those cows up close in the dark were a big sow bear and her two cubs eating blackberries. Sammy tells her little girl how two skinny scratched kids were no longer so braggerty.

In the dark, or when I close my eye, fluid pressing on the eyeball is seen as a kind of firelight.

Wind chinkles metal against metal; sumac leaves shift shades of late summer red. Brambly stalks slender as a boy's wrists, thorns able to catch hold of a boy's coat or scratch at a girl's legs, these blackberries, are seen now as the perfections they are. The men that they were, were bigger and better men. This land was clear cut to pasture. Stone was dug from the ground, fired, broken. Stone was walked from side to side then stepped into place as wall. Stone was dragged on boats by horses and stacked as foundation later cobwebbed and cool as the dirt floor of the cellar where a boy played with chipped glass aggies once his mother's girlish treasures, where the same boy piffed BBs from his Red Ryder air rifle at rats hiding between jars of seedy jam, behind a tin crusted on top with dripped sap house syrup that grandfather as a boy helped boil down; where sisters squatted and

spooned dirt playing tea while sheltered by stone once the break-
er of plow and harrow blade, by stone holding the sills of small
houses.

Lives are stacked on lives.

Sam's little girl may some day live in this house. Sammy's
little girl grown to have children, or her children's children, a boy
wandering in the woods, may some day know the smell of wild
lilac come to him for the first time, or taste the tart taste of blackberries found while hiding in play behind heaps of stone, or see
his bigger, older people on a leafy summer night while they burn
brush cleared from this land; a boy seeing the fire-lit faces of his
loved ones in the long splendor of our dying.

CAMPFIRES OF
THE DEAD

Campfires of the Dead was originally
published in 1989 by Alfred A. Knopf
and has been out of print since the first
printing.

BLOOD AND SEED

Maggie, Mom tells me she sees you now and again at the market with your husband and your two boys. Mom tells me you stop and ask how she is, how we all are, while your husband pushes the cart and your two boys shout, "Mom! Hey, Mom!"

Maggie, what is asked in your heart's heart these years later is answered—Yes, Maggie still.

This life those years ago, Maggie, is how I still see you. I can still see you waiting for me, football jacket tailed-out behind me running to you. The window light behind you is blocks and bars through the yellow kitchen curtains, on the kitchen floor, on the mouth of you telling me, "Mom comes home at two."

The home sick talk of television in the day is what still comes from the other room, Maggie, that talk, and the smell of toast, toast rims on the plate on the couch. You sit, handing the plate down to the carpet. You undo your robe, looking me your look.

Maggie, your mouth is still toast, tongue, girl. You are still the smell of girl sleep. You are soft robe bunched under me and, under the robe, the heat and smooth of a girl unfolding.

A car that is maybe your mom's car, outside and under the talking low of the television, is heard driving up and by the house where you live. You pull me neck down from behind, lettered football jacket and all, to where we fit as if born for this.

Maggie, I can still see your dark hair golding, your hair on the corduroy ribbing-up of couch, on and over my hand. I can still see your bubs out flat, the dark of the bull's-eyes centered. Shadowed lines, thumb-traced by God, parcel out your small ribs. Your lean girl legs come up, apart. The hair down there is darker, pointed as goateed beard. My knob-on is out. My football jacket is rucked up, the snaps unsnapped and shirts yanked up for skin on skin, for the knobbed poke-bobbing of me inside you.

Maggie, there is no going back now. Breaking you open, the fear is you will not heal better than before. I can still see what looks like fear, your head back, your eyelids pinching, your lips rounding out O . . . after O . . . Maggie, the gathering of that vowel over and over is what brings me on, that and seeing you in the breaking and making of this, our lives.

The yellow light crosses the kitchen floor to poke the carpeted dark. The talk of daytime television talks on. I can still smell the smell of blood and seed. I can still see the red-knobbed slit with pearly gloss spun out of me come out of you. Gobbed, glossy strands hang shining from me to you, from yours to mine, from your two boys and their bluish bloodied heads pushing out of you to the red-glazed daughter of mine the doctor holds up by her feet, the same daughter soon to be home waiting while a boy runs to her as fast as he can run.

Maggie, when you again see Mom and she tells you, "Fine, we are all fine," know that what is asked in your heart's heart is answered—Yes, Maggie, still, Maggie, it is still gobbed and shining between us.

ROSIE AND DELLA, SANDY AND BESSIE, SISTER AND DINAH

The flies have found her. All winter, the only flies were those dead in the cold of the window sills. Now the cold has turned to warm, the days are longer, and flies tick the window glass. The windows are raised. The front door is held open by daughters bringing clean nightgowns and cake, by granddaughters afraid to come in and happy to go home. The flies land here, loop there, find her and the others rocking and dozing. A fly lights on the back of her hand and walks a blue vein. The flies circle the rocking Mrs. Podolski and Mrs. Hatch and Mrs. Keck. Flies light on her sleeping face. Susan keeps the flies from the lips. One lights on the nose. Susan waves that fly away, then soft whaps a fly on the sofa with a rolled-up newspaper. The old woman comes awake.

"Flies," Susan says to her. "Just some flies. Go back to sleep."

Summers, when her and her grandmother and Tops the dog fought the flies, is where she goes: those summers of Granddaddy coming in hatted and dusty for his noonday meal. Granddaddy makes sure the screen door is closed tight so no more flies get in. Somehow, more flies get in; get on: flies that are walking specks on the basin where Granddaddy washes his hands, on the crockery in the cupboard, on the white-painted walls and the lace-trimmed curtains, on the black of the Kalamazoo stove. Flies are over Granddaddy's noonday meal of chipped beef and cream gravy. Flies are on the blue stitching of the linen covering the buttermilk biscuits. Flies are in the melting brick of Brownie Girl's butter. The flies are everywhere in the farmhouse so that Grandmother says, "Claire, I will give you a penny for every twenty flies that you catch me and bring me."

After the last of the red-chipped beef and the buttered buttermilk biscuits, after the rice pudding with raisins she at first thinks are flies, after hatted Granddaddy has smoked his pipe and gone back to mowing the fields, she and Tops stalk the kitchen. She sweeps down a fly with Grandmother's fly swatter. Tops eats the fly, still buzzing, and looks like he wants more.

"Grandmother," she says to Grandmother pumping water over the plates from the noonday meal. "Tops is eating my money."

After her and Tops finish patrolling the kitchen, they go into the parlor. Flies are on the sheeted sofa and chairs. Flies are on the piano keys. Flies are on the family photographs of the newborn, the baptized, the gone to school, the graduated, the married, the gone to war, the come back from war, the once living, the once dying, the all dead. The flies are stirred from the faces dead before she was born. The flies come back.

Her and Tops go back through the kitchen and out to the closed-in porch. Flies are on the screen door's screen. Flies are up on the glass of the tall porch windows, too high up for her to reach. Flies are down in the porch window corners, flies already dead, the leftover meals of spiders. One by one she picks the flies up by crooked wings and legs. One by one she drops the flies in the dab of soap on Grandmother's cracked bone saucer. She shows Grandmother the twenty-two flies that Grandmother counts out. She reminds Grandmother about the flies Tops has snapped up.

Grandmother says, "Claire Fagan, you will soon be as wealthy a girl as you are already rich."

Some summer mornings of fighting the flies Grandmother says the kitchen is too hot. The heat of the kitchen will have Granddaddy sweating more than his work in the fields, Grandmother says. The heat of the Kalamazoo stove will have Granddaddy sweating more than the horses Pat and Young Ned, Grandmother says, and so, Granddaddy's noonday meal is taken outside.

Under the cool of the two pine trees, Grandmother floats a quilt down. Grandmother lifts the quilt back up before the quilt can touch the dead pine needles, then lets the quilt again float down.

The plates and pitcher of milk are handed over from out of the apple-picking basket. The knives and linen napkins are laid down. When Grandmother sees the hatted coming of Granddaddy she uncovers the sliced chicken, the peas, the boiled potatoes, the rhubarb pie sprinkled with powdered sugar. Grandmother napkin wipes away the droplets on the pitcher of Brownie Girl's milk while Tops, on the quilt at Grandmother's feet, snaps at the flies and the yellow jackets.

Grandmother and Granddaddy and her take their time with the noonday meal. When they are done, Grandmother clears away the plates and lifts aside the pitcher so they can all lie out on the quilt. They lie on their sides, on their backs, in the creaking and sighing of the two old pine trees above. They lie in the pine needle smell. They lie with Grandmother and Granddaddy holding hands. They lie with Granddaddy talking farm talk up through the straw of his hat. They lie with her petting Tops. They lie dozing until Tops rolls up and snaps at the buzzing of a big horsefly. Tops misses, tries again, misses again.

Later, after Granddaddy has gone back to the fields with Pat and Young Ned, after Grandmother has flapped the dead pine needles from the quilt, after Grandmother and her have gone inside and Grandmother has washed the plates and started supper, after supper is done, after all that and before her bedtime, her and Granddaddy do the last of the day's chores. Her and Granddaddy go out to the barn and to Granddaddy's calling Brownie Girl. The flycatchers swoop out from the loft of the barn, circle in the getting dark sky, swoop down and around her and Granddaddy. Granddaddy claps and calls for his good Brownie Girl. Granddaddy calls with his voice carrying over the pasture where Pat and Young Ned fly shiver in their skin. Granddaddy's voice carries over the granite stone wall going up the hill, up across the cleared land to the high pasture and to the bell clanking of Brownie Girl coming. She runs to her chore of getting Granddaddy's milking chair. Granddaddy sets down his milking chair near the tie-up rail worn smooth by the neck rubbing of long dead cows named Rosie and Della, Sandy and Bessie, Sister and Dinah. Dinah's Brownie Girl looks in, her Brownie Girl head big in the closeness of the barn.

Granddaddy says, "Come on, Brownie Girl. It's me and Claire." Brownie Girl slow clanks her way into the barn and over to the tie-up. Granddaddy, tipping his straw hat up with the resting of his head on Brownie Girl's side, begins milking. While Granddaddy does the milking, she goes over near Granddaddy's workbench and looks at the long-handled screwdrivers lined up from smaller to larger. She looks at the sharp teeth of the saws in the last of the day's light coming in through the window over Granddaddy's workbench. She looks at the curling yellow chaff of flypaper slow twisting in the last of the day's light. The flypaper is thick with flies, thick with the dead. She looks at the sticky curl of flypaper and listens to Granddaddy strip the warm spurts of milk from Brownie Girl. Brownie Girl's tail swishes up the flies to buzzing around Brownie Girl and her and Granddaddy. The flycatchers swoop into the dark of the barn from the almost all dark outside and hollow flap around Brownie Girl and her and Grand-daddy. A flycatcher, seeing what is left of the day's light in the window over Granddaddy's workbench, thumps against the glass.

"Granddaddy," she says.

Granddaddy keeps the one-two count of Brownie Girl's milk filling the bucket.

"Granddaddy," she says louder, "there is a hurt bird over here."

The strip strup of the milking stops.

The flycatcher, beak open, lies still in the wood shavings on Granddaddy's workbench. She hears Brownie Girl's bell clank. She hears Brownie Girl's milk foaming in the bucket. She hears Granddaddy set the bucket aside. She hears Granddaddy scrape back his chair. She sees Granddaddy loom over from out of the dark. Granddaddy takes the flycatcher into his hands and smooths the dark feathers down.

Granddaddy says, "Poor thing, it broke its neck."

Granddaddy says, "Don't cry, Claire, it did not suffer long."

There is also the summer of fighting the flies when Grand-daddy takes to his bed with the sickness in his throat, stays in his bed, suffers long.

173

In the upstairs of during the day, she hears Granddaddy trying to cough out the sickness in his throat. She hears Granddaddy cough as she looks for flies in the upstairs hall. She swishes the fly swatter down the hall until coming to the open door of Granddaddy's room. The shades are drawn and the room is dark. Tops, on the bed at Granddaddy's feet, thumps his tail.

"Shhh, Tops," she says.

Tops quits thumping.

Granddaddy lies there gasping. Granddaddy lies in the sheet that Grandmother has floated down cool and clean.

The wind creaks and sighs the two old pines outside of Granddaddy's window. The wind lifts the drawn shade, letting her look at Granddaddy not wearing his straw hat, the first time she can remember Granddaddy not wearing his straw hat. The wind keeps the shade lifted. She looks at the blue veins clumped on the back of Granddaddy's hands. She looks at the rings turned around on Granddaddy's fingers. She looks at Granddaddy's closed eyes and open lips. She looks at Granddaddy's lips working as if trying to tell her and Tops something. She looks at the thinness of Granddaddy's face. A fly lights on Granddaddy's face. The fly walks across Granddaddy's cheek. The fly walks over to Granddaddy's lips, trying to tell her something. The fly is on Granddaddy's lips when the shade flaps down and Granddaddy's room goes dark.

She hears the drawn shade tapping against the wood of the window sill: She hears Granddaddy gasping. She hears Granddaddy telling her. She hears Granddaddy telling her how she will join him beyond the waters of the Deerfield River flowing down below the farm. She hears Granddaddy telling her how she will join him, and how they will walk together up the hill, up through the summer green pasture where Brownie Girl and Pat and Young Ned graze. She hears Granddaddy telling her how they will walk together once more as if after chores, and how they will walk together to where Grandmother and all her others wait for her, to where she hears the welcoming drone of her dead.

THE CAREERIST

Ever think what do chicken-sexers think all day?

Well, this chicken-sexer thinks mostly him and me and Sweet Miss Stringbean. Make him Billy Boillit, sometime mill rat, most time drunk, my best friend. Make me Sarno, chicken-sexer. Make Sweet Miss Stringbean Billy's sweetheart.

I think mostly of Billy and me and Sweet Miss Stringbean and working as a chicken-sexer all . . . make that as a chicken-sexer all night. I work the night shift. Working the night shift, once you know what you are doing, once you tune out the peeping, allows plenty of time for thinking. Mostly me thinking how Billy, my forever best friend, does what he wants whether he wants to or not.

I am almost happy when bow-hunting, although I never get anything bow-hunting, or watching TV over at Sweet Miss Stringbean's, although I never get anything over at Sweet Miss Stringbean's, either.

Sweet Miss Stringbean is almost happy when her kids, who likely will make her a grandmother before she is thirty, are also almost happy.

In other words, like everybody else we know, none of us are happy. If we are, none of us know we are. And that, chicken-sexer or not, is plenty to think about.

But there is always the Legion and who goes to the Legion.

This chicken-sexer goes to the Legion before going home to. . . make that to supper and sleep.

The Legion's the same as most legions—the same dark, the same smells, the same smoke, the same TV shows on the same TV always on the same kind of shelf sticking out over the same kind of stick.

What makes the Legion different is Desperado and Billy.

Desperado, who works behind the stick, is what everybody at the Legion calls him. The unclean rag he wears to cover his mouth and everything right up to his eyes is why.

Billy, who everybody calls Billy, slumps on the stick doing shots and beers and watching Desperado's unclean rag suck in, blow out, suck in, blow out.

Billy watches and weeps.

"Billy," says I, "what's up with you?"

"Me and Sweet Miss Stringbean," Billy says. "I say marry me to Sweet Miss Stringbean and she says to me she will when I quit drinking and getting marihoochied up and getting otherwise crazier than I get."

"Oh no," says I.

"Oh yes," Billy says. "I say marry me to Sweet Miss Stringbean, or else."

"Aw, Billy," says I, not knowing what else to say to Billy.

"I say marry me," Billy says, "or else I'll get drunk and marihoochied up and otherwise crazier than I've ever gotten before, whether I want to or not."

"Aw, Billy," says I, because what else can anyone say to Billy?

You know where and when I do most of my thinking? When I am wearing egg-white booties, egg-white jumpsuit, egg-white shower cap in a just-hosed-down room full of peeping.

Other than the peeping, which you tune out after a while, there is no noise except the noise of what you could hear if you could hear us chicken-sexers thinking and looking for the tiny bump that means a boy chicken. Looking for the tiny bump is, I like to say, eggciting work.

This is the kind of yoke—make that joke—that us chicken-sexers say when us chicken-sexers say anything. Most chicken-sexers do not say anything while sexing, at least not the good chicken-sexers. The good chicken-sexers, like Emile and unlike me, sex about nine hundred chicks an hour. Every joke amounts to almost twenty chicks and forty cents less.

This chicken-sexer would rather have forty cents less—make that a whole lot less—than think what this chicken-sexer is thinking.

Everybody at the Legion knows everybody else from going to the same grade school, to the same junior high school, to the same high school.

As long as everybody has known Desperado, we have never heard him say much. Now he says even less. Now Desperado works the stick without saying anything.

After work and before going you-know-where, I watch Desperado's unclean rag suck in, blow out, day in, day out. I watch Desperado's unclean rag suck in, blow out of the place where Desperado's nose used to be, until Billy, drunk and marihoochied up at the Legion's New Year's Eve party two New Year's Eves ago, bit Desperado's nose off.

This chicken-sexer usually goes over to Sweet Miss Stringbean's before going to work. Me and Sweet Miss Stringbean and Sweet Miss Stringbean's two kids sit on the couch watching family-type game shows.

The couch and TV are just about all the furniture Sweet

Miss Stringbean owns. We sit on the couch with the two kids, with Danny and Dana crawling over each other and over us. Dana, the kid who is the youngest kid, wriggles around and yells out the right answers before the people on the shows can yell them out and way before I could ever do it. It takes me too long to think. It is me mostly trying to think and wrestling around with the kids with Sweet Miss Stringbean yelling for us to stop.

In other words, going over to Sweet Miss String-bean's before going to work is like bow-hunting, with me never getting anything and being almost happy anyway.

Desperado is what everybody at the Legion calls Desperado.

Billy is what everybody calls Billy.

Sweet Miss Stringbean is what Billy and me call Sweet Miss Stringbean.

Billy started calling Sweet Miss Stringbean Sweet Miss Stringbean first, saying she was so skinny and her legs were so long and she was so young and fresh as to remind him of a young, fresh stringbean.

Sweet Miss Stringbean's sweetest feature, Billy says, is how those long stringbean legs of hers lead all the way up to her snap.

The best thing about bow-hunting is time in the woods. Time in the woods, going around with a bow in my hand, makes me feel, well . . . make that almost happy.

I think getting something, getting anything, must be like getting to be something you are not.

Except when she yells, Sweet Miss Stringbean is sweet.

Sweet Miss Stringbean is sweet for a brick-eater.

Brick-eater is what Billy and me call women with no teeth. Sweet Miss Stringbean has teeth, just not her upper teeth, the big ones in front.

Billy, my forever best friend, punched out Sweet Miss Stringbean's teeth on Sweet Miss Stringbean's fifteenth birthday. What Billy's present to Sweet Miss Stringbean was was to wait until me and the kids were not looking when he punched her teeth out.

Except for what Billy says and for what everybody at the Legion wonders out loud, how would I know?

"What do you mean?" says I.

"What do you think I mean?" Billy says.

"Aw, Billy, I'm not sure," says I.

"Are you Sarno the chicken-sexer?" Billy says.

"Sure," says I.

"Then think, you chicken-sexer you," Billy says.

"Think what the bump that means a boy chick feels like, but think of that bump as big as the end of your little finger, and right in all that snap."

"Aw, Billy," says I, thinking of all that peeping.

I am in my skivvies making ready for sleep when I hear knocking on the door.

"Sarno, it's me! Come quick!"

It is Sweet Miss Stringbean, sobbing and sucking in her top lip where her teeth are missing.

"It's Billy," Sweet Miss Stringbean sobs. "Billy's gotten drunk and marihoochied up and otherwise crazier than he's ever gotten."

"Oh no," says I.

"Oh yes," Sweet Miss Stringbean sobs. "And he's got Dana. Billy's got Dana and says he's not giving her back except in pieces until I say I do."

"Call the staties," says I, putting on what is handy.

What is handy are the day's—make that the night's—egg-white booties, egg-white jumpsuit, egg-white shower cap.

"Get your bow!" Sweet Miss Stringbean sobs. "There's no telling what Billy will do!" she sobs.

"Call the staties!" says I, getting my bow and a handful of broadheads and going out into the light.

"Hey, Emile," says I during last night's shift.

Emile looks up, but keeps on sexing.

"Emile," says I, "want to hear a poem?"

Emile keeps on sexing.

"Here goes," says I. "Had a little chicken, she wouldn't lay an egg, I poured hot water up and down her leg. Little chicken cried, little chicken begged, little chicken laid a hard-boiled egg."

That fucking Emile just keeps on sexing.

I live crawling distance from the Legion.

Outside the Legion, in the light, is Billy's old ride.

Inside the Legion is the same dark, the same smells, the same smoke, the same TV shows on the same TV, and behind the stick, suck-smelling it all and watching it all, is the same Desperado.

Slumped at the stick doing shots and beers, watching Desperado suck in, blow out, suck in, blow out, is Billy.

"Aw, Billy," says I. "What's up with you?"

"Me and Sweet Miss Stringbean and Sweet Miss Stringbean's Dana," Billy says.

"Where's Dana?" says I.

"Dana's at my place asleep," Billy says. "Dana was watching TV and wriggling around and yelling out the right answers before the people on the shows could do it and now she's asleep."

"Oh no," says I.

"Oh yes," Billy says. "And now she's asleep."

"Aw, Billy," says I. "In how many pieces?"

"In one piece," Billy says.

"Hey, Emile," says I during last night's shift.

That fucking Emile looks up, but keeps on sexing.

"Ever hear the one about the two chickens sitting together in the chicken coop?" says I.

That fucking Emile never stops sexing.

"Well, there's two chickens sitting together in the chicken coop," says I. "The first chicken says, 'Bawk, bawk, bawk,' and lays a fifty-cent egg."

That fucker.

"The second chicken says, 'Bawk, bawk, bawk, bawk,' and lays a fifty-five-cent egg," says I. "The first chicken says to the second chicken, 'So? For a nickel more, for a lousy five cents more, I should break my ass?'

Hey, let us not even talk about that Emile, okay?

Not knowing what else to say to Billy, I do not say anything to Billy, just look at him and at Desperado and around the smoky darkness of the Legion.

But Billy, he looks at my egg-whites and bow.

"Sarno, you chicken-sexer you," Billy says. "Are you my best friend?"

"Sure," says I. "I'm your forever best friend, Billy."

"Then load your bow and do me," Billy says.

"Aw, Billy," says I. "You're my forever bestfriend."

"Then do him," Desperado says.

"What?" says I, not sure I am hearing Desperado say anything.

"Do him," Desperado says, his unclean rag sucking in, staying in, blowing out, blowing all the way out.

"Do me," Billy says. "Whether you want to or not."

"Aw, Billy," says I, loading my bow and weeping.

I tug back the bowstring and broadhead and take aim. I hold back while the shakes set in, hold back some more, then let the broadhead fly.

"Hey, Sarno," Emile says to me during last night's shift.

I look up from sexing. I look up, thinking I am hearing something other than peeping.

"Sarno," Emile says, "why does the chicken cross the road?"

"What?" says I, not sure I am hearing that fucker say anything.

"Why does the chicken cross the road?" Emile says.

"I'm not sure," says I.

"The chicken crosses the road because the chicken can," Emile says.

The broadhead thunks deep into the stick and wide of Billy.

"Aw, Sarno, you chicken-sexer you," Billy says.

"No wonder you never get anything. Try again."

"Aw, Billy," says I, weeping and loading my bow again. I tug back the bowstring and broadhead and take aim. I hold back until the shakes and the ringing set in.

The ringing rings more while I hold the bowstring and the broadhead back until I am unable to hold anything back.

"Hold it until I get the phone," says I, tramping over in my egg-white booties, my egg-white jumpsuit, my egg-white shower cap to the pay phone.

"The Legion," says I, getting the pay phone.

"Sarno?" Sweet Miss Stringbean sobs.

"Sweet Miss Stringbean," weeps I.

"Where's Dana?" Sweet Miss Stringbean sobs.

"Dana's at Billy's asleep," says I.

"In how many pieces?" Sweet Miss Stringbean sobs.

"In one piece," says I.

Sweet Miss Stringbean sobs and I just listen to her sob. Oh God, she's such a Sweet Miss Stringbean, thinks I.

"Tell Billy I will say I do when Billy quits getting drunk and marihoochied up and getting otherwise crazier than he gets," Sweet Miss Stringbean sobs. "Tell Billy now, Sarno."

"Hold on," says I.

"Billy," says I, tramping back to the stick in my you-know-whats. "Sweet Miss Stringbean says she will say I do when you quit getting drunk and marihoochied up and getting otherwise crazier than you do."

"Aw, Sarno," Billy says.

‘   "Aw, Billy," says I.

"Do him," Desperado says.

"Don't think," Billy says. "Do me."

I do Billy. Just as quick as that, I thwack a broadhead into Billy.

Billy, looking surprised, looks at the broadhead feathering his blue jeans.

"Billy!" says I, weeping and amazed.

Billy fingers the blood darkening his jeans, then holds the fingers up. Billy looks like he just made the discovery of his life. Billy gives me, then Desperado, that look—then looks once more at the broadhead—then passes right the fuck out.

Ever think what do cow-manicurists think all day?

Well, this cow-manicurist thinks mostly him and me and Sweet Miss Stringbean.

Make him Billy "The Gimp" Boillit, full-time mill rat, most time sober, my best friend. Make me Sarno, cow-manicurist. Make Sweet Miss Stringbean Sweet Mrs. Stringbean Boillit.

I think mostly of Billy and me and Sweet Mrs. Stringbean

Boillit and working as a cow-manicurist all...make that all day. Working all day, manicuring cow hooves with wood chisels and mallet, allows me to go over to Billy's after work.

Billy's is the same as Sweet Miss Stringbean's was before she became Sweet Mrs. Stringbean Boillit, or I guess I should say almost the same except for the new big couch I bought us when they exchanged the I-dos. It is almost the same, with us sitting on the new big couch, watching the same TV with the same two kids, Danny and Dana, crawling over each other and over us.

In other words, it is almost the same except for the couch and for Billy and Sweet Mrs. Stringbean Boillit and me almost happy. And me—once I tune out the mooing—as almost happy as I have ever been, and that is plenty to think about, whether you want to or not.

CAMPFIRES OF
THE DEAD

In this long low slant of hill country twilight they have gathered, all at one time, now, her living blood out of the going-back and the going-back. Grandma Julia May goes back the longest, and looks and talks it with the flesh wrinkling off her bones, with the skin where she knuckles the same brown as the skin of the piglet the men have spit turned, Grandma Julia May says, way too long.

"Come here, Sarah, and see your grandma!" Grandma Julia May says.

Sarah goes over and into and is surrounded by the old woman's warmth and smell. Sarah holds her breath in the smell of housedress in the hamper and feels the flaking skin, the sway of the big hanging bosoms when Sarah pulls herself out from Grandma Julia May, sigh breathes out, and looks up at the spittle strings twisting in Grandma Julia May's mouth.

"You are almost as tall now, Sarah, as when your Grandma first rode under most of the bad men and too few of the good ones," Grandma Julia May says. "Of course, that was when both bad and good were not riding the real loves of their lives, their

Steel Dust and Wink, their Lady Ghost and Raleigh."

Mama, taking in the big macaroni bowl, says, "All right, Ma, that's enough of that now. You, Sarah Caron, find yourself somewhere else."

In the hill hollow of backyard where the late summer cool and dark first settles, Sarah finds Uncle Brayton off and away by himself. Between sips and carefully setting the bottle down, Uncle Brayton cranks the ride-around Lawn Boy. Uncle Brayton holds back long enough to say, "Hey, Sarah Bear. How about... ?" with the rest lost in tug and roar. Uncle Brayton holds onto the Lawn Boy while bending for and feeling for and finding his bottle. He steps on and swings over and sits on the Lawn Boy while holding the bottle chin-high. The Lawn Boy sends beer shakes out of the bottle's top. Uncle Brayton puts a stop to the getting-away beer by sipping some more. He lets go of the handlebars long enough for a back swipe, then gases the Lawn Boy out into the growing dark.

Back over in the last of the after-supper shadows of the China willow on the shed, in the snap of the coiled blue bug-zapper hanging Daddy head-high, Sarah is knees-to-chin slung down in the strap-busted lawn chair with Grandma Rose saying, "Watch yourself, Sarah, or you will jackknife all the way through and hurt yourself good!" Grandma Rose and Aunt Phil and Uncle John make three away from Grandma Julia May, all sitting around the supper table set outside for today. Sarah watches Aunt Connie help clear away the bowls and the tins and the waxpaper-covered plates of what is left of the black-bonnet beans, of the salt-pork-fried-string beans, of the zucchini breads and pumpkin breads, of the last of the brought-up-through-the-field slices of tiger-cat-striped pig, of Aunt Connie's corn-flaked chicken and maple-sugared yams, of there-is-a-lot-of-Grandma-Rose's-chickadee polenta left, of the two ears of the husked and blackened Indian corn, of the sliced tomatoes and cukes taken from Mama's garden of the raised polebean flags—and Cousin Walter's run-down-your-chin-

and-down-your-wrists watermelon, and, "Aunt Connie, is it time for Mama's pie yet?"

"Not yet, Sarah Bear!" Aunt Connie says in a voice busy with the wiping of the checkered oilcloth. "But it's time for you, if you would, to go get little Marlaina and Stevie and tell them to come now and get washed up for bed."

"Go now, Sarah, sweetheart," Grandma Rose says.

"And watch you don't hurt yourself getting out of that darn chair."

Outside the supper table and the circle of trying-to-remember old ones is dark now. Sarah runs through the dew already down and past Uncle Brayton's shirt riding in the steady of the going around and around roar of the Lawn Boy. Sarah runs down the deer trail, down through the over and over of the crickets, past the floating-up little ghost faces of the burst-open milkweed, down to where the trail bends near the big woods and where there hangs the coming-on of night meadow haze. Sarah hurry-now-run-flies with the fear at her back until reaching the fallen-down stone wall and thrust up darker than the night line of trees. Sarah tastes the wood smoke and sees the half-dark, half-firelit shadow casting tallness of Daddy and Cousin Walter and Uncle Baptiste and Rico and Stevie army-blanketed up and little Marlaina sleep-slung in her daddy Charlie's arms. Sarah runs up to and against Daddy, who, without looking away from talking Uncle Baptiste, strokes the hair away from Sarah Bear's face. Sarah stands with one dirty bare foot on top of her other foot in the safe, tall warmth of Daddy, in the talking and laughing low of the men above.

"Sarah, it must almost be time for some of your Mama's deep peach pie," Cousin Walter says after a not long enough time of her standing close to Daddy, of her looking up at Daddy and at these men with her last name.

"Even if it isn't, it's anyway time to head up," Charlie says. "This little one has had it."

Rico pours what is left of his beer into what is left of the banked-down fire. Daddy moves his feet in a way that makes you think he does not want to be anywhere other than talking and laughing soft with Uncle Baptiste. Rico starts out followed by Charlie cradling and murmuring to his little Marlaina. Stevie, army blanket all wrapped up, gets to pony ride Cousin Walter. They pass from the smoky clearing into the darkness of the trees. Daddy takes Sarah's hand still talking with Uncle Baptiste. Uncle Baptiste goes up the narrow deer trail followed by Daddy followed by Sarah with the bigness of the darkness at her back.

Up ahead of Daddy is Uncle Baptiste, making the dark between him and Daddy wider. Up ahead more is the bobbing-blur-of-Stevie face riding the up and down dark gray that is Cousin Walter's white shirt.

Daddy and Sarah move on, more idly than before. The night haze is almost all around them now, hanging low to the belly-high grass. Daddy stops and waits for the others to get on way ahead, while Sarah comes around and stands inside the safe tallness of him, with her back to the tallness and the strength of him resting his big Daddy hands on her shoulders. They stand quiet while the field haze moves around them with the feel of large animals slowly moving, the ghosts of the horses Grandma Julia May named maybe, or cattle maybe, or deer coming up from down below the big woods, stopping and grazing, switching their ears and tails as they come.

Daddy looks straight up, and so Sarah looks straight up, out of the drifting-in haze at what Sarah once heard Daddy say Indians say are the campfires of the dead. They stay looking, heads back, his hands on her shoulders, until that swimming-in-the-stars feeling overcomes her and only his hands keep her from swim-falling away.

When she is again steady on the no longer springing diving board of deer trail, Daddy lifts his hands from her shoulders and they go on through the rhythm of night-bug sounds, up the hoof- and foot-worn way to the backyard slip of wet grass. They go on through the just-cut grass and gasoline smell to where they can see Uncle Brayton mowing away.

"Go run for your Uncle Brayton," Daddy says. "Go on now."

Hair bouncing, Sarah runs in the slippery grass to Uncle Brayton hunched over white in the roar of the Lawn Boy, to careful now, to shouting, "Uncle Brayton!" to Uncle Brayton hunched over and not hearing, to running alongside and again shouting, "Uncle Brayton!" to Uncle Brayton looking up and seeing Sarah, to Uncle Brayton gentling the Lawn Boy down enough to hear Sarah shout, "Come on, Uncle Brayton!" to Uncle Brayton shaking his head yes back at Sarah and shouting back for Sarah to go on over, that he will soon be over.

Carrying the news Uncle Brayton is coming, Sarah runs until reaching the shed. Tapping the weathered-smooth planks, humming to herself, she stops before stepping out into the backyard light, into the voices and the laughter; stops humming and holds herself back in the slanting shed shadow where she watches without being watched.

In the backyard light falling from up on the pole through the darkness all around her, through the shadowed trailing down of the China willow tree, Sarah watches Grandma Julia May in her red-holey-grandma sweater telling something to Grandma Rose that Grandma Rose's face says Grandma Rose does not want to hear but is listening close to anyway, and Uncle John *puff-puff* starting one of his cigars, and Stevie no longer blanket wrapped up and eating some of Mama's deep peach pie, and Mama and Aunt Connie and Aunt Phil laughing over something while watching Stevie eat, and Aunt Ellyn with her head leaned down on Charlie's arm with both Aunt Ellyn and Charlie peaceful looking down at their sleeping little Marlaina, and Cousin Walter and

Rico laughing out open-laughs, and Daddy listening to Uncle Baptiste, and they are all there, all of them but Uncle Brayton who says he is coming over soon, soon, soon.

As she watches them all coming, she says, "Almighty God, Father of all mercies, forever bless and keep my loved ones. Forever bless them in their loving gentleness and goodness. Bless us all, O Lord, with Thy love everlasting."

HUNGRY IN
AMERICA

You start out hungry for a little cuntlet other than the little cuntlet you have waiting for you at home, and the next thing you know you are with a lot of cuntlet not your wife, a lot of woman who is a vision such as she is, who heats you even when you are alone, who Says she does hoodoo you do not believe in, do not want to believe in, are afraid of even if you do not believe in, only hoodoo or not, believe or not, afraid or not, the next thing you know you are far from where you started out, far from the wife no longer waiting for you at home with the no longer long hair: far from her and at the place in yourself where all you have left is the knowing that nobody, that no little cuntlet, no lot of cuntlet, no hoodoo: not that you believe in hoodoo, and even if you did, that nothing other than yourself is ever going to save you from yourself.

How I first met Sansaray—that is this whole lot of other woman's name, Sansaray—was while I was working the Pussy Galore and the DinoSores gig and standing down in front of the stage in front of the wall-high, wall-wide boom boxes: standing around in my grays, my Shadow Security gray pants, my Shadow Security gray shirt, with the Shadow Security patch on the sleeve, and looking at all the jail-quail-little-cuntlet with the rock-and-roll look, with the rock-and-roll-all-in-black-come-here-and-take-a-look look, with the little-black-under-things-worn-as-over-things, with the high black hump-pumps, with the gold and silver sparkling on their necks, on their wrists, on their fingers: looking at all the kid-little cuntlet wearing what they wear, while me and the other men and women of Shadow Security were wearing what we wear: wearing our Shadow Security grays and standing between the kids and Pussy Galore's roadies with the tobacco chaws wadding their cheeks, with the ponytails hanging down the back of their Pussy Galore and the DinoSores T-shirts, with the belly rolls jiggling over their cowboy belt buckles as they swung hammers down on the fingers of the shake-and-make-kid-little cuntlets making it to the stage despite the men and women of Shadow Security, making it to the stage and trying to get up and over to Pussy to come away with fingers pointing several ways at the same time. Many of the roadies, at least many of the roadies I could see from where I was standing, stopped swinging their hammers when seeing this one womanly lot of cuntlet, this one womanly lot of something that from where I was standing looked to me like she was a lot of anything she wanted to be and later turned out to be Sansaray: that whole-lot-of-make-you-want-to-gobble-her-up-kind of woman; that whole-lot-of-make-you-want-to-jack-rabbit-yourself-until-your-fillings-fall-out kind of woman; that whole-lot-of-want-to-make-you-whip-up-some-hasty-pudding-using-only-yourself kind of woman; that kind of woman in her black hump-pumps, in her black stockings with the rhinestones running up the seams, in her little black-and-white undersomething spotted and striped as if once belonging to some big make-believe animal, some big make-believe cat maybe crawling around in some make-believe jungle somewhere, and now, and then, crawling all over her, crawling up her, crawling up Sansaray's vajaguar so you could see the groove of Sansaray's vajaguar; see that while seeing her big, her gigundo slurpies leaping all over, and her hair—man, what hair, hair black and curly and out twice as far, blow-dried out at least twice as wild as any hair at the gig—her hair was almost as long as my wife's long hair was, but black and blow-dried way out; and there was also the gold and silver sparkling on her neck, on her wrists, on her fingers, sparkling all over her, while she, while Sansaray, sort of humped, sort of rode the blast of sound until Sansaray, this whole-lot-of-hoodoo-or-so-she-later-said kind of woman, this table-grade kind of woman, this schtupperwear kind of woman with her vajaguar and her slurpies giddyapping all over her, reached up under her little black-and-white-spotted-and-striped under-something worn as outersomething—but going down so far, just crawling over and up her vajaguar so far—reached up and yanked down her little V-sheath of panty undersomething, which she then stepped out of, which she then balled up in one bejeweled *uh, uh, uh* hand and sort of sissy-tossed toward Pussy Galore and the DinoSores for the lacy little V-sheath of a panty undersomething to then float, to then barely carry, to then unball and land *right... on... my... head*, with me looking out one of the leg holes at her, at Sansaray humping the sound with ten thousand million other screaming and singing Pussy Galore fans, not to mention the men and women of Shadow Security in their Shadow Security grays.

Meanwhile, the little wife at home at the time with her then long hair was trying despite herself, trying despite myself, trying with among other things notes left on the kitchen table starting with "Dear Fuckface" and ending with "Love, your wife, who loves you despite myself, despite yourself, and who is at least trying, which is more than can be said for some of us"—and despite the despites, she did try—among other things, tried pulling me into the shower with the hot water sliding down us, with the shower drain clogged and the warm and the soapy and the scummy water rising up us, with my wife's long wet hair all over us, with my mouth on my wife's mouth, with my hands on my wife's soaped-up slurpies, with my wife's hands on my soaped-up Elijajuan. With all the soap, with all the trying, there was still no "*Oh, Jesus, oh*" from my wife, just more trying with the running-out hot water sliding down us, with the scummy water with the strings of dirt and with the clots of Elijajuan juice rising up us, with the look in my wife's wife eyes turning from *I'm trying, Chet*, to *What the fuck are we doing, Chet?* until that *we*, until that us, became that *I*. . . starting out, going out, ordering out for a side order of what I started telling you about.

I was looking at Sansaray, the most lot of cuntlet looked at outside of a bone book, the most lot of anything I have looked at while looking out the leg hole of a little undersomething, while then taking Sansaray's little V-sheath of a panty undersomething off my head, while then handing the little undersomething back to her, to which she says, "Thank you," says, "Look at the big spook over there, look, coming over here with three beers in each hand"; says, "The big black giant of a son-of-a-bitch, Dacey, that Dace, the motherfucker is driving me to hoodoo!"—while slipping around behind me, while holding on with both hands, while holding onto her little V-sheath of black panty undersomething while holding onto my arm, the arm with the Shadow Security patch on the gray sleeve; the arm that in high school almost had a muscle, just the one arm and just the one muscle from scooping, from using just the one arm to scoop ice cream after school; that soft but official arm under Sansaray's bejeweled *uh, uh, uh* fingers, when the big black fucking spook with muscles all over, with big muscles in places I did not have places to have muscles in, when the big black fucking spook of a man came over and says, "Occifer," this is the way he said officer, says, "Occifer, whatever the probem," this is the way he said problem, says, "Occifer, whatever the probem, I so big, so black, so giant of a spook son-of-a-bitch, that no probem, that no nothing, that no nobody wants to waste whatever little they got fucking with me"; and I say, "Yes, sir, only this woman, sir, this whole lot of heat-and-eat woman here, sir, is now in the custody of Shadow Security for, for, for indecisive exposure in a public place with an occupancy of more than ten thousand million people, sir, Dacey sir, if I may call you Dacey or Dace, sir, if I may call you sir, sir"—when the spook says real soft, says, "Occifer, who's zooming who, okay?"—and this officer, me, I say nothing, not one word more, while putting on my best I'm-bending-over-and-cracking-a-smile smile, while giving him that smile with the lower lip up over the upper teeth, while backing up, while inching back, with Sansaray holding onto the back of my Shadow Security belt, with us—notice that *us*—with *us* inching back, tripping back over some of the screaming kids with their kid faces locked on Pussy Galore and the DinoSores, with *us* moving as quick-footed as *we* could move backward with Sansaray in her hump-pumps, with *me* looking at the giant spook, at the big black muscle of a man standing looking at *us* tripping back through the crowd with *me* yelling, "*Shadow Security backing through!*"—until getting through and *around* and *backstage* to the band's way out, which was guarded by at least ten, maybe more, Shadow Security men and women, who let *us* back *by* and *through* and *down* the hall—and *out* the back way to the parking lot and over to the Shadow Security jeep, when Sansaray, holding on to the back of my Shadow Security belt, says, "How about a lift home"; says, "You look married"; says, "The hoodoo works in strange ways"; says, "Uh-oh"; says, "Look"; says, "Here comes the fucking spook"; says, "Drive, Mr. Shadow Security, drive."

I drove—headlong.

Sansaray sometimes, one time, talked hoodoo in a way that was enough to make you wonder when she talked about causing snakes and spiders to spring up inside the body of somebody, although Sansaray said she only talked that kind of hoodoo and was not into that kind of hoodoo and that she was mostly, really, only, into uncrossing hoodoo, into doing hoodoo that was against hoodoo, and not really into snakes or spiders or anything like that, although Sansaray did say she once did use a catfish that she had her brother Levon catch and hold while she clipped off the three sharp spikes on the catfish's back, which she dried over a flame, which she crushed into powder, which she mixed with white pepper and then, she said, and then she then wrote the name of the somebody, the name of Sansaray's second-semester math teacher. You see, Sansaray was in her second semester at Apex Tech at the time I am telling you about—or so she said, and that she also said that she would never do any hoodoo like this now, or like that now, although Sansaray said she did once do this kind of hoodoo to get a good lock on a neighbor's insides, so the insides of this neighbor could not even come across with a Hershey squirt or anything for the rest of his fucking life. Then she wrote on a slip of paper the name of the somebody, this Mr. Amato, her second-semester math teacher at Apex Tech. She wrote his name three times across itself, then folded up the powdered catfish spikes and white pepper inside the paper and put the paper into the mouth of the catfish, then had her brother Levon throw the catfish back into the same part of the river Levon had first got the fucking catfish out of, and within a week, or so Sansaray said to me, this Mr. Amato was teaching second-semester math fucking naked from the waist down: naked with his little hairy woman-bait hanging down, fucking naked like that, until Mr. Sullivan, Apex Tech chancellor, and Mr. Lemoyne, Apex Tech custodian, hustled Mr. Amato out; and that was the one time, that and her neighbor's locked insides, that Sansaray said she did that kind of hoodoo to anybody, and she was now into uncrossing hoodoo, using roots to uncross hoodoo, using, she said, red coon root, Solomon's red root, Come Back In One Piece root, Cast Off root, Hurry Up root, yaw root, Jinx Killer root, and some other roots I do not remember, because by then Sansaray was making me think only of my Elijajuan root, more than she had already been making me think of it.

Meanwhile, the little wife said what she said by leaving off the light, so coming home late, coming home early, there was no light for me to see to put the key in the lock as quietly as possible, to close the door as quietly as possible, to tiptoe down the hall as quietly as possible, to heel off my Shadow Security boots, to tiptoe in my socks into the kitchen for a slug of milk straight out of the carton and down my chin and down my Shadow Security gray shirt to drip all over the goddamn kitchen floor, to read in the light of the open fridge the note left on the kitchen table starting with "Dear Numbnuts" and ending with "You and your secret Shadow Security night assignments, come on, Chet, who is zooming who?" to put the milk carton away as quietly as possible, to tiptoe back down the hall as quietly as possible, to leave my Shadow Security grays on the living room rug as neat as possible, to lower my 157 pounds of no muscles whatsoever into bed so as not to disturb the person then sleeping the way she then slept, with her then still long hair spread out on the pillow, with her a sleep-breathing the one sound other than the sound of the fucking fridge, with the set of her chin saying to me in in the dark, *Yes, Chet, you have pissed what we had away, Chet!*

When you find a little cuntlet that turns out to be a lot of cuntlet, the next thing you know you want to do, you want to go a little somewhere, like to Pizza My Heart on a slow Tuesday night to order the Heart Stopper, which, by the way, is seven dollars and change a slice. You order a slice of the Heart Stopper for her and a tall water for you, and you watch as the olives, as the hot sausage, as the shrooms ooze off onto her sweater-covered slurpies at their slurpies-at-ease, which you offer to clean off without using your hands, and to which she says, Yeah? So... then... you... figure you will take her to Donut Master for donut holes, and watch as she scarfs down maybe half a dozen at three-and-change a dozen before heading back out to the Shadow Security jeep and to sitting and telling her how *you have never felt like this before* and how you are going crazy to take her to some really special place, like probably to a Brew & Trough, but, hey, you are a right-to-a the-point kind of guy, with the point suddenly being that you have got to slap a little Elijajuan on her right this very instant; then you say, in all *seriousness* now, with all *kidding aside* now, that what you really want is for her to throw a crotch-lock on your face until either her legs go numb and turn blue or until you drop dead from suffocation, whatever comes first, and this is exactly what the game plan was on that slow Tuesday night, with me wearing my best Shadow Security grays and driving the Shadow Security jeep, when suddenly I am out front of where Sansaray lives with her father, her mother, her grandmother, her four sisters, her brother Levon; out front looking in the bay window dark but for the flicker of blue on the glass, and me honk-honking for Sansaray, for that whole-lot-of-hurt-me-good kind of woman, for that whole-lot-of-even-learn-ballroom-dancing-if-that-is-what-she-wanted kind of woman, for that whole-lot-of-spank-and-serve-fucking woman, and then that woman letting the screen door whack shut behind her while she clacks down the steps in her hump-pumps, then clicks down the walk with all the sparkle sparkling on her neck, on her wrists, on her *uh, uh, uh* fingers holding a little kimono something or other up close to her as she clicks. I reach over and snap open the door to give Sansaray a hand in, as it were, when she says, "You know, you still look married, but not as married as you looked before, Chet"; says, "We're staying right here, Chet"; says, "You can meet my father, my mother, my grandmother, my four sisters, my brother Levon, and some others I want you to meet, Chet."

We Stay.

I figure I saved big bucks by not going to Pizza My Heart, by not going to Donut Master, by not going to Brew & Trough and by going inside instead, but that leaves out, of course, totaling up certain costs, which you will see are to come later.

All the while, of course, less and less of the little woman was at home, less and less of the little wife—less like no washing dishes, like no washing clothes, like no cooking food, like no talking words, like no leaving notes anymore, like no fucking for the idea of home and hearth.

But I still come home and give her the "Honey, I'm home," and get back just the sound of running water until, after an hour of getting that sound, I go in and see her sitting in the tub with a scissors in one hand and a clump of long hair in the other hand, sitting with the shower water shooting down at her, her face all twisted up in the weeping way she has, sitting with clumps of long hair floating all around her on the rising, scummy, too-cool-by-then water.

We were inside, in the living room dark except for the big TV flickering *Fantasy Island* all over the walls, all over the ceiling, all over the faces and the hands of Sansaray's father, Sansaray's mother, her grand-mother, her four sisters, her brother Levon, all watching *Fantasy Island* with none of them even looking up to see me when Sansaray says, "This is Chet of Shadow Security," with none of them even looking away from *Fantasy Island* when we go into Sansaray's room with Sansaray clunking the door and snickering the dead bolt behind us, locking in what looks to me like a big wind had come through and blown all of Sansaray's shit all over the floor, all over the chair, all over the unmade bed, all over and hanging off the antenna of the little TV rolling *Fantasy Island* we are now watching while sitting on Sansaray's bed, that little TV that Sansaray is watching while I help her take off the kimono sort of outersomething worn as outersomething over her white-turned-blue-with-*Fantasy Island* shoulders, over her strapless, shoulderless, cut way-low-way-down-to-there little pushup of a little undersomething worn as under-something, while I help her unzip the pushup little undersomething's zipper, letting loose her humongous slurpies, while I help her slide down her little V-sheath of panty undersomething hiding her groove, her slice of hairy vajaguar, while I help me unbutton, unzip, let drop my Shadow Security gray pants, while I help slide down my Shadow Security gray skivvies, when Sansaray, without for one instant looking away from *Fantasy Island* rolling blue over her white arms, over her white belly, over her red slice of vajaguar, says, "Wait, Chet"; says, "*Fantasy Island* ain't over, Chet"; says, "Dincha hear the door, Chet?" when I hear *thud, thud* on the door and I hear her brother Levon, shouting, "The big black giant of a spook is out here with a whole lot of others, and the spook and the others want to fucking talk to what's his name!" and Sansaray says, "Tell the big black giant of a spook and all the others that we are watching *Fantasy Island!*" and Levon shouts, "You tell them yourself!" and Sansaray, without taking her eyes off *Fantasy Island*, gets up off the unmade bed and goes over to the little TV and turns up the sound and comes back over to the bed, when there is a *thud, thud* on the door and a *deep, deep* voice on the other side of the door says, "Occifer, I want to talk to you," and Sansaray, without looking away *from Fantasy Island*, says, "Talk to him, Chet"; and the deep, deep voice on the other side of the door says, "Occifer, there is no probem that we cannot take care of if we put our minds to it"; and Sansaray, without looking away from *Fantasy Island*, says, "Put your mind to it, Chet"; and the *deep, deep* voice on the other side of the door says, "Sansaray, unlock the door"; and Sansaray gets up off the bed without looking away from *Fantasy Island* and goes over to the door and grabs the dead bolt . . . when I shout, "*Wait!*"

About my wife, you should know so much less of the less of the little woman was no longer at home that there was just a note left on the kitchen table with nothing written on either side of the plain white notepaper other than "Dear Geekmonger."

As I was saying, Sansaray was waiting when I shouted, "Wait!" and holding on to the dead bolt and watching *Fantasy Island* when the *deep, deep* voice on the other side of the door says, "Occifer, it is nearly time"; and no sooner does the *deep, deep* voice on the other side of the door say that than the theme music for *Fantasy Island* cranks up and Sansaray snickers back the dead bolt and comes back over to the bed, while the doorknob on the door slowly turns, while the door slowly opens, while the door slowly opens all the way for Dacey, for Dace, for the pumped-up, veined-up spook of a Dacey spook wearing *whites*, wearing Universal Security Service *whites*, Universal Security Service *white* gloves, Universal Security Service *white* pants, a Universal Security Service *white* shirt with the Universal Security Service patch on the sleeve; and from what I can see from standing with my Shadow Security *gray* pants and my Shadow Security *gray* skivvies down around the tops of my Shadow Security boots, out behind Dacey is Pussy Galore and the DinoSores, and out behind Pussy Galore and the DinoSores are Pussy Galore's roadies, and lined up and stretching out behind the roadies are the kid-little-cuntlets with their rock-and-roll look, and behind the kid-little-cuntlets are the men and women of Shadow Security, and from what I can see from standing where I am standing, out behind the Shadow Security men and women is a pizza delivery man fucking naked from the waist down, naked with his little hairy woman-bait standing out like a shroom, and behind the pizza delivery man is a man standing with his legs crossed, and lined up behind that man is Sansaray's father, Sansaray's mother, her grandmother, her four sisters, her brother Levon, and behind her brother Levon is a man, no make that a woman, a woman that is—my God—that woman is my wife— when Sansaray, spreading herself, spreading her vajaguar wide, says, "Now, lover, eat now."

THE REPORTER

"Jesus wept" is the way Jim puts it.

"Jesus wept, all right," is the way Paley puts it. Paley puts it the way Paley puts it while waiting for Jim. Jim types his obit. Jim cranks the sheet of paper out of the typewriter. Jim stacks the sheet of paper with the other sheets of paper. Jim hands the paper to Paley. Paley reads out loud.

James Peter Kittridge today joined the do-it-yourselfer club. Membership, as far as he knew, was a family first. The father he never knew, he was told, pneumonia-wheezed his last. The mother and two older sisters died from cancers and kidneys and hearts too big. The mother and two sisters he knew best rose in the dark and the cold of that mill town. They walked the nearly four miles to work. They worked twelve hours in the roar of the looms. They walked the nearly four miles back. Home was the flapping of shirts frozen between tenements. Home was waiting in the dark for their coming home. When they came home, there was the light and the stirring of the potato soup. There was the reading of the Bible out loud while they ate. There was the threading of the rosaries in bed. There was the dying in bed. There was the dying under the gaze of Jesus. A kind of living was had from the freights along that mill town siding. That, and shouldering beef. That, and stacking cinder block. That, and finding a man as good as a good man. The good man put him to work pasting up, running copy, setting type. When none of the others were around to send, the good man sent him. He crossed the ice of the pond. He bellied to where the hunter clawed black water. He held on to the hunter and prayed. Dusk seeped over the cornfield. Dusk seeped over the pond. He held on and prayed, until the others came running down through the corn-stubbled dark.

After that, the good man showed him. He typed with two fingers while the good man said, "Jesus wept. Got it? Try again."

There was trying on the four-alarm fire so hot he heard the teeth popping of those trapped inside. There was the four-year-old found at the dump. There was the driver headless after driving into a tree.

When the war came in four-inch headlines, he jumped from airplanes at night. He watched for Arabs standing on high ground. He learned how it was to be afraid for so long.

Back from the war, he learned to think of his wounds, once they scabbed over brown and hard, as medals bestowed for living. Back all the way was living with his wife-to-be and her two daughters. That, and the wedding. That, and the sleeping with his medaled leg between the legs of his wife.

Given time, there was the sleeplessness. There was the trying day after day in the name of Jesus.

There were the cancers and kidneys. There was the wanting to-do-it himself. The wanting grew, indifferent to family and prayer and trying again. The wanting grew, until the wanting was all that was left. That, and the question when.

Older versions of himself could be found most nights at the end of the bar, in the column three times a week, in all the usual lies. He lied that he was doing some good. He lied that he had given back all that he was given. The truth was, he was tired of lying.

He typed his obit.

He drove to where they lived.

He looked in on his wife sleeping.

He took the Colt from the desk.

He waited.

He waited in the dark, until knowing no one was coming.

"Nope" is the way Paley puts it. Paley puts it the way Paley puts it while handing back the paper. "Nope, and it is going to stay nope until you get it right. Got it?"

Jim laughs.

"That son-of-a-bitch laughed" is the way Paley later put it.

WAYS OF SEEING

Who of us trusts his own way of seeing?

For instance, from where he whomped down on the water mattress, Bolio can see past the drunken faces. Bolio sees past the insect-charged halo of the parking lot lights to the sky and a few summer stars. As a boy, Bolio imagined the stars were pinholes in the painted-Easter-eggshell-dome of Heaven letting in the light from a room pale and bare except for the egg-enclosed universe and a huge sun bulb. Now, for the first time in a long time, Bolio again imagines seeing the stars as such, one of his few inventions, while seeing the gacked-up faces surrounding him, the owner hustling over with the tape measure. Moving anything other than his head would disqualify the toss. Bolio raises only his head and eyeball estimates twenty-two feet, five inches.

"I would say twenty-four feet, four inches," says the owner of this tavern.

The owner runs the tape measure from the foul line to Bolio's closest body part, which, for this toss, is the second toe of his right foot. On both of Bolio's feet, the second toe is bigger than the big toe.

"Mark that twenty-four feet, six inches," the owner says, drawing applause, huzzahs from the whooped-up young.

Lifted from the water mattress to his outsized feet, Bolio runs back to Ermack. Bolio lies on the mat at Ermack's feet. The mat is the same kind of mat you knew in high school or junior high school gym. Remember those mats? Remember what looks like horsehair stuffing sticking out? Remember when you were next to somersault or cartwheel and you were not ready? Remember feeling you would never be ready? Remember feeling the sweat roll down your ribs?

"Are you ready, Bolio?" Ermack asks.

From down on the mat, Bolio can see Ermack's white high tops with the looping purple laces. Bolio can see Ermack's mismatched tube socks stretching over freckled calves.

"Yes," Bolio lies, raising an arm and a leg.

Bolio closes his eyes as Ermack grabs Bolio's upraised wrist and ankle. Bolio listens.

"Errr-mack! Errr-mack! Errr-mack!" the crowd chants.

Ermack's lift shifts into crow hop, spin, launch as he slings Bolio skyward. Bolio sees spinning stars and meteor showers riddling the black eggshell dome of his eyelids.

Ermack's best invention may be Ermack.

"My eyes are as piercing as coat-hanger darts tufted with cotton balls lung heaved from a glass blowgun," Ermack says.

"My breath is the exhaust from a fifty-five Caddie doing eighty on open road," Ermack says.

"My will is a pack of starving dogs let loose in a butcher shop," Ermack says.

"My heart is the sound of the late night train moving through the town and sleep of your childhood," Ermack says.

"My mind is a boomerang to throw farther and farther until I am afraid it will not come back, and then, when it does, I throw it again," Ermack says.

Ermack has his invention while Bolio has his feet. Bolio's

feet are too long and too big for his three-foot, seven-inch length. Bolio's feet are too big for his ninety-eight-pound body.

"Your long toes with the second toes bigger than the big toes is where you began," Ermack says.

"All that egg-growth spurted down to your feet, exploded down to your toes in an all-out effort to make you big, bigger," Ermack says.

Ermack may be right, Bolio thinks. Maybe Bolio began with his feet, Bolio thinks. Maybe Bolio ends at his feet. When Bolio cums, that electric-urge twitches down his little legs to arc and sputter in his big feet.

"A zillion little Bolios turning cold on your belly," Ermack says.

"A zillion little protozoan Bolios with big heads and big hands and big feet somersaulting in your Milky Way spill," Ermack says.

Walking to the tavern, Bolio sees many of the same young cruising up and down the strip.

"The same young faces cruise up and down this strip like pharaohs on the Nile," Ermack says.

"At the same time, youth to the young seems shuffling, barely able," Ermack says.

"Youth is a tyrant, a small tyrant to the young, a large tyrant to the old," Ermack says.

"The young are like you, Bolio, with your body a tyrant to your mind," Ermack says.

Ermack may be right, and yet, Ermack has plenty of youth cruising for him.

"My joy is winter light snapping off a fast-moving stream," Ermack says.

"My anger is the anger of a whore, cold and sad," Ermack says.

"My arrogance is the arrogance of dreams," Ermack says.

"My past is the town where you grew up, which is now just somewhere on the way to somewhere else," Ermack says.

"My present is returning home from a cold night to the warmth of a sleeping child you love," Ermack says.

"My future is a too short fucking drive over a fast new road," Ermack says.

When you get this low you really get to see the summer sky.

"Are you ready, Bolio?" Ermack asks.

Bolio raises his head and sees the faces of the young.

Bolio sees the owner ready with the tape measure for Ermack's last toss. Ermack needs a toss of more than twenty-eight feet, five inches to win tonight.

"Yes," Bolio lies, raising his arm and leg starward.

"No, Bolio," Ermack says.

"Something new, Bolio," Ermack says, his face souped-up with all his youth, all his will.

"On your back, Bolio," Ermack says. "Roll on your back and cross your arms like so."

Bolio rolls on his back and crosses his arms. Ermack takes hold of Bolio's feet.

"Not my feet," Bolio says.

"Yes, Bolio," Ermack says. "You will see."

Bolio closes his eyes. Bolio listens.

"Errr-mack! Errr-mack! Errr-mack!"

Ermack's lift glides to spin, another spin, snap as he boomerangs Bolio nightward.

Bolio spins over the upraised faces, over the thirty-foot mark, out over the water mattress. Bolio spins in the stars squint-seen as a sieve of light slanting, cart-wheeling, exploding. Bolio spins on until seeing, finally, how suited the heart is for this life's ride.

FLAMINGOS AND OTHER SELF-CURES, ALMOST

I knew something was needed so I planted one on top of Zio Frank. It was hard finding something that spoke to me. Once found, the something was harder to steal. I am talking one of these Day-Glo plastic flamingos with a black hook of a beak and a neck like a question mark. The neck curves down to a molded hollow body and a folded black-tipped wings. The legs are two-foot-long wire rods sticking into underbelly bearing the words MADE IN LEOMINSTER, MASS. I am talking simple and complete, ready to plant when and where you want. I planted one on top of Zio Frank.

Mornings I am not buzzed I go out driving around. Driving around, seeing what is available, is something we used to do. We meaning me and Zio Frank. It is how I found the flamingo. It is how I spend my mornings. I get behind the wheel of Zio Frank's big Impala, one of the old ones with the manta-ray fins and roomy, you forget how roomy, interior. Since my butt has come to resemble gnawed pig knuckle, I get behind the wheel of the Impala as carefully as I can. What hurts most is knowing how Elaine, Zio Frank's wife, my aunt, will call the cops if she catches me. She has already. She has promised to do so again. I wait until she goes to dancercize class to schmooze and wiggle her wide butt—no pig knuckle there—schmooze and wiggle between the hours of ten and two Monday through Friday. I wait until she goes to class before flashing the spare key she does not know about. I inch my tender, runny butt behind the wheel. I sit until I am used to the pain again. I sit smelling Zio Frank's smell, his brand of smokes and after-shave. I sit until I am used to the pain again before sliding down, sliding slowly down until as little of the raw as possible is left on the front seat. I slide down until I can barely see over the dash.

Half sitting, half lying down, I start up the big Impala and ease it down the driveway. I ease the Impala faster along the back roads and through the spreading subdivisions. The Impala almost seems to take over, leaving me in my butt-chewed-way to see what is available. Available is his word, Zio Frank's word. Driving around, seeing what is available, was his big thing, the thing that almost cured him. I said almost. The flamingo is mine.

Most of the time you have to cure yourself. This is true, is it not? Zio Frank tried. He tried to cure himself of a lot of things. It beat hell out of coming home from the plumbing and machine shop the way he did: the same plumbing and machine shop he worked at thirty-six years: coming home all private and sulky and stay out of my way. Nights he came home like this, the first thing he did was galumph sulky and pissed-off to the fridge. This and hook back a cold longneck and roll his eyes up until they looked like the eyeholes in a mask. This and blow out as if he just surfaced from the cold, cold bottom of a lake. All this paved the way for the rest of the night: a night in his easy chair smoking and killing a six of longnecks and watching TV: a night of watching the same news over and over followed by comedy shows where the women are jiggle and shriek. All this sitting and smoking and killing and watching pretty well poleaxed him, put him under until the smoke between his fingers burned down to the knuckles. Other than sulk there was no complaint, not to me, so I can only guess he was worn down working through the morning, through the day, through the thirty-six years: worn down working just to pay the bills: worn down watching TV and waking up with knuckles on fire until it was either do something different or die. The truth is he did both, and the way he began was by driving around seeing what else was available.

Me, I drive around because I am not smart enough to think of anything else; getting buzzed takes no genius. Mornings I am not buzzed I go out driving around. I drove almost two weeks' worth of sober mornings before finding the Day-Glo. It was hard. It took me two weeks to see beyond the usual. I am talking the usual gas-fed barbecues, wishing wells, and such. None of the usual spoke to me, so I drove more. I drove until I saw something that spoke to me, something as in lawn jockeys, lawn jockeys both white and black. I am talking concrete lawn jockeys with caps and painted silks and knee-high black boots: the ones holding lanterns as if looking for someone or something. This is what spoke to me, this meaning the looking part. That is until getting close and really seeing the look. Both lawn jockey races, white and black, have the same look. Look closely next time you see a lawn jockey and you will see what I mean. It is a baring of teeth and it spooks me. It spooks me in that it reminds me of when I could look in the rearview. Before my butt was chewed and I could look in the rearview, this look was the same as mine.

When Zio Frank began, he began big. I am talking big and then some. I am talking life-size. I am talking a day or two after he started driving around seeing what is available, she appeared out behind the garage. I saw her while mowing the lawn. She is hard to miss. I said life-size. I am talking statuesque. I am talking biggest I have seen. I am talking bigger than me and when buzzed I feel almost life-size. She is, the Bathtub Virgin that is.

Standing barefoot on a half-globe base, the Bathtub Virgin is protected by an upright quarter-buried bath-tub covered with concrete and strings of blue lights; the same color blue as the long concrete veil covering her head and shoulders: the same sky blue as her Heaven-raised eyes that say to me, Yes, I have known both beauty and shit.

Imagine. Imagine all this. Imagine all this and then some as in bare white feet and hands emerging from the concrete folds of a long white robe: a robe like the one Elaine, Zio Frank's wife, my aunt, sometimes wears, only with Elaine's robe you can see the outline of her nips.

As far as I can tell, and I have looked closely, the Bathtub Virgin does not have any, nips that is. She does not have any nips or tits or butt, not that I should talk, not about butts, not anymore, but the Bathtub Virgin has no butt, especially when matched against Elaine. When Elaine wears a skirt, her wide butt looks like two small dogs fighting in a bag. She was some beginning, the Bathtub Virgin that is. Elaine came later.

Me, I took my time. I took almost two weeks' worth of mornings easing the big Impala around the back roads and through the spreading subdivisions. Besides the usual, I saw lions and porcelain rooster planters filled with mums. I saw pipe-sucking leprechauns and ceramic donkeys on power mower chassis. None of these spoke to me, so I drove. I drove sober and it seemed a long time. I drove until something spoke to me. Something spoke to me at the Mohawk Mobile Home Adult Park, speed limit ten miles per. I drove within the speed limit around the park's roads: a grid of roads named after famous Indians and Indian tribes: Pocahontas Place, Cheyenne Way, Tecumseh Court.

On Tecumseh Court I heard. In the fenced-in yard of a small black and white mobile home I saw. I saw a flock of half a dozen Day-Glos with their lovely questing necks, their molded plastic bodies with that little event of upturned tail, their delicate wire legs. Every bird was simple and complete in a way that, well, you know. I parked. I parked the Impala out front of the small black and white mobile home surrounded by nip-high wire- mesh fence. Two signs were on the fence: BEWARE OF DOG and THE DEMPSEYS.

I could see Mrs. Dempsey, or rather a boiled ham face with a smoke angling out of the mouth. She was at a window of the mobile home, stiff-arming a Venetian blind. I could see the white flesh sagging at the back of her arm, flesh as white as marble set off against the meat color of her face. I could see her head juke trying to see between the Venetian blind slats. She juked while barking hammered over and over inside the mobile home. I am talking barking that meant business. I am talking barking that made me know something else besides the first something I told you about was needed.

Then there was then some, then some after the Bathtub Virgin and before Elaine. I am talking Zio Frank driving around, seeing what is available. I am talking Zio Frank driving around before work as well as after work. I am talking Zio Frank driving around and seeing and then some, then some as in patio. I am talking marble patio.

"The best that is available," Zio Frank said; Zio Frank, who once came home from the plumbing and machine shop all private and sulky and stay out of my way. I am talking once, once in that he quit. He quit working and sulking and took to driving around, seeing what is available, full time.

"The best that is available," Zio Frank said. He was talking patio. He was talking marble patio, midnight chill and quiet. Us sweating despite the chill. Us meaning me and Zio Frank. Us sweating while heaving marble slabs into the back seat of the Impala: marble slabs wrecking the shocks and filling the Impala's interior, you forget how roomy interior, with the smell of damp and moss: these same marble slabs now planted around our pool. Sitting around our pool killing longnecks you can read as in JASON COCKBURN or LUCILLE ASHTON 1846-1902 or JOHN CHILSON BELOVED BROTHER AND DEVOTED SON. You can read all this, all this and then some.

The flamingos and Mrs. Dempsey can keep a while longer. Let us talk Elaine, Zio Frank's wife, my aunt: the same Elaine who called the cops on me and said she will do so again: the same Elaine who until a short time ago was not Zio Frank's wife, was not my aunt: the same Elaine I first met while mowing the lawn around our marble patio and pool. She said Frank said come over any time and use the pool. She came over. She came over more.

I did not mind her coming over, not even with her wide no-pig-knuckle butt, not that I should talk, not anymore, not about butts, but I did not mind, even with her wide butt she can barely keep in her zebrastriped bikini: more butt than bikini, more butt and then some. I am talking low rider. I am talking varicose veins. I am talking fleshy butt.

As soft and as wide and as fleshy as Elaine is you know where, her face is hard. It is hard in a way you might think stupid. It is not. It is not unkind either, even after calling the cops on me. It is a face with a slash of red lipstick and eyes that look at me like she knows I would not mind sticking whatever instinct I own between those red lipsticked lips.

I guess Zio Frank felt the same way. He said come over any time. She came over. She came over more. She stayed. They married.

While killing longnecks and watching some jiggle and shriek, I could sometimes hear them upstairs. I could hear them going at it with all the wherewithal lips and mouths and bellies and whatever else can muster. When Zio Frank did, muster that is, I could hear him moan like he was gut shot.

I am talking Tecumseh Court again. I am talking looking at the imprisoned flock and listening to the barking and knowing: knowing something was needed: knowing I needed something else to get that first something. I am talking just one and not a longneck, not my well-known mean drunk act either, not my stay too long and fall down thing, not my sick dog stuff. I am talking none of that, well, almost none of that, and just one. Knowing what I knew, I opened the door of the Impala and got out. Mrs. Dempsey of THE DEMPSEYS, meat face at the window, left the blind to appear at the mobile home's screen door. A dog, a barking silhouette of doggy fury, appeared with her.

"Is this the Dempsey residence?" I asked.

Mrs. Dempsey stared while the dog boomed his voice around the inside of the mobile home and bounced himself off the screen door Mrs. Dempsey kept closed with both white-as-marble arms.

"Is the mister in?" I asked, pitching my voice down like a fat TV detective.

The woman and the dog stared more; she with smoke curling around that face; the dog with ears raised.

"No need to worry, ma'am," I said. "I am here to tell you there have been reports of high levels of radiation found in some lawn ornaments, especially flamingos. Don't worry, ma'am, not yet, but I do have to look at your flock."

I said what I said while closing the gate behind me, while trying not to step in the dog's huge shit piles. It was useless, the shit piles were huge and all over. I thought of the Bathtub Virgin. I thought of her covered with concrete and strings of blue lights, the same sky blue as her Heaven-raised eyes. I thought of the Bathtub Virgin and, this is the truth, got down on my knees in the shit piles and crawled all around and made a little show of looking at each flamingo.

By the time I crawled all around, going so far as taking a pad out of my back pocket and pretending to take notes, by the time I crawled all around to the last flamingo smaller and more Day-Glo than the others, I knew.

"I will have to take this one in," I said, meaning the one slightly smaller and more Day-Glo than the other ones.

"I am talking about having to take this one in now," I said, getting to my feet. As I lifted the plastic bird off its wire legs, Mrs. Dempsey swung open the screen door.

Zio Frank got his walking their bed. I was downstairs killing and watching some more you know what when instead of a moan, a moan like I told you about, I heard a cough. Zio Frank coughed like somebody trying to swallow a fleshy hairball.

Elaine, her hard face even harder in her seriousness, padded naked into the living room. She came downstairs serious and naked and rippling and butt and said call an ambulance. When the ambulance arrived, Zio Frank's eyes were open, but he was not awake.

Me, I felt sleepy with fear. Mrs. Dempsey swung open the screen door and I asked myself whether I was too sleepy to try. I was not too sleepy to try, and made it out the gate and almost halfway across Tecumseh Court. I was almost halfway, when I turned and saw the white in the muzzle. I saw the white and how one of the eyelids was torn off showing a white ball looking straight up. The other eye was red and big as a big dog's eye. I looked into that eye and knew that I was a doomed pretender.

Me on my knees on the examining table in the emergency room. Me more hurt and bloody than I knew.

"This looks like pig knuckle," the doctor said while tweezing away strips of bloody underwear and blue jean. He tweezed away while I passed out of me.

When I came to, and this is something, I felt pretty good. But for the pain in my butt, I felt pretty good. What I mean is, but for the pain, I felt as pretty good as I can ever remember feeling.

I felt pretty good right up to when the cops stopped by: the same cops Elaine, Zio Frank's wife, my aunt, called. The cops stopped by and we talked. We talked Impala. We talked bloody front seat. We talked flamingo and all. We talked and I lied. The cops laughed and told me unlicensed, unregistered and uninsured use of a motor vehicle.

Elaine's, Zio Frank's wife's, my aunt's unauthorized use charge was dropped after I told her I would not take the Impala out again until all this was straightened out. I lied to her too. You know. You know mornings I am not buzzed I go out driving around between the hours of ten and two. Mornings I am not buzzed, and it has been almost six weeks' worth now, I go out driving around. Six weeks and I still know. I still know so I inch my tender, runny butt behind the wheel and go out driving around, seeing what is available.

Sometimes I stop by and see Zio Frank and the flamingo. The flamingo is a little unsteady on TV antenna wire legs: a little unsteady so I lean the flamingo against Zio Frank's half-ton marble marker: a marble marker I know nothing short of four-wheel drive and winch will move.

This is not all I know. I know this is no cure, but maybe it is a beginning, maybe even a beginning and then some.

DEAR TO WHOEVER FINDS AND READS THIS SO THAT YOU SHOULD KNOW DOZIER AND ME ARE NOT ALL BAD, AT LEASTWISE NOT DOZIER

Anything can happen now that everything has.

Don't you wish it is you who says this? I wish it is me who says this, only it is Dozier who says this. I cannot think of a single anything to say since writing this down is not my idea in the first place and is Dozier's idea, with Dozier saying to me, La-Donna darling, be my writing-down angel and write all this down like you are an angel come to earth. Some angel I am, not even knowing what to write down first. I say to Dozier, What should I write down first? Dozier does not say anything, only is keeping his hands on the steering wheel and is keeping his eyes straight ahead on the road with the bugs shooting white out from the black from the both sides of the road like they are shooting at us. I wonder maybe Dozier is thinking about the same what I am thinking about and is not hearing me, only Dozier hears me all right, for after I watch the bugs shoot out some more and after I nearly quit thinking what I was thinking about I told you about, and after I start getting asleepier and asleepier, which is the why this writing is slanting down now the way it is slanting down, Dozier says to me, LaDonna darling, write this, write anything can happen now that everything has. As you can see, I wrote this down and also write what I just wrote.

This is maybe not what Dozier had in mind when he asked me to be his writing-down angel, only Dozier is the only this I can think of right now to write down about. This is Dozier road mapped out for you as Dozier is right now, starting with the nothing Dozier has on what he calls his mechanic tan southernmosts. Take Dozier's closest bare southernmost, the one on the gas pedal, and jump your mind up from the toe traffic jam to the squiggly green veins under what was Dozier's inside-all-day skin as if somebody started squiggly drawing a road map using his skin and a green crayon to draw with. The little squiggle of highway goes in under the underside of anklebone before starting up again to spread out from the higher-up muscle bunch of down under Dozier. From the bunch of muscle-up, the in and out of vein gets bigger, at leastwise looks bigger, gets to be what could be interstates shooting up to the outside of what could be a side of the road rest stop on top of Dozier's old baldy knee worn bald by the rubbing of Dozier's jeans when Dozier is wearing jeans, only now Dozier is wearing baggy army cutoffs and a T. From under the sleeves of Dozier's T, the big see-able, what I call interstates, start up again, bulk squiggling out again at the big humped-out arm muscle half mechanic tanned and half sunburned. These interstates squiggly dip down, up, into the nearly all sunburned before becoming four-lane divided dividing out into the crowded underside of elbow to wrist before tunneling under Dozier's watchband. The back of Dozier's sunburned hand, the one on the steering wheel, has the veins forking out and running over themselves into a kind of downtown busy-ness ending with Dozier's fingernails rimmed in tarred parking lot black. Next comes Dozier's scenic overlook, starting with the sunburn riding up his neck to his clean-shaven unpaved Dozier says he shaves every other day for me. Next comes Dozier's wooded parkland of curly black hair that if you were me you would not mind camping out in and maybe getting lost in. Talking about getting lost in, Dozier's toll-limited lips let me in in a way that I never wanted in before and do not want out of until what is the innermost of me is tongue driving around down inside Dozier, driving down Dozier's throat and down inside Dozier until I am looking out Dozier's eyes at what is the outermost of me writing all this down.

Already the everything that happened seems so long ago, although in trying to figure back I guess it was only, if today is already Friday, was only Tuesday, Wednesday, Thursday, three days ago. Three days and another me, or so it seems ago, when the me that is me now awoke up out of myself asleep walking through my life in a way I did not even know about until the everything that happened to us happened. Maybe you know what I mean? Maybe something has happened to you to all of a sudden make you say to yourself, Where have I been until now? How did I get anything done until now? How did I get to where I am now? Three days and a lifetime ago and here I am now with the heat rising wrinkly off the road the way it is and whip-shaking the hair on the off sides of our heads the way it is and sucking in hot over us the way it is and sticking us to these seats the way it is so every time one of us moves it sounds like somebody tearing tape. This wrinkly and this whip-shaking straight and this sucking in hot and this tearing tape of our skin means I am wide awake, at leastwise I think I am wide awake, although the truth is it does seem a little like dreaming with Dozier riding us to the anything that can happen next.

All the what Dozier is about on the outside I road mapped out for you is one thing. All the what Dozier is about on the inside is another thing. What Dozier is on the inside is not as easy to write down about as the what on the outside, not that that was easy, only with me, what you see, which is not much, is what you get. With Dozier, what you see, at leastwise what you see on the outside, seems a whole lot different than what is on the inside. On the outside, Dozier looks like he can take care of himself and anybody and anything else needing to be taken care of. On the inside, Dozier is . . . Dozier. What this girl is trying to say to you the best I know how, which I know is none too good, is that inside of Dozier, in spite of what you might first think on first seeing Dozier, and in spite of what Dozier did or does, is a lot of something making somebody like me want to do for Dozier the best I can. At the same time, something else in me wants to say I most likely will never be able to do for Dozier, at leastwise not in the way Dozier most wants, whatever that way is. Maybe this is true for all of us and those we love the most.

. . .

This is written down in the dark with Dozier having us settled in on sixty, only with the dark the way the dark is, you, dear whoever you are reading this, will have to forgive me if this writing down is not on the lines and is all over instead, only I have to write down to you now so you should know to forget about most of the whatever you might hear about what Dozier and me did or did not do and about the everything that did or did not happen. The truth is, who other than Dozier and me and maybe Stepdaddy really cares about the everything that happened? More of the truth is but for Stepdaddy's seventy-three-and-whatever-the-change-was, I bet, and maybe you can hear Dozier doing the talking and me trying to pass it off a little that it is me doing the talking, only we bet Stepdaddy does not really care much about what happened. Everybody we meet seems to only care about and is only talking about this weather, talking this sit-on-you heat and how no end to the heat is in sight. To tell you the truth some more, sometimes Dozier starts the weather talk himself by saying in his best-natured-Dozier way, Lots of weather we're having lately. Dozier says you can tell a lot about a person from the way they answer that, if they bother answering. Knowing this, I say to you whatever you likely hear about Dozier and me and about what Dozier and me did or did not do and about the everything that did or did not happen is not worth knowing much about and just is.

Dozier believes in getting up early, getting up either with first light or a little before to see the sun light up as far as you can see. Dozier says there is something about that light and about that time of day that gives a someone a kind of hope, a kind of promise of what the day might bring. I say let me asleep, although the only time I have ever gotten up that early, at leastwise after awhile after the only one time I have ever gotten up that early, there was, and there most likely still is, if I could only get up, all the not having to go anywhere we do not want to go, or do anything we do not want to do, and if we want we can spend the whole day out of this heat somewhere, stopping out at some spinachy sump hole somewhere to laze around in the choked-off shallows talking about what we want and what we will do and where we will go, or if we want we can go, go five hundred miles north, south, east, west to see some of the nearly everything I have never seen and most likely will never see again. Along with all of Dozier himself, all this is nearly enough to make me maybe think Dozier is right about what Dozier says about getting up with first light.

This is again maybe not what Dozier most likely had in mind for me to write down about when he asked me to be his writing-down angel, so this will be just between you and me, not that you might likely will want any of it anywhere near you once you know what it is. It can happen anywhere at any time just like it happened now with Dozier cruising Dozier and me who cares where with my hand cramping up with my writing all this down when Dozier gets his little look to himself like Dozier is amusing himself, not as if there is anything bad about amusing yourself, or even so bad about Dozier's little look to himself so much as what comes after his little look. What comes after his little look is a kind of bark or a string of barks, and I do not mean a kind of bark the same as the bulldog's bark so much as a ripping-out-fast bark followed by Dozier saying, Uh-oh, trouser mice, or Uh-oh, listen to these trouser mice barking it up. Dozier's saying what he says is a not as bad as what Dozier does next, especially in this heat sticking us to these seats as it is already and sweating us through what little we have on. After Dozier does what he does, Dozier says, LaDonna darling, I know these trouser mice are loud, only don't you know the louder the better since the louder ones don't smell as bad as the softer ones smell. When this does not work Dozier says, La-Donna, between you and me, darling, trouser mice between a man and a woman is the highest kind of closeness. When this does not work either, Dozier says, LaDonna honey, do you think I would do this if I did not want to share with you the all of me there is to share, both the good and the bad all of me. Only trouser mice are somehow not what I had in mind when Dozier long ago already said to me, Are you coming? I am coming and going and trying to write all this down the best I can and trying to love Dozier, the all of Dozier, the all of the good and the all of the bad of Dozier the best I can.

You are always in more shit than you think you are in.

You can guess who it is who says this and you can also guess the other who it is who wishes she does not have to say this, only now does have to say this. You remember what I wrote you about hearing about the what seemed like the everything Dozier and me did that really seemed like everything, and in some ways was, only with nobody but Dozier and me and maybe Stepdaddy really caring? Now some others care about what happens and about what Dozier and me do or do not do. I do not mean the same some others as maybe you who might have been wondering all along now how we have been getting along asleeping and eating. The answer to your wondering is we have been getting along better than all right, asleeping in the back or on the roof of the van and eating wherever we can find salad bars where you most likely already know you can fill up a tray all glopped over with all the chunked-up creamy that you could want. Anyway, to make a short story shorter, seventy-three-and-whatever-the-change-was, as much money as this is, was, does not go as far as you might think, even asleeping in the van and eating glopped-over salad sometimes three times a day. To tell you the truth some more, even with our doing all what we are doing, I did not think much about where the seventy-three-and-whatever-the-change-was was going, even when we pulled up at one of these self-serves. This self-serve is run by a fat guy so fat it makes you wonder about laying off the chunked-up creamy, not that I have anything against fat guys or fat anyones or fat anythings, at leastwise not that I know that I do, only this fat guy is so fat sitting inside the little glassed-in and cinder-blocked self-serve with all the ciggies and with all the candy bars and with the little TV on and with his two big fans blowing right on all his fat, that it has to make you wonder. Now this fat guy, although I suppose it is not his fault he is fat, is so fat that just sitting and not doing anything other than just sitting is enough to make his fat tremble. This fat guy with his fat trembles more when his fat-guy hand and his fat-guy fingers push out the spring-loaded drawer at Dozier with Dozier putting in a five and saying, Hidy, lots of weather we're having lately. This fat guy, with even his hair slicked straight back looking fat, trembles around the lower half of his face with the word regular coming out. Dozier is not saying anything until I start wondering maybe Dozier is not hearing the fat guy, only Dozier is hearing the fat guy all right with Dozier saying, Regular, along with this lady, meaning me, would like to use your dumper. This fat guy, fat lips, fat chin, fat everything I can see gone trembling to fat says, There is a faucet out back. Dozier says, This lady, meaning me, don't need to use a faucet, if you know what I mean. The fat guy trembles back how the faucet out back is all there is to use. Dozier says, Then what do you use when you have to use the dumper? Before the fat guy can say something back for me to hear, I am on my way out back to over near where the faucet is where nobody if they were around could really see me anyway, and squat down with my sun dress up in my arm crooks and watch the trickle thread itself out through the dust before skinning over to a stop. I try twisting the faucet on, only this faucet has not been used in awhile, or if it has been used, whoever used it last really twisted the faucet off tight. Using both hands I cannot even start twisting the faucet on. I go back around to tell Dozier watching the PAY THIS AMOUNT rolling up, and tell him, when Dozier says all short, You do this! I am doing the pumping with Dozier sticky popping over the hot sticky tar over to the glassed-in fat guy again when I notice besides the sticky popping of Dozier's flip-flops, that Dozier has the bull-dog stuck barrel down and mostly hanging out of the back pocket of Dozier's cutoffs drooping way low down in back. The PAY THIS AMOUNT starts slowing down some with me clicking and squeezing out every last all what I can. I only half hear Dozier say something to the cinder-blocked and glassed-in fat guy about how YOU, meaning the fat guy, really better take a look, when I half see the fat guy take his fat old time tremble heave himself off whatever he is sitting on and tremble huff himself the way really fat guys do over to the door and let himself out with a key and with the same key lock the door behind him when Dozier has the bulldog out. The fat guy, tremble huffing and rolling from side to side the way really fat guys do, looks back and sees Dozier has the bulldog out. I look around and see nobody else around, only me and Dozier and the fat guy unlocking the door again, only this time to let in himself and Dozier. I clank up the nozzle seven cents over and twist on the cap and go around and get in. In the little glassed-over, and with the way Dozier and the fat guy seem to be moving so slow, they look to me as if they are moving underwater. Dozier and the fat guy look to me as if they are talking underwater with me not able to hear what they are talking about, only I bet it is not the weather, only with Dozier you never really know. They are talking with the fat guy doing most of the talking when Dozier, just as slow and as calm as Dozier can be, blaps the fat guy a slow one with the bulldog. Something black starts slow down the fat guy's no longer-combed-straight-back fat-looking hair and the fat guy is doing something slow and underwater with his hands I cannot see, while as calm as can be, as slow as can be, Dozier is slow stuffing, with his hand not holding the bulldog, something into the pockets of his bagging-out cutoffs. Dozier stops his slow underwater stuffing and, as easygoing as Dozier gets, backs out the door. The hand not holding the bulldog is in Dozier's pocket while the other hand is dangling, pointing the bulldog down at the sitting-down fat guy. I can only say pointing though I am seeing this all the while and not seeing or hearing the bulldog go off once, never mind the twice the newspaper says, only I did see the fat guy all of a sudden look up at Dozier in a way I knew the fat guy knew that whatever much shit he thought he was in before, that he was in a lot more shit now.

The feeling of having just awoke up out of myself that seems long ago already, and is long ago already, grows dreamier and dreamier with this going and going and with this fun-house-mirror-making-everything heat and with this knowing heavy up inside me now that the some others, whoever they are, are coming. Dozier says the some others are not the same some others I most likely think they are, and how they always come for you with smiles, and how they always come for you as friends, and how they always come for you at a time when you are at your weakest. Dozier says the only what we can do is keep doing what we are doing, keep going and going, keep trying to get around this heat, keep the bulldog wrapped up in the greasy rag on the seat between us, keep writing all this down to keep the feeling of having just awoke up out of ourselves from getting away from ourselves.

This is us, Dozier and me, and the more that is the us together and how most nights we try and get around this heat lay-over-your-face hot. This is the more that is us, with nothing other than a few jacks around and with nobody we know of around and with nothing on, other than sweat, up on top of the van on top of Dozier's old asleeping bag. This is the more of us together, cooking in our own juices after making more than either of us alone could make. This is the bigger us, cooking and watching off at the thin wires of lightning lighting up the clouds and the dark. Down below us, Dozier has the game on the radio with the talk of whoever that is talking now as almost close as somebody you have known a long time, an uncle on your mama's side you love and you see once a year and has come to visit now and is in the room next to your room talking low. This is all of us, cooking through Dozier's old asleeping bag with this all-over-us heat, only with all our cooking through, only with all the more that is the us together, there is still not enough us for me with me wanting and with me having Dozier's arm and Dozier's hand around and over and on me. This is me, tracing down from Dozier's snugged-down watchband without seeing anything about Dozier but the what is Dozier that is in my head. This is me, blind tracing the hairs on the back of

Dozier's hand to the bumped-up smooth of Dozier's crossing over and fanning out interstate offshoots I now trace back the other way as far as I can trace back with me inside my head wanting to be inside Dozier tracing all the way around the inside of Dozier until tracing, finding, and staying forever safe in the heart of Dozier's heart.

Those some others coming for us came. Up in these hills is already cooler with the one way up hairpinning around and up past the sliders, past the snow fields, until we are in the climbed-up-coolness with either going all the way back down into the heat the same hair-pinning way we came up, or going on. Those some others, two of them, are a him sitting inside collecting, and a her standing outside wearing a wide-brimmed hat and an open heavy coat the same as he is wearing, only her open heavy coat is humped up in back by a holster with her looking in the cars, nodding in and saying something in to the each of the three cars ahead, then two, then our van with the wrapped-up bulldog on the seat between us with her nodding in and looking in at Dozier with Dozier saying, Lots of weather we're having lately, and her not saying anything, only looking in at Dozier with her face having lost all her how-do. Dozier's face has his little look like he is amusing himself until her finally saying, Enough weather to suit me, with Dozier then holding out the five and the two ones and her saying to Dozier, Hand it to him, and Dozier pulling up and handing him the five and the two ones and me looking and finding one quarter, another quarter to make the fifty, and me handing the fifty to Dozier with Dozier handing the fifty to him with him saying, Thank you, and with Dozier not saying anything more, only going and going until we are gone.

Dozier and me are fat wrapped in the all we have to put on put on against this watch-yourself-smoke-out-the-inside-of-yourself cold. Dozier is still asleeping down in the tunneled-down warm of us caterpillared together down inside Dozier's old asleeping bag. That was us, until me awaking up and wriggling up and unzipping and rolling out and zipping Dozier back up. The moon was ghosting down enough for me to see by to get out this notepad and to open to this page only without me writing anything down to you without first watching the soft asleeping little hills that was and is Dozier still asleeping, watching the rest of what I can watch from up on top of the van of the lake below, of the moonlit snow, of the black of these surrounding hills that I watch until nearly all the moonlight ghosting down has all but ghosted away leaving the rounded backs of these hills rimmed with day. This is when I start writing this what I just wrote down to you with me knowing what you are most likely thinking about now and have most likely been thinking about for a long time now. I say to you do not worry the way I am no longer worried for I know no matter what happens from here on in that at least-wise Dozier has already been delivered and saved, if only because I have been Dozier's writing-down angel.

THE MAN WHO
FAILED TO
WHACK OFF

Among the LIVE GIRLS, SEE LIVE GIRLS, LIVE GIRLS HERE, he is Gramps, Casabas, Blinkers, Humpers, Jugs, Early Bird. Little and bent, he shuffles in after the eleven-to-oners, before the four-to-sixers. Going deep into pocket, he draws out four singles counted and folded.

"Four will get you two," Luis says, sliding over two brass tokens.

With tokens in shaking hand, he drags muscle and bone and brain giving way after eighty-three years to the REAL LIVE GIRLS, LIVE-ALL-LIVE-GIRLS, LIVE COLLEGE GIRLS calling, "Yo, Gramps! Bumpers! Get a load of these garbos, creamers, bonkers, congas, rib-bangers!"

The PACING LIVE GIRLS, LEANING LIVE GIRLS, SITTING LIVE GIRLS check polish on broken nails, eat beef lo-mein, squeeze pimples, call, "Yo, Jugs! Try petting these paw patties, oompapas, jemimas, pagodas, gob stoppers, flapjacks!"

Brass tokens clinking in hand, he looks at the GAZING LIVE GIRLS, BUBBLE-GUM-BUBBLE-BLOWING LIVE GIRLS, SMOKING LIVE GIRLS in red-curtained booths, waiting in lace and little else.

"Come on, Gramps! You ain't got forever! Get yourself some fresh chimichangas, balboas, chihuahuas, sweet rolls, sweater meat!"

In this staring time, take-as-long-as-you-want-just-hurry-it-up-time, honey-I-could-use-your-token-time, he looks for her, the ONE LIVE GIRL, the ONE PARTICULAR LIVE GIRL, the ONE-AND-ONLY-THIS-ONE LIVE GIRL named Misty, named Ginger, named Brandy, named whatever he wants to name her.

The other LIVE-AND-KICKING GIRLS, GET YOUR LIVE GIRLS, LIVE GIRLS RIGHT HERE RIGHT NOW see their chance, take the chance.

"She's working, Gramps, so try these hush puppies on for size, these peepers, wahwahs, wobblers, umlauts."

Counting his brass tokens, he smells his own smell sucked into lungs, sees the line of light under the door of the booth she uses, sees the door open to the ONE LIVE GIRL, ONE SPECIAL LIVE GIRL, ONE-AND-ONLY-THIS-ONE LIVE GIRL saying to him,

"Hey, Gramps, howse it hanging?"

In the closeness of the booth where his bony narrowness is almost too big, he waits. Knowing the quickness of two minutes, of eighty-three years, he unbuttons, un-zips, lets his pants fall to the sticky floor.

The clinking down of brass token becomes shade rolling up: becomes legs of a high stool: becomes dirty soles of open-toed heels on the other side of the glass: becomes stockinged legs: becomes shaved pussy flaps: becomes smooth jump of white belly:

becomes breasts covered up by hands: becomes the ONE-LIVE GIRL, the BEST LIVE GIRL, the IF-YOU'VE-GOT-THE-MONEY-I'VE-GOT-THE-TIME-HONEY-LIVE-GIRL.

In the heat raising sweat on his brow, above his lip, under his arms, through his shirt, he holds both hands around his nodding cock as if in prayer.

The ONE LIVE GIRL, THIS ONE REAL LIVE GIRL, THIS ALWAYS THE SAME ONE LIVE GIRL helps him with, "Come on, Gramps! Come on, Grampers!"

Mouth-breathing the heat, he tries. The shade un-winds as he pumps faster, as he drops the brass token. Reaching for the token becomes stabbing behind eye: becomes dizziness: becomes sitting down hard: becomes sucking the ammonia smell: becomes sucking the cool floor: becomes suck, suck, suck.

Among the LIVE GIRLS, REAL LIVE GIRLS, LIVE GIRLS HERE is another old man who is gagas, twofers, twangers, floaters, goners.

INDIA, WHEN YOUR PHONE DOESN'T RING, IT'S ME, POMP

It is thoughts of her doing the everyday that sets Pomp off.

It is Pomp, small-town lawyer, one-time Baptist, volunteer fire fighter, pork-and-beaner until the day I die whose insides seize up into a morning-after when walking into the bank or the hardware store or the wherever and seeing someone with hair like her hair.

Yes, it is Pomp picking his nose meat in the checkout line at the all-night Stop & Rob while football cradling a box of chocolate-covered donuts and reading through one of these newspapers, this one newspaper with the headline: I WANT BIGFOOT'S BABY, and me wanting her to have my baby.

Back at the house, it is the same old Pomp staring in the toothpaste-spotted mirror at the same old face belonging to a middling, small-town bachelor with dark quarter moons under his eyes and a mustache that looks pasted on crooked.

It is Pomp staring back at Pomp that leads him wandering back, crawling back around to the what was, to the her, to the let us say, yes, it was true, to the her washing her face in this same spotted mirror.

Her face was as wondrous as her name.

India. India Early.

Not bad, huh?

You bet your bung-foddered patoot not bad. Her face and the rest of her were just as wondrous: the long tallness of her, the tangle of dark hair lifting out behind her when she walked, the forgiving heart, unlike my heart.

Now not-so-good old Pomp says a lot of things, but Pomp was as there with her with his heart as he was ever anywhere. Pomp saw her wondrous beauty and the rest of her stop the half-gone party goings-on. You say beauty is no guarantee of happiness. Pomp says back to you, I know, but it is something. Think of yourself at a party full of people like me putting what we think are our most charming mustached faces and the rest of our charming middling selves forward. Think of India coming into the room with her wondrously beautiful name and face and all the rest. Think of Pomp watching the men watch her while the women watch the men, then everybody watching her long enough for everybody to wonder or know. Think of India coming through the room, parting the just-trying-to-get-by shitsuckers like me with her wondrous India face full of her look saying, Well, there you are, and there you are, you, Pomp.

Well, wherever you are, India, and whatever you are doing, it is Pomp, crawling back through the what is left me of the everyday you.

Her doing her everyday wondrous was nothing compared to her doing the other.

Pomp supposes you might be wondering a little about this other because old Pomp has wondered about it more than a little hisself. Using his eight years of land-grant schooling, and his just about fourteen years now of lawyering, his thirty-nine years on this great engine earth, what Pomp comes up with is every want gives rise to the opposite want, what Pomp calls this other.

Not much, is it?

Not much considering the higher schooling, these years.

Pomp did say middling. Pomp meant middling. Middling as Pomp is in looks and lawyering and all the rest, Pomp had India, at least for a while. Pomp wanders back to that while. Pomp often wanders back to that while when India was stretched out with nothing on on the bed. Pomp was eating an orange and listening to her breathing as she slept. There she was, and there she was, stretched out sleeping and adding up to wondrous. Yes, Pomp was eating the pulpy orange and listening to her and wanting her, wanting to be inside her and wanting her inside Pomp more than she was already. Pomp, the long ago fallen away Baptist, the not so good old good old boy, slipped some pulped-up orange up inside her, way up inside her, before stroking her all over, letting the orange squish around in our love juices before getting the orange back out and eating it.

Pretty good, huh? Pomp can even wander back so far as to tell you the special taste of that orange. Pomp can wander that far back, and Pomp can tell you how that pulped-up orange tasted like cuntsicle.

If you think that is something, think about this. Think about how Pomp's doing what he did gave rise to other wants, others he supposes should not happen, but do, and did.

Sometimes when Pomp is not able to sleep he heads down to the all-night Stop & Rob.

No doubt you already guessed why Pomp is not able to

sleep, and yes, you are right, it is not the lawyering. The lawyering rolls along with little help from this lawyer. All Pomp does is tear out a few forms, hand them over to one of his girls, put on his best lawyering suit looking like it should belong to some lawyer somebody else, head down to the courthouse, talk his lawyer talk, stack up the checks.

It is not Pomp's health keeping Pomp from sleeping at night like a person should sleep. Considering the speed bump around his middle, some needed gum and crown work, his habit of trying to find some peace and sleep with the help of a George Dickel, or three, or more, his health is healthy enough. No, you are right, it is not the lawyering or his health that has him finding his not-so-good-old self all hours of the night at the all-night Stop & Rob.

At these hours, the wide and well-lit aisles are usually empty but for the working pimply high-school boy or the somebody shoplifting something or the other sort of somebody bored shitless come in to handle frozen chicken parts or the middling sort of nobody called Pomp who usually ends up with these chocolate-covered donuts reading these newspapers. Pomp knows you know what newspapers. These ones with the headlines and stories like: GIANT CATFISH ATTACKS SLEEPING BABY or MEN WHO DON'T BATHE ARE SEXIER SAYS SHRINK.

Check out the newspaper with the story about a three-hundred-year marriage where the couple were wed in nine past lives. Her and this life and wander-crawling around in the what was come to mind.

Well, maybe it is thinking such thoughts that will help Pomp close the gap on all the time we have been apart, put an end to this crawling back and thinking and feeling sick and feeling like a nobody who finds his shitsuckering self all hours of the night at the all-night Stop & Rob.

The same as Pomp said to you, there was this other.

We did other wants at Pomp's wanting. It was not the same as Pomp pressing his thirty-eight to India's wondrous head, although India certainly had her times of doubt. Like the time Pomp asked her to dress up in her black silk dress with the white polka dots, long black stockings held up with nothing other than a black garter belt, black shiny patent leather heels. She dressed up, and I drove us the next town over for what you can now stay home to see on your VCR, although back not so long ago you had to go over to the next town over late Friday nights.

The mayor, police chief and some others we knew were let in the side door while we were told to go in the front way. India balked at first, seeing those she knew and who knew her and knew her daddy and knew her daddy's daddy, but I wanted to, said I wanted to front way in or not, and in we went.

We sat in the dark with all those men knowing her and hers without any one of them saying anything to her other than what they said by not looking at us, by not looking at India's wondrous any time, but especially then.

After watching what was going on up on the big screen for a while, Pomp slipped his hand up India's long-stockinged legs, found her and brunswicked her the same as some hairy bowling ball until the mayor and those other men, most with eyes staring and mouths open the same as something murdered, were watching us instead.

The best part, the worst part, is India loving it all.

Feeling sorry for hisself and wandering some more back around in such thoughts and doing what Pomp told you Pomp does gets Pomp to work early. Pomp is in before his girls and while all is quiet except Pomp's heart and lungs, which are pumping away the same as if Pomp is running up the courthouse steps late in filing some high-paying company's claim.

Hearing his huff-pumping self like this and the whirring sound of the number going through the glass and copper telephone lines has Pomp wondering what to say.

"Hello, India's mom," Pomp says, trying not to show right off how Pomp is a professional something, mainly the professional horse's patoot Pomp knows hisself to be.

"Who's this?" asks India's mom in her voice like India's voice except more mom-like.

"Pomp," Pomp says, waiting for the hang-up sound, the sound of hard plastic on hard plastic. The hang-up sound does not happen. Pomp tells India's mom how the lawyering is going, without adding, with the no help from Pomp.

India's mom tells Pomp how the wedding went, how India married a Jew doctor, how India is studying to be a doctor herself.

Pomp does not remember hearing much after married except Pomp saying how a big case requires Pomp's traveling near to where India now lives, wherever that is, and how he would sure like to give India a call.

India's mom asks if Pomp is married.

Like the good lawyer Pomp is not, Pomp sidesteps the question by ignoring it and asking a question of his own. Pomp asks India's mom if she ever reads any of those Stop & Rob newspapers, the ones with the stories like: LIGHTNING MELTS ZIPPER, LOCKS MAN INSIDE PANTS.

Long quiet follows.

Long quiet follows before India's mom gives Pomp India's married-and-you-better-believe-Jew-sounding last name and India's telephone number.

By not saying good-by, Pomp makes it to the shitter without getting too much on his lawyering shoes, wing tips lightly chunked with chocolate-covered donut.

You remember Pomp telling you of the Pomp forgets whose party it was with everybody putting what they think, Pomp especially, were our most charming selves forward, and India with all her wondrous beauty coming in and putting a stop to it? Well, maybe this is what Pomp hopes in traveling to where India now calls home. In case it is not, there is always the thirty-eight.

Maybe Pomp will get his old self invited to supper using some of his lawyering, soft-talking skills.

Maybe Pomp will show his thirty-eight, putting the fear of something, the fear of a horse's patoot, in her Jew doctor husband.

Maybe, maybe not.

Maybe not since the thirty-eight is just the thirty-eight and nothing compared to memory. Think of India excusing herself from supper and old Pomp here asking Doc if he ever puts fruit way the hell up the wife. If Doc does, can Doc tell Pomp the taste of the fruit after Doc fishes the fruit back?

If this does not do the trick, maybe Pomp will tell Doc how Pomp can and watch Doc's expression go out.

Yes, yes, it is you know who, at his lawyering desk where all is quiet but for the chirping of these little birds ruining an all-night numbing, and the turning-over sound of the pages of one of these Stop & Rob newspapers, this newspaper with the headline: MAN GIVES BIRTH TO HIMSELF.

What do you make of that?

What do you make of you know who, hearing his heart and lungs sprinting and feeling his insides start to go while doing the dialing and hearing the whirring sound?

It is him, hearing two rings, then it is her.

"Hello," India says in her sleepy India voice with Pomp nearly losing some of his insides and what little purchase on anything he has.

"Hello," India says again with this Pomp supposing her sleepy lying beside her successful-as-all-hell-doctor husband in all her everyday wondrous, all the wondrous Pomp once had until wanting some other, until wanting her past too, and then Pomp having her past too, Pomp having it all by having her tell me, despite tears and pleas, everything she ever did with anybody. No little anything was too little. What she wore when, their smells, her wishes, their sounds, until even with all her wondrous, all of India was not enough.

India forgave me.

India forgave me in her knowing what has taken all my years of schooling, lawyering, crawling around to right now come to know, and this is love like ours, love like mine, is its own undoing.

"Who's this?" India says.

Me, Pomp, not saying anything before softly hanging up.

LEGENDS

My boy reels his line in through the dark from the trees on the bank. He reels in and up a bare hook.

"Dad," my boy says, laying down his rod. "Who is the best, you know, you ever saw?"

"You, boy."

"Be serious, Dad," my boy says.

We drift over the slow opening ring of a single rise.

"Someone I served with," I say.

We drift on with the spoken part left at that.

What was never spoken by any of us who knew and were afraid to blunt it, or spook it, was that the Wiz was the best you ever saw. You knew the Wiz was the shit starting with what was inked on his helmet, those block letters spelling out SHAMAN, and THE WIZ. You knew seeing the long tube rig the Wiz carried on his back, what you first thought might be some sort of shoulder rocket, or maybe a long map case, and turned out to be the tube for what he called his ugly stick. See the Wiz—with the ground all blackened over and still smoking-up white—join up that nine-foot ugly stick of a smoke pole and head for the nearest bomb crater filled with a week's worth of monsoon rain, or a burned-off rice paddy, or some still burning river to false cast like a trick-rope artist at a rodeo. See him do that three or four times, then see him crank out fish, flop out some big bigmouth bass, and believe me, you knew.

We were almost all boys, not much older than my boy, but with nothing like boy lasting very long, at least not in those of us stepping in it every day. While the Wiz stepped in it the same as the rest of us, you could somehow never think of seeing him clothes-still-smoking dead. Seeing yourself dead is why most of us started drinking first thing, washing down the opium balls rolled around in your palm, doing what you had to do to dull the edge, to chill it so you would not have to feel sorry for anyone, mostly for yourself. The fear really came on when you turned around to see the sled you flew in on rear straight up, dip, then seemingly disappear as fast as light over the jungle.

We waited for after nightfall when Hand Job shagged us through the wire, kept us going out into the jungle until saying, "Get some."

We all clumped around the Wiz until Hand Job put his side piece in Okie Dokie's mouth and hiss-whispered, "Spread out!"

None of us who knew what we knew got far from the Wiz with his big night scope and his ugly stick and his all the rest of what he had. I went into some lie down and went to my place of no difference between awake and asleep. I went to my place for who knows how long before coming back to the Wiz working on his fly-tying knots close enough to reach over and touch him. The others were stretched out on their bellies with their hands and their faces night-painted up so the only white was the white of their eyes rolling like the eyes of scared ponies.

You listen to the soft patter drip of the jungle. You listen to the ticking of Light Bulb's watch. You smell the deep green rot the rain brings out. You smell your own breath smelling like a dead snake sealed up in a jar while trying to settle back into your place. You hold yourself still in that place until something, until hearing that suddenly-too-quiet-somewhere-deep-in-your-head, until seeing something move in the clearing. Chill it. Hold it. Chill it down while seeing something move again. Lord, please make that something a monkey. Make it some kind of night bird. Please make whatever it is, Lord, anything other than what I know it is. Somebody else sees it moving too and puts out a Fourth of July sputtering-up that sends you back to being a boy sitting on your sleeping bag spread out on the hood of Daddy's car. Daddy and Mama and Sammy girl are right next to you again, with all of us eating deviled-ham-and-cheese sandwiches, slow chewing Mama's sandwiches with upturned faces dead white in the fire-work sizzle, flash, boom. Lay it back now. Hold it back. It is all right. The Wiz man is right beside you, while in the dead light of the floating-down flare, the snaketail shower of sparks, the quiet of no lying to yourself now, it is them. It is them and they are coming for you, slow coming right at you, these three, four bareheaded and barefoot boys with death held at the ready for you with this being the one where you know you get it, Wiz or no Wiz. See him screwing together his nine-foot rig, his ugly stick. See how they are now so close there is no time to get up, to run, to go so bad. You have to go so bad the same as when you were a boy burrowed under the pricker briars catching in your hair and on your shirt. You have to go so bad burrowed down in these briars there is no way you can hold it, and, somehow, you hold it. You hold it and see Sammy girl run by without her seeing you. You hear Sammy girl's voice calling, "Olley, olley all come free." You stay burrowed down in these briars in your own let-go warmth and wet when somebody, the Canj Man maybe, lays out some heat and light. The others do and you do too, too fast squeezing off at the boys caught out in the open, caught in the rolling flash of man-made lightning, in the walking all around them of the Willie Peters, in the up above of the ghost-making flares in the great field of monsoon-clouded night. The boys are caught by our little high winds puffed into them and into the muck all around them. Our little winds jerk-blow them down into the muck where the boys stay. We pour more little wind into them, puffing up their hair and clothes and the muck around them. It stops with another flare parachute-sputtering down. The pock, pock of one of theirs starts up. Three or four of ours put out our answer back, sweeping back the dark until it stops, all of it, but for the crying out in the pillared-up white smoke of the Willie Peters, the over and over crying of what sounds like a little girl crying out.

I will thank you, Lord, by taking it, and taking it, and promising to make the most of every second of it, Lord . . . Where is the Wiz?

Another flare sparks over the clearing with two of ours crouch-running out, flopping down, getting up, running more into the hanging smoke. A burst of back and forth flash and the little girl crying stops.

"Okie Dokie, where's the Wiz?"

"Beats me, Wes, but look here," Okie Dokie says.

"Looks like old Hand Job caught some."

The second lieutenant is a curled-up little boy. His helmet is overturned and the back of his head is a raised-up clot of chewed-up licorice.

"Thataway," Light Bulb says, looking at the boy lieutenant while pointing his sixteen behind us down a strip of muck.

You ease on down the slide of trail. You slip through the soft drip from up high. Easy does it over the little roots and the wait-a-minute vines. Hold your breath past the freeze-you-to-the-bone of what looks like a face and is a knot in a rocket-shattered tree. Ease down to the rushing-off of monsooned river.

Up to his knees in the sweeping through of the risen-up river is the Wiz doing the ancient waving of his wand. The Wiz lets the leader settle in first. The line snaps straight and the ugly stick spring bows with the Wiz coming up hard. Water streams up the leader, up the three feet of shearing, twisting, stopping, shaking the Wiz starts reeling in, cranking in, until the Wiz bends and one hand reaches under the rolling surge of river to raise high by the gills the biggest freshwater-finned-anything you ever saw. The Wiz—some sort of black statue in the deep jungle night—holds the fish up and out at arm's length. The Wiz dips that one-time fish back into the sweeping away river, and, with one quick twist, sets the fish free.

The yelp-barking of a fox somewhere in this moonlit night is what brings me back.

We have wind drifted out to the deepest part of the pond.

My boy is asleep among the everywhere risings. My boy, a gift better than I deserve, is asleep in the now so still I can hear the soft sucking sound of the big slow takes.

It was wasted lifetimes worth of being back before thinking of writing the Wiz and asking him how big he thought that fish was, and, then, never writing him or any of the others.

It was Light Bulb who wrote me. Light Bulb boy-scrawled how the Wiz was missing, could-be caught, could-be killed, and how there were rumors, and then how a brother in Recon told Light Bulb about seeing a naked black American boy way out in the boonies. That tall black American boy was fly whipping the night with the biggest damn ugly stick of a pole you ever saw. That black boy pulled out some kind of jump-up slippery water-god when the brother in Recon called out, yelled out, and that black boy was gone.

I reach for and pick up my boy's little pole, untwist the line, swing back as far as I can swing back and whir the weighted popper out and out into the night.

for Dort

ON RISING
AND SINGING:
A GUIDE TO
WHALE RIDING

The way in is first through the ear—the late summer night bug-buzzing on high. Underneath the buzzing is the clicking and whistling of the killers, their one to the other squeaking and lowing. The killers' language pulls the ears and the eyes down to the cement plot of blacker-than-night seawater. Under the topsoil of nightwater heaven showing the stars upside down are deep water moves. A shadow glides surface near before spiraling away, around, back again to bubble trails of breaking through, to plowing the three-acre grid of star field with six feet of notched-twice fin.

The two killers furrow on in their nightwater work: blowing saltwater smoke, rowing an eye upward, baring teeth as long and as white as sharpened piano keys.

You know their tune: hand signals, belly scratching, hunks of salmon helping you forget the National Geographic photographs of one of these killers blow-heaving himself onto an ice floe, his six tons tipping up the drifting ice table, sliding the white fur and the skittering black claw of polar bear down to the waiting snap and crunch of no more.

Knowing this, you make your way from the bug-buzzing of the grandstand down past the row upon row of no one here other than you and the killers, swoops of white saddle.

Up and out on the edge of the stage is the seawater-iron-smell of upturned earth after a spring rain; the up-closeness of these immense, snow-patched shadows.

Anything darker than star brings the killers up from trout-shadow size to what? To midget-submarine-size only longer, more tapered than the captured Japanese sub now landlocked-up out on the hometown green.

That size, but with none of the sub's slow-go hulk.

That size, but flash-squirming-quick-dwindle-diving back down to trout-fingerling size with you on the mark now, getting set now, letting go.

In this underwater world of no man breath, the dark and the cold are pulled on like another flapping tweed. Hair and the length of silk knotted about neck float loose, reminding you how living is a thing learned.

Follow your hair, break dark plane and float on your back.

The two killers are behind you with the star-diamonded water layering over the shiny black domes of their heads.

Slow bicycle-ride the legs.

Slap the night-cellophaned surface and the twice-notched killer, the bigger of the two, passes slab-solid and slick under palm.

Keep water-pedal pumping.

Keep slap-splashing until again, rising fast in boiling water, fish breath is blow-spraying forth in living song. The six-foot dorsal is now in hand and flying you up and through the saltwatery-silver foam cresting shoulders and chest in what feels like a dream of soaring and soaring until a headswing off and a rollover later and you are pedal-bobbing once again.

Swim over and along to the man-made edge with an ol-ley-oop up to the weight and the drip of standing, to the listening and the looking for six-foot-notched sickle mowing black swells.

Here comes, up alongside here. Step on, hold on to the slip and smooth of Old Topnotch sliding away sea swell smooth and fast. You will not believe how fast, with the fear and the joy stretching you from the back of your shoulders to your belly to the all the way through and down you, with the night wind flapping your hair and silk and tweed, with the killers surrounding you with their bellows and clicks while dipping you away and keeling you over into splash.

In the darkness down on you, in the salt-soil layers of colder and colder, is silence.

The oldest way out makes you feel that you move at the heart of the world.

That is until a killer slides his six tons of deep-cave black and arctic-white swoop between your legs, slips notched hook into the groove of your spine before sea-bronc blasting droplets of sil-ver into the star-flecked night where you are the rising and rising king of forever.

PASTORAL

Farmer Brown is a big man. We are speaking now of the Farmer Brown who, from what I can tell, is no longer a farmer, although he always says to call him Farmer Brown. I do. I call him Farmer Brown, and I say to you he is one big man.

Now as big a man as Farmer Brown is, and I do mean big, he is not as big as he once was. For that matter, none of us are as big as we once were. By us, I mean the porcupines and me and Farmer Brown. Other than the porcupines, none of us are as big as we once were, and we are getting smaller.

Let us, us meaning you and me, let us back up a little to when Farmer Brown first started getting smaller, which was when Farmer Brown's big foot started getting bigger.

Farmer Brown's big foot, from his big toes to his big knob of anklebone and up, started swelling up with the skin going from white to yellowish to yellowish-green. His big foot swelled up until the skin split.

About a day and a half later was when the sores started eating at the wetness down inside where the skin split.

Three days later, the sores were mostly black. By then,

there was also the stink. When the stink got to be too much for Farmer Brown, Farmer Brown drove himself in his Corvette over to the hospital where Farmer Brown's big toes were taken. Farmer Brown's big foot was taken. Farmer Brown's big leg up to the big knee was taken until some, not much, just enough to mention of Farmer Brown's big leg was left. Farmer Brown says the doctors took what they had to take and sent the big rest of him back.

I know it is hard to believe, but Farmer Brown's Corvette is also getting smaller.

You may have seen Farmer Brown's Corvette out along one of these snowy back roads. If you have not seen the Corvette by now, the one parked over near the snowed-over and fallen-in chicken coop, you better hurry, for as we speak now, Farmer Brown's Corvette is getting smaller.

Farmer Brown is soon up, hopping around, sucking his crutches out of the mud and snow in the yard. Farmer Brown is lowering his big what is left of himself into what is left of his chewed-through Corvette.

Lowering himself is about as far as Farmer Brown gets with the Corvette until we fix Farmer Brown up with a sawed-off pool stick belted with two army web belts to the some, not much, just enough to mention stump of bandaged leg. By using the pool stick's bigger end, Farmer Brown can pretty much work the clutch and the brake.

Farmer Brown works the clutch and the brake the best Farmer Brown can.

Have you ever seen a grunting porcupine up close? Have you ever seen a porcupine in a Corvette up close? At this time of year with the snow drifting deep against the fallen-in chicken coop, the porcupines come out at night from wherever the porcupines come out from. Click on the yard light and the porcupines are all over the Corvette.

"Leave the porcupines alone," Farmer Brown yells from his big bed.

Left alone, the porcupines keep coming back night after night. With the day-to-day smaller of the way the Corvette is now, smaller with most of the rubber on the windshield wipers eaten away, and a lot of the leather seats and armrests eaten away, the porcupines keep coming back.

Have you ever seen a porcupine through a peephole rear sight on a Gook piece?

You can pretty much guess how driving the getting smaller and smaller Corvette with a sawed-off pool stick for a leg is not easy.

Driving the Corvette paid for with the bundle Farmer Brown says he saved up from his two loops—the same Corvette that just this morning I discovered has some of the wiring under the dash eaten away, the knobs on the radio chewed off, the belt part of the seat belts gnawed through—is now less easy for Farmer Brown to drive, and not just because of the porcupines.

I guess it has been about three weeks since Farmer Brown's big hairy hand, big hairy wrist, big hairy arm right up to Farmer Brown's big elbow were taken at the hospital.

It was this morning that Farmer Brown asked me to hack-saw the seven iron at the kitchen table.

If you think driving a disappearing Corvette with a pool stick for a leg is hard, you should see somebody try it with a pool stick for a leg and a golf club for a hand.

Jacob Bronstein is what is written in black pen on the photograph taken from the top drawer of the dresser near Farmer Brown's big bed.

What is anybody, other than Farmer Brown, doing going through the drawers of somebody else's dresser? Looking for ammo. Finding ammo. Finding a clip of long points for the big light Gook piece on the big bed that might be the same Gook piece in the photograph.

Jacob Bronstein is what is written on the back of the photograph of the young and gangly big Farmer Brown with the gangly neck and the gangly wrists. The gangly young Farmer Brown in the photograph is squatting on a tank or a half-track or whatever it is. The big light Gook piece Farmer Brown is holding up, the one that might be the same piece on the bed, looks tiny next to Farmer Brown. Farmer Brown is holding up the Gook piece and squinting up his big handsome face into a Gook sun. Farmer Brown is squinting up his big handsome face at whoever it is taking the photograph.

You can tell him whatever you want to call him, Jacob Bronstein or Farmer Brown, I call him Farmer Brown with the big handsome face that was big and handsome right up to when the sores set in.

Farmer Brown sleeps in the light from the moon looking as if the moon crawled into the snow-covered branches of one of the big dead elms. The wind blowing in the dead elms waves the shadows of the creaking branches on Farmer Brown's big bed. The shadows wave on Farmer Brown. The shadows wave on those raised-up sores on what is left of Farmer Brown after more of Farmer Brown has been taken.

The shadows waving on Farmer Brown are about as big as his big other leg that has been taken all the way up to Farmer Brown's big hipbone. Watching the shadow branches wave over Farmer Brown makes it easy to almost believe the shadows are the big arm, the big leg, the other big leg that Farmer Brown no longer has.

Farmer Brown whimpers in his sleep while the shadows

wave over my holding him, shushing him back to quiet.

"I hate to ask you only would you drive me" is all Farmer Brown says.

Outside is one of those winter mornings bright with the sun on new-fallen snow. Looking down I see the tracks from the night before. The tracks are all over the yard with the toed-in mark that could almost be the track of a barefoot boy.

The tracks all over the yard go up and on and inside the snow-covered Corvette through the big hole eaten through the ragtop. The tracks go in to where the three-spoke steering wheel is eaten away.

Back upstairs, Farmer Brown has already worked out what we will do.

Farmer Brown is on the big bed. Farmer Brown's good one big arm is almost all the way in the big sleeve of his big army jacket. Farmer Brown's stink is worse than the stink has ever been. Farmer Brown stares at the water stains on the ceiling. Farmer Brown has worked out, even if I could have, me not having to drive Farmer Brown anywhere.

Sometimes, like times like tonight, when the blowing snow is a grainy sound against the farmhouse, in the big dead elms, against the snowed-under chicken coop, you can also hear the sound of grunting.

The grunting stops when you start crunching over and through the snow. The grunting stops when you get close enough to count the two, the four, the five porcupines. The porcupines look as big tonight as the porcupines have ever looked with their big porcupine eyes and their big porcupine yellow teeth and their big porcupine stink all over the next to nothing that is left of the Corvette.

Move in closer until the big stink rising off the porcupines is too much. Move in until the big porcupine stink is enough to keep you from moving in any closer, then move in closer. Move in until you are afraid to move in more without having something, a piece, in your hand. Hold the piece out until the barrel almost touches quill. Hold it and listen to the blowing grainy sound. Listen to the sound of the wind in the big dead elms. Listen to the big sound no matter how small you are of yourself still living.

I DON'T CARE IF

I EVER GET BACK

We are in the rest of the world. The heat baby blankets me. The heat, the light are in the white stones of the parking lot. The stones chalk my hands.

"Put those down and give me your hand," my father says to me. The stones click back to stones. My hands are patted on my seat. The some small of me that is not my father is given to my father.

My father walks us over the hot of the dusted stones, around the silvered-glint off the cars. I am no bigger than where my father bends his legs. My shadow is a small shadow of his. His big shadow walks us, hand in hand, to these other boys as small as me, and bigger boys, and men in hats waiting in this light. The men smell of sweat, of hair under hats, of my Uncle Johnny Del's cigars. These men hold tickets the same as the blue ticket my father holds out. The man bigger on the wooden box than even my father's bigness takes our ticket. My father walks our big shadow over the bigger shadow of that man onto the cinder track. This width and grit of track widens over to the patter of water fountained, curves narrow around the green of the outfield curving around the closer red-clayed infield, comes wide back to this, our cinder-black self.

"What?" my father says to me. "What are you pointing at? Water? You want some water?"

My father has us in this world of mud. Water plops on puddled water, on mud, on dust. Bigger boys than me call at other bigger boys, splash and spray. A man, big in his white-whites, in his black shoes cleating the cinders says, "Watch it, boys!" The bigger boys than me scatter back. The man spreads his big cleated shoes, bends. His cap is sideways on his big sweated head. His big throat apple is swallowed, and swallowed, and swallowed. The man bends up, sleeves his big man mouth, says to my father, "Go ahead, I'll hold it while you hold him."

My father flies me. My Red Ball Jets fly over rivers, lakes, pebbled boulders. Watered silver rains the dust of deserts. I close my eyes, reach with my mouth. The wet is slurped, breathed. Slurp this geyser again. This wet is too fast and much, bubbled big and much up my nose.

"Too much," my father says for me, saving me back down to the heat and light of standing. In this light, we are so clearly seen for what we are.

The world is bleachered. My Red Ball Jets kick the darkness under the bleachers. Potato chip bags and paper cups spook white in the darkness under us. Spooking bigger boys than me call at one another, at me. My smallness of hand is inside the knuckle knots of my father's bigness of hand. My father is the rope keeping me from falling into the open darkness under us.

I watch up at my father's bigness watching out at the sun-lit grass, the base paths where the men run in their white-whites. I watch up past my father's big face to the shadows under the roof. Birds coo white up in those shadows, birds, or the Father, the Son, the Holy Ghosts of spooking dead boys flapping on to Heaven. The Holy Ghosts of the boys wing through the pole of light hung across the shadows. The light is a giant's flashlight. The giant is looking for the Holy Ghost souls of boys the same as me, me, when my father lets go my hand to cup his big father mouth to shout, "Take him out, coach!" The Holy Ghost in me flaps out of me. The ghost of me rises near the birds watching me fly away from the beamed light of the giant. The calling boy souls in the darkness under my father's feet call at me more. I fly out from under the wide-slanted roof.

I float up in this blowing world of blue sky and light. I see down on my father in the bleachered rows, on the still living other boys, the bigger boys and the men in hats all toy-soldiered down. The men in their white-whites are smaller too. Those men run in and out of the big box shadows, over the greened-flat of the grass. I see the little rain of the small small boys spraying. I can see the ribbon of cindered track. I can see the whiteness of the parking lot, the sunlight off our car waiting for my father and for me.

Beyond our car, roads game board. Trees rug up green. Up from the green of the trees is the giant pencil point writing this is where God lives on Sundays. Tree tops nub under me. The whole world dollhouses down small.

Where we live is small fence, tarred roof, small-windowed. Rusty dog is smalled out in our yard. Rusty far away bark-barks up at me and is the only one not a giant, or God, who can see me now.

Mama—small as can be and still the Mama I came out of—comes out the back door of our house with a basket of what we wear. I can see my mama carry the basket past my barking brother. Mama's yellowed mama hair blows, as does what Mama clothespins up. Mama will save me. Mama of mine will wrap me saved in the socks, shirts, sheets Mama clothespins out. My Rusty dog brother will bite the giant, bark-bark at the calling boy souls lost in the darkness under the bleachers. What about my father? Mama will save the flying Holy Ghost me and say to me, "Who will save your father?"

Mama and Rusty and where we live littles all the way away. The world is sidewalk blurred under me as when my father carries me upside down. The world is blowing blue, clouds, light up above those tiny bugged-down men catching the tiny ball, those tiny men in their tiny men hats, these tiny boys smaller than me, small as me, the man my father and the afraid for him that is me beside him.

"I'm here" is what I say up to my father.

My father's bigness of arm hugs me into the darkness that is the father smell that is Mama's wash and him. My father hugs me safe in the sound of the world that is my father's heart.

ACKNOWLEDGMENTS

Grateful acknowledgment is made to the following publications where these stories first appeared: *The Quarterly, StoryQuarterly, Story, Raritan, The Antioch Review, Harper's Magazine, American Literary Review, The Nebraska Review, New Letters, Bridge, Alaska Quarterly Review, Carriage House Review, Midnight Mind, Plazm, Chelsea, Failbetter*. Stories in *CAMPFIRES OF THE DEAD* were originally published by *ALFRED A. KNOPF* in 1989.

ABOUT THE AUTHOR

Peter Christopher was an award-winning author and journalist. He was a writer-in-residence for the Writers Voice Workshop and a guest lecturer at Columbia University, New York University, University of Florida, and Portland State University's Haystack Program in the Arts. Peter curated a reading series for the New York Public Library and La Mama La Gallerica Second Classe. He joined the faculty of the Georgia Southern Writing and Linguistics Department in 1998, where he was instrumental in establishing and building the creative writing program. Peter inspired countless students, winning Georgia Southern University's Dorothy Smith Golden Award for Excellence in Teaching. He also was awarded a grant from the National Endowment for the Arts and took first place in Story's Naked Fiction Competition. Peter passed away in 2008 at the age of 52.

11:11 Press is an American independent literary
publisher based in Minneapolis, MN.
Founded in 2018, 11:11 publishes innovative
literature of all forms and varieties. We believe
in the freedom of artistic expression, the
realization of creative potential, and the
transcendental power of stories.

Printed in the USA
CPSIA information can be obtained
at www.ICGtesting.com
LVHW090818221023
761714LV00028B/127